B

RESCUED BY LOVE

THE RYDERS

LOVE IN BLOOM SERIES

MELISSA FOSTER

ISBN-10: 1941480578
ISBN-13: 9781941480571

This is a work of fiction. The events and characters described herein are imaginary and are not intended to refer to specific places or living persons. The opinions expressed in this manuscript are solely the opinions of the author and do not represent the opinions or thoughts of the publisher. The author has represented and warranted full ownership and/or legal right to publish all the materials in this book.

RESCUED BY LOVE

V1.0

Cover Design: Elizabeth Mackey Designs

WORLD LITERARY PRESS
PRINTED IN THE UNITED STATES OF AMERICA

A Note from Melissa

The best way to stay up to date on my releases is to sign up for my newsletter:
www.MelissaFoster.com/News

I've been excited to bring you Jake and Addy's story since I first met them. I knew they were not going to fall easily, and it was so much fun watching them fight the sparks we all knew would fly. I hope you enjoy them as much as I do. Be sure to read past the end of the book for news about Gage and Sally's book, as well as sneak peeks to more upcoming novels.

About the Ryders

The Ryders are a series of stand-alone romances that may be enjoyed in any order or as part of the larger Love in Bloom big-family romance collection (40+ awesome books). You can jump into the series anywhere. The characters from each family appear in other Love in Bloom subseries, so you never miss an engagement, wedding, or birth. For more information on the Love in Bloom series visit: www.melissafoster.com/LIB

THE RYDERS
Seized by Love (Blue & Lizzie)
Claimed by Love (Duke & Gabriella)
Chased by Love (Trish & Boone)
Rescued by Love (Jake & Addy)
Swept into Love (Gage & Sally)

Download a FREE Love in Bloom series list:
www.MelissaFoster.com/SO
Download a FREE family tree and more here:
www.MelissaFoster.com/RG

CHAPTER ONE

ADDISON DAHL LEANED against the outdoor bar, surrounded by all the beauty an evening wedding on Elpitha Island, a small stretch of land off the coast of South Carolina, had to offer. Couples danced beneath twinkling lights, children darted across the lawn with sparklers in hand, laughing and making designs against the night sky. With ocean views as far as the eye could see, island music sailing through the air, and a lighthouse standing sentinel, Addy's best friend, Gabriella, married her forever love, investor Duke Ryder. Tonight was bittersweet. Addison had worked as Gabriella's legal assistant for several years, and now Gabriella was talking about starting a family and cutting back on her practice. She and Duke were leaving for their honeymoon in a couple days, and Addy was leaving for ten days of soul-searching in the mountains of Upstate New York. She couldn't help wondering how different their lives would be when they returned from their trips.

"They look happy, don't they?" Trish, Duke's younger sister and Addy's friend, joined her by the bar. A lock of her dark hair swept across her cheek with the breeze, and she tucked it behind her ear, her eyes dancing with excitement. She'd been absolutely glowing since her fiancé, rock star Boone Stryker, had proposed to her earlier in the evening. He'd surprised her not only with a ring, but also with a wedding that was scheduled to take place the day after tomorrow right there on the island.

"Blissfully happy," Addy agreed. Duke, an investor, was beautifying Elpitha, where Gabriella had grown up. He was single-handedly making all of Gabriella's dreams come true. Addy was happy for her friend, but her needs were vastly different. As the daughter of a world-renowned fashion designer, she didn't want or need a man to take care of her. She'd had enough of that for a lifetime. At almost thirty years old, she doubted she'd ever meet a man fierce, smart, and passionate enough to hold her interest for a week, much less forever. Addy had never felt anything beyond turned on for any man, and at this point she assumed it was just how she was wired. Which, apparently, was vastly different from the head-over-heels-in-love women she was currently surrounded by.

"I'm so glad Boone decided to get married here," Trish said dreamily. "I couldn't have asked for a more romantic setting."

Elpitha was the epitome of romantic, but life moved too slow for Addy on the tiny island, and the Internet moved even slower. She needed excitement the way others craved downtime, which was what she loved most about living in New York City.

"Speaking of romance," Trish said conspiratorially, "Jake hasn't taken his eyes off of you all night."

Addy forced herself not to glance at Trish's older, arrogant, fast-talking, hotter-than-sin brother she'd been hard-core fantasizing about since she'd met him several months ago. She really needed to get him out of her head once and for all, because he was starting to mess with her mind. It didn't help that he hit on her every time they were together, which was often, because Addy joined Gabriella and Duke, along with several of his siblings—almost always including Jake—for drinks or dinner about every other week. Hopefully her ten days away would get the sexy player out of her head for good.

"Oh!" Trish exclaimed. "My *fiancé* is finally done dancing with my mom." She lowered her voice and said, "I can't get enough of saying that. *My fiancé*. I'll catch up with you soon. I want to get in his arms before one of Gabriella's pretty cousins tries to snatch him up."

Trish crossed the lawn with a bounce in her step, leaving Addy alone with her thoughts. A cool breeze swept up the bluff, lifting the hem of her royal-blue halter dress clear across her thighs. She felt the heat of Jake's gaze before she raised her eyes, catching sight of him striding confidently in her direction. Chin held high, eyes dark as night, every step full of potent male swagger, he zeroed in for another round of innuendos. The man had a homing device for all things sexual. Pretending not to notice the heat of his stare searing through her normally impenetrable nerves, she looked around for something to distract herself, wishing she had her phone so she could at least scroll through Tumblr. She'd spent more than a handful of nights trolling the naughty pages of nearly naked—*okay, and maybe a few naked*—men as a distraction from the one coming closer by the second.

Jake moved like a lion, stealthy and powerful, seemingly oblivious to the excited voices and laughter all around him as he patiently stalked his prey. Being hunted by a man who looked like he could take down a predator with one hand tied behind his back was an exhilaratingly dangerous feeling. And *hunted* was the only way to describe the way he came just close enough to mark his territory without physically staking claim. Not that Addy wanted him to stake claim.

That's not entirely true.

She'd like him to drive his stake into her but not *claim* her.

They'd been playing this seductive game for months, giving her plenty of time to decipher her feelings. Or rather, her *impulses.* Addy didn't *do* feelings toward men. But she couldn't deny that over the past few months she'd seen more in Jake than just his badassery and ability to weaken knees with a single glance. She'd come to admire the way he protected his siblings, was always there for his brothers' significant others, and the way he acknowledged the accomplishments of others, both male and female. Addy was used to working with men who were too wrapped up in themselves to see past their own noses, and she'd grown up with a father who had never allowed women the *need* to make decisions, much less accomplish anything significant.

She couldn't help comparing her understated father, who moved like the wind, silently handling every aspect of her and her mother's lives before they even had a chance to think, to Jake, a bull in a china shop with no airs about him. She admired Jake's open appreciation for both beauty and brains as much as she admired his brooding, alpha tendencies. She'd *love* to know if he packed the same dose of virility in between the sheets as he did when he was flirting. He had an edge about him that never seemed to soften. Even the appearance of a smile on his impossibly chiseled face knocked her off-kilter. It came across as a wicked invitation, one she'd like to take him up on, if not for the fact that he scared the shit out of her.

The spicy scent of Jake's cologne overrode the aroma of grilled meats and casseroles Gabriella's relatives had spent all day preparing. Jake rested his elbow on the bar beside her, brushing his muscular forearm against hers and sending ripples of awareness to her core.

Who was she kidding? There was no distracting herself from the biggest distraction of them all.

"I think there are still a few guys you haven't danced with."

Of course Jake would go straight to pushing her buttons.

"I'll have to take care of that, won't I? Gab's brother, Niko, is looking awfully hot tonight." Niko was the epitome of a Greek heartthrob. Tall, dark, handsome, and as touchy-feely as the rest of Gabriella's warm and loving family. He was also a shameless flirt.

Jake ground his teeth together, nearly paralyzing her with a blistering stare.

"I haven't seen you dance all night. What's the matter? Not into sexy island girls? Because I'm pretty sure that guy over there by the tree bats for the other team." She enjoyed taunting the lion, even if she didn't want to get too close. Her pulse beat wildly, and her fingers ached to grab him by the collar of his dress shirt and yank him down for what she knew would be an incredibly hot kiss. She tried to keep from dropping her eyes lower, but she was no match for the enticing ever-present bulge beneath his zipper. The one that became even more prominent when they were near. And damn, she liked knowing she had that effect on him.

He leaned in close, his warm breath coasting over her cheek. "I'm not into dancing, but if you keep looking at me like that you might find yourself getting up close and personal with more than you can handle."

She lifted her eyes to his, which had gone coal black, and she swallowed hard against the lust threatening to pour out of her mouth. Addy was used to controlling every interaction and reveled in holding her own and taking what she wanted where men were concerned. Or at least she always had, until the King of Hotness standing next to her came into the picture. Jake definitely threw her off her game. Lately, when they were together, she caught herself wondering if what she was experiencing were actual emotions rather than impulses. That was one thing that had kept her from taking their flirting to the next level. His relationship to her best friend was the other. But boy did she want to cross that line. It had been way too long since she had been with a man, thanks to *Jake*. Every time she came close to satisfying the urge to feel the weight of a man pressing down on her and get lost in the throes of passion, goddamn Jake swam into her mind, stealing her focus *and* killing the moment. Her fantasy had become her own personal cockblocker.

In an effort to reclaim the upper hand and prove he did *not* rattle her, she dragged her eyes over his chest again and said, "I have yet to meet a man who comes close to being *what* I can handle, much less *more*."

The edge of his lips twitched as if they might quirk up, but he clenched his jaw, making the muscles beneath his dark scruff jump. He shifted his eyes away just as Niko headed toward them with a warm and inviting smile, making those jaw muscles work double time.

Niko nodded at Jake and offered his hand to Addy. "What kind of brother would I be if I didn't dance with my sister's beautiful best friend? Care to join me?"

"I'd love to." Addy reached for his hand, taking pleasure in the tension rolling off of the man who had yet to ask her for a single dance but had no trouble inviting her into his bed.

IF JAKE HAD to watch one more guy dance with Addison he was going to murder someone. His hands fisted at his sides as yet *another* of Gabriella's relatives put his hands around

Addison's slim waist, holding her so close she could probably taste his breath. That thought grated like sandpaper beneath his skin. The only breath he wanted her thinking about was *his*. Between her thighs, preferably. Which was precisely why he needed to stop watching her.

He loosened his tie, forcing his eyes away from the woman who was seriously screwing with his mind. Jake wasn't big on weddings, but Duke had gone all out. The ceremony had taken place on a bluff overlooking the ocean, surrounded by their families and what seemed like the entire close-knit island community. Strings of sparkling white lights stretched clear across the bluff, illuminating the dance area, dozens of tables with floral centerpieces, and the awesome gazebo their brother, Blue, had built for the occasion. Hell if something inside Jake hadn't unexpectedly softened at the sight of his teary-eyed eldest brother pledging his eternal devotion to the woman he loved.

His eyes drifted back to Addison, dancing in a blue halter dress that hugged every inch of her slim, sexy body. *Just like Niko is doing.* Yet another tall, dark, and built dude to yank Jake's chain. Not that she was his to drool over. A relationship was definitely not in his plans. But that didn't stop the woman from sticking in his mind like an itch he couldn't scratch since the very first time he'd set eyes on her. Maybe it was her full, tempting lips that gave her a starring role in his dirty midnight fantasies. *Or maybe it's your goddamn vehemence about not needing a man in your life.*

Or, more specifically, not needing *him*.

Wanting, he corrected himself. Not *wanting* him.

Damn that stung.

Over the past several months, she'd met each of his innuendos with one of her own but had no trouble walking away without taking him up on them. That was probably a good thing since she was Gabriella's best friend, and he knew she was totally off-limits for a one-time hookup. But for some reason, he couldn't back off.

"You could ask her to dance."

Jake glanced at his older brother Cash. He'd been so lost in thought he hadn't even heard him approaching. He took in his serious brown eyes and his I-know-what-I'm-talking-about expression. Cash and his wife, Siena, had two-month-old twins, Charlotte "Coco" Rose and Seth, and somehow, when Jake added *father* to his brother's already impressive repertoire—fireman, loving husband, and protective older brother—it gave that look in his eyes even more credence. And that bugged Jake, too, because of his five siblings Cash had always been one of the easier kids. A *good* one. While Jake was definitely…*not.* Following in Cash's shadow had not been easy. His older brother's good-boy behavior made Jake's rebellious nature stand out even more. Usually Jake was cool with that, but tonight he was too irritated to be okay with anything short of Addison Dahl lying naked beneath him. Or maybe on her knees. *Yeah, that'd do just fine, too.*

"I'd ask her to dance if I *wanted* to dance, but the only kind of dancing I want to do is horizontal." He wasn't about to make his attraction to Addy out to be something it wasn't, despite the way she became tangled in his every thought. She was a hot chick he wanted to bang. An unattainable challenge. Nothing more.

At least that's what he told himself.

Lucky, Boone's eighteen-year-old brother, joined them at the bar. He had that bad-boy attitude girls his age dug, and his dark hair and eyes gave him an edgy biker look. The kid was brilliant, too. In the span of a few short hours he'd chatted Duke up about online marketing, told Blue about a software program he could tweak to maximize efficiency for his business, and gave Gage tips on how to fix his computer issues.

"Seriously?" Cash laughed. "Jake, you've been drooling over her for months, and you haven't been with another woman in how long, exactly?"

Long enough that hearing you say it makes me want to throttle you.

"You've gotta be talking about Addison." Lucky smirked. "She is so freaking hot, and man, Jake, if you don't want her..."

"Back off," Jake growled.

He never said he didn't *want* her. Addy was as frustrating as she was beautiful. He didn't know a woman alive who didn't need a man in her life. As an independent search and rescue professional handling rescues all over the United States, he knew all too well that there were times that called for sheer strength. But Addy had something to prove—to herself or to her family, Jake wasn't sure. She was also the complete opposite of the women he usually went for. Tall, blonde, a nice rack, and a firm ass were pretty much mandatory in his bed. Or at least they had been until he'd set eyes on the petite, small-breasted, sassy brunette who looked like she should be treated like fine china but spoke as though she could hold her own in a biker bar. Her no-bullshit attitude should probably turn him off, but it had the complete opposite effect. He could barely look at her without getting turned on, and Addy knew it. She taunted him as if she were offering honey to a bee—only she was the one with the stinger, and she never hesitated to use it. And now she'd gotten a bug up her sexy little butt about roughing it in the wilderness. She was leaving the day after tomorrow. That gave Jake two days to talk Addy out of her crazy plan so her stubborn, sexy ass didn't get injured, or lost. *Or picked up by a forest ranger.*

"*That's* how I know you're not just looking to get laid," Cash said.

Jake scoffed. "Getting laid is *exactly* what I'm looking for with Addy, only as Gabriella's best friend, she's not exactly fair game for a good time." *Good time?* He tried to ignore the voice in his head telling him that he wasn't fooling himself any more than he was fooling Cash. Addy's eyes found his, igniting the torch she'd planted the first time they'd met.

Niko's hand moved south, his fingertips grazing the base of her spine. Jake's gut knotted. *One more inch and I'll break those fingers.*

"She's only off-limits if she's not on the same page," Lucky said with a smirk.

Cash's pinched expression told Jake he did not agree, but Jake had already latched on to Lucky's nudge, and his mind was running with it.

"Better think long and hard about it, bro," Cash said. "If you make a move, don't make the wrong one."

Jake's gaze darted back to the woman toying with his emotions. Addy flashed a coy smile, licking her luscious lips and sending heat straight to his groin. Was she on the same page? After months of flirting to the point of leaving him blue-balled, could this be his lucky night? It was no secret that she talked about sex like she thrived on pushing her boundaries—boundaries Jake would be all too happy to shatter. Was Lucky right? If she was cool with a one-night stand, could he take her friendship with Gabriella off the table? Adrenaline coursed through him with the thought, followed closely by Cash's comment. Was there a right or wrong move when it came to a one-night stand?

Niko's hand slid lower. Addy's narrowing eyes were still glued to Jake. She arched a brow. The little minx. Casting a last taunting look at Jake, she flashed one of her gorgeous smiles up at Niko. Jake should look away, drown his desires in more alcohol, or hit on one of Gabriella's hot cousins to distract himself from whatever game she was playing. But his eyes were riveted to Addison moving sensually in another man's arms while she sent him challenging looks.

Fuck this shit. He set his glass on the bar.

"Where are you going?" Cash asked.

"To play librarian," Lucky answered for him.

"Damn straight." He was done dicking around. It was time to see exactly what page Addy was on.

CHAPTER TWO

ADDISON WAS PLAYING with fire and she knew it. Her breathing quickened with every determined step Jake took as he crossed the grass with a pissed-off, predatory look in his eyes. And hell if that didn't practically melt her panties right off. For months she'd done so well at refusing to cross the line between flirting with and fucking Gabriella's new brother-in-law. He was the last man she should even be thinking about in that way. But inevitably, her mind circled back to the big, brooding hunk who was currently eyeing Niko like he wanted to tear him to shreds. It wasn't Niko's fault she was flirting with Jake while dancing with him. *God, what is wrong with me?*

"Mind if I cut in?" Jake's deep voice left no room for opposition.

Niko glanced down at Addy. "You okay with that, Addy?"

Ever the gentleman.

She stared at Jake for a long moment before answering, reminding herself that all she had to do was make it for a couple more nights. Then she'd be on a mountain, away from their flirtatious banter, away from his piercing stare. And then she'd be back at home, where she could have her pick of willing men who were *not* related to her best friend.

Men who aren't you.

She swallowed hard, but the jagged image stuck with her.

That had been the problem for the past several months. She'd tried to work Jake out of her system, but it always came down to a competition between her fantasies of Jake and the men she chose as substitutes. Even never having shared one blessed kiss with him, Jake always won.

Jake's gaze never wavered from hers. She was surprised Niko's hands weren't burned by the electricity sizzling between them. They really needed to just get down and dirty once and for all, to get it out of their systems before they spontaneously combusted.

Jake narrowed his eyes, silently willing her to respond.

She let the silence linger for another minute, torturing them both. When the song came to an end, she went up on her toes and kissed Niko's cheek, earning another death stare from Jake. "Thanks, Niko. I enjoyed our dance."

"Anytime, beautiful." Niko nodded at Jake. "She's a great dancer. Hope you don't have two left feet."

The semi grunt coming from Jake as he tugged Addy against him pretty much said it all. *Whoa.* Not quite as well as his hard body did.

"Thought you didn't dance," she said as *he* positioned her hands around his neck. She stifled a laugh as she lowered them to his waist. *Controlling much?*

"I said I wasn't *into* dancing." He moved her hands around his neck again. "But I want to get *into* you."

Holy cow. It was one thing to hear his tempting teases when they were in a crowded bar with Gabriella and a group of friends, but to be in his arms, so close she could feel every inch of his arousal against her? She needed some serious Jake repellant to withstand this type of torture.

He flattened his hand on her lower back as the next song

began. His long fingers splayed over the curve of her ass. His eyes remained trained on hers as he led their sensual moves. Addy loved to dance. She'd honed the ability to seduce a man from across the room with nothing more than a few dirty-dancing moves. But, good Lord, she had nothing on Jake. The man moved like he owned her. His hips rocked in slow, sensual, and precise thrusts, smooth as butter and wicked as sin. One hand remained on her back, the other slid to the top of her spine, his fingers pressing into the base of her neck, holding her body flush with his in all the best places. Every move brought slithers of heat, ramping up her arousal. No wonder he didn't want her hands around his waist. This position gave Jake full control. Sliding his knee between Addy's legs, he created delicious friction. And his eyes…They were merciless, caressing her, sending silent messages of wanton thoughts directly to her brain that made her want to give in.

He towered over her, even bigger and broader than he appeared. She'd stood beside him dozens of times and had no trouble verbally sparring and walking away. But now, dancing within his strong embrace, feeling his glorious muscles pressed against her, his intoxicating scent infiltrating her lungs, her *skin*, her very being, she felt herself falling under his spell. No woman was strong enough to resist six plus feet of pure, unadulterated seduction.

He lowered his face until his hot breath whispered over her cheek, as he'd done earlier. He was a master at this. The *king* of seduction. They probably had his picture in the dictionary as the definition of the word.

"Ready to stop playing games with boys and take it from a real man?"

His cockiness snapped her mind back into gear—and

turned her on beyond belief. She liked a man who knew how to give and take in equal measure. *Real* men were few and far between. Most men turned into kittens looking for direction when they hit the mattress. Or they hurried through sex like it was a race instead of what could be the most pleasurable experience of a lifetime. Not that she had yet experienced the dirtiest-talking, most multi-orgasm-inducing, thrilling man on the planet, but she knew he had to exist. After all, Gabriella had found Duke, and from what her bestie had told her, he was as naughty as he was nice. Even still, Duke was a little *too* nice for Addy's tastes.

As if he'd read her mind, Jake tugged her harder against him, flashing another haughty grin. "Not up for the challenge? I figured your imagination was too big for your—"

She slid her hand from his neck to his cheek. She'd been dying to touch his sexy scruff for months. The muscles in his jaw softened against her palm, erasing his arrogant grin, and his touch lightened against her skin. Oh, her big, brooding alpha turned soft when faced with feminine wiles. *Good to know.*

"My imagination is *wilder…*" she said in a husky whisper, drawing out the last word into two, lustful syllables. "*Hotter…*" She ran her finger along his jaw to his lower lip. "Than you could even *begin* to toy with."

His lips pressed into a tight line, but his eyes turned to liquid heat. Desire pooled low in her belly, sizzling and rising as she continued taunting him, tracing her finger along the seam of his lips. When his lips parted, she touched the center of them, and slowly—*torturously* slowly—went up on her tiptoes as he bent toward her. Her lips hovered a breath beneath his. In her peripheral vision she caught a glimpse of Gabriella dancing with Duke. Guilt whirled inside her, battling against the urge to take the kiss she so desperately wanted. Gabriella knew Addy enjoyed a healthy sex life that didn't often include repeats. Or at least she had, before Jake came into the picture. But getting down and dirty with her brother-in-law might be crossing a line, and the consequences could hit too close to home.

Jake held her tighter. The length of his arousal pressed into her belly, tempting her even more. Addy was prepared for their incessant flirting. It had become a game between them, one she craved and revisited often in the darkness of her bedroom, where she took the flirting even further, to where she could feel his long, hard cock in her hands, her mouth, between her legs, pushing inside of her, filling her so completely—

"You know you want this, Addison." Jake's lips brushed over her cheek, snapping her mind back to the moment.

She'd been so lost in her fantasy her cheeks burned. Her eyes darted beneath the shimmering lights to the couples dancing around them. What was she thinking? Everyone could see them. There would be uncomfortable questions to answer if she continued to get lost in him. Straightening her spine, she placed her hands on his cheeks, taking one last, long feel of them before sliding her hands to his chest. His heart thundered against her palms, mimicking the erratic beat of her own. His fingers pressed into her skin so hard she wondered if she'd have marks tomorrow, piquing her interest even further. This man was no kitten. It was all right there within her grasp. One night with a real man, a man who knew how to push all her buttons. One night with the man of her dreams.

Anticipation trickled in, bringing pinpricks to her flesh. But what if they somehow didn't have a good time? What if they pissed each other off, and then things were awkward tomorrow? She couldn't chance it. They saw each other too often with

Gabriella and Duke and the others. She loved being part of that close-knit group. She'd come to depend on the friendships she'd developed with Trish and Cash's wife, Siena. Even the few times his brother Blue and Blue's fiancée, Lizzie, had joined them they'd hit it off right away. She couldn't risk all of that for one night of hot sex.

She noticed Gabriella and Duke were no longer slow dancing but dancing to a faster beat. *Great.* The song had changed and she hadn't even noticed. She and Jake were still dancing like they were naked and he was about to bend her over for a hard, thrusting *dip*!

His mother waved as she and his father danced by. "You two dance like you've been partners forever."

Oh God, your parents! She loved his parents. They were down-to-earth and funny and…*so* not going to like it if she toyed with their boy. Everyone knew mommy claws were deadly regardless of how grown up their children were. Well, everyone except her own mother, who never had a chance to worry her pretty little head about anything.

Jake's breath slid between her lips, bringing with it the taste of alcohol, reeling her fuzzy mind toward submission. What the hell? Addison Dahl did not *submit* to any man.

Pressing hard against his iron pecs, she forced space between them. His eyes filled with confusion and, seconds later, annoyance, which only made him look hotter. Yeah, she was totally screwed up, and not because of alcohol. She'd had too much Jake-flavored Kool-Aid. Time to pull her head out of her ovaries and regain control.

Squaring her shoulders, she put on her best not-interested smile, which at the moment felt more like I-want-to-lick-every-inch-of-you, and said, "Thanks for the dance, Jake."

She spun on her heels and made a beeline for the bar.

THE NIGHT CRAWLED by like a three-legged centipede. Cash and Siena took off early to put the twins to bed, and the dance floor remained packed until close to midnight, when Duke and Gabriella finally called it a night. Amid a flurry of cheers and rose petals thrown from baskets Gabriella's aunts had prepared, they walked down the hill toward their bungalow hand in hand. That started a long, slow procession of each of Gabriella's extended family—apparently all Elpitha residents are considered related—hugging and thanking each of the Ryders. Jake had never been embraced by so many handsy women in his life. Each whispered bits of advice he'd never asked for. *Time for you to find a wife. A handsome man like you? Single? I have a beautiful niece for you to meet.* They were not exactly subtle, and from what Jake could discern, his older brother Gage was getting an earful as well. Only Gage's advice was focused on his relationship with Sally, his longtime best friend and coworker at No Limitz, a community center in Colorado, *and* his wedding date, whom everyone knew he was desperately in love with. Everyone except maybe Sally. If you asked Jake, it was time for Gage to stop dicking around and make a move. But Gage didn't talk about his relationship with Sally, and Jake wasn't about to push his way into his brother's business. Gage was another of the Ryder *good boys*, or that's what everyone thought. Sure, he and Duke had spent as much time with their noses in books as they had with their appendages in women when they were younger, but they were discreet about their extracurricular activities, whereas Jake had never seen a need to be discreet. He took what he wanted with consenting adult women, when he wanted it, and didn't care what anyone thought.

Except when it came to Addy.

Pushing the thought he didn't want to analyze aside, he focused on Blue, who was crouched beside a buffet table, inspecting its broken leg. He, Boone, and Jake had carried the broken table inside the villa to check it out after two of Gabriella's cousins had knocked into it when they were horsing around.

"We can shore this up in no time tomorrow." Blue pushed to his feet and patted Boone's shoulder. "Just in time for your wedding."

Boone grinned like a fool in love, which was fitting since he was marrying their sister. Boone had met Trish on the set of his first film, *No Strings*, in which Trish had a starring role. It was no surprise that the media was buzzing about Trish's Oscar-winning performance, but it had shocked everyone when Boone had knocked his debut role out of the park and his name had been added to the award-worthy gossip. Boone, it seemed from what he'd shared with them, had endured a torturous revisiting of his past, and he credited Trish for having helped him bring those emotions into his acting. Knowing Jake's pushy sister, Jake was sure he was right.

"We don't need a buffet table," Boone said. "All we need is someone to pronounce us husband and wife—and to blow up that boat full of paparazzi. Man, I feel horrible about them stalking Duke's wedding. I hope our plan works." He nodded toward the ocean as they headed back outside. The paparazzi had caught wind of Trish and Boone on the island, and although they had security on the perimeter, a single boat of reporters lingered offshore. Duke and Boone had arranged for two models to arrive on the island later that morning, and at some point before dawn tomorrow, disguised as Boone and Trish, they would leave on a boat, with plans to hop from boat to plane to boat, and run the press around until well after Trish and Boone's wedding took place.

They stepped outdoors, and Jake was glad the party had finally cleared out. His gaze immediately found Addy sitting between Lizzie and Niko at a table with Trish, Sally, and Gage. It had been hours since Addy had walked away from their dance and his proposition. She'd spent the last few hours drinking and dancing with the girls, except for now, when she was all fluttery lashes and sexy smiles aimed at Niko.

Niko leaned closer to her and said something that made her laugh.

Her laugh was a little breathy and melodic, and it made Jake's stomach go funky.

"Liar!" Addy pushed a shot glass toward Niko. "Drink up."

Things just got a little more interesting.

Niko splayed his hands, his dark eyes dancing around the table. "Me? A liar? What about you?" he asked Addy. "Have *you* had sex on a beach?"

"It's not her turn," Trish answered.

Jake looked at the two open bottles of tequila and the shot glasses strewn across the table and realized they were playing a drinking game. How long had he been inside the villa? He homed in on Addy, awaiting her answer and praying it was *no*, because there was a hell of a lot of beach just waiting to be christened. And he knew the perfect man for the job.

"Finally something I've done!" Lizzie clapped.

"Jesus." Blue moved behind Lizzie and whispered something in her ear that made her giggle. Helping her to her feet, he said,

"I think my girl's had enough to drink. We'll see you guys tomorrow."

"Drink up, Niko." Trish pushed to her feet to hug Lizzie, wobbling a little. "See you guys tomorrow."

"Looks like I better take Trish home, too," Boone said. "Before she needs to be carried down the hill."

Lizzie snuggled against Blue as they walked toward the dirt road. There were no cars on the island, only bicycles and golf carts, which suited Jake just fine. He hated to feel confined, and at around eight square miles, the island was barely big enough for a good run.

Trish wrapped her arms around Boone's neck and hung on him. "You love carrying me. *Fake impregnator.*"

Jake raised a brow in question.

"Don't ask." Boone swept Trish into his arms and followed Blue and Lizzie.

Gage pushed another shot across the table to Niko. "There's no way you've never done it on the beach. You *live* on the beach."

"Yeah, with an island full of nosy relatives. But if you don't believe me, I'll take the hit." Niko tossed back both shots and turned a heated, glassy gaze on Addy. "You could help me change my answer."

Over my dead body.

Jake was beside Addy in half a second and sank down into the seat Lizzie had vacated next to her, draping a proprietary arm around the back of her chair. He scoffed at the icy stare Addy pinned on him and palmed the curve of her shoulder. Oh yeah, that felt nice.

"Sorry, man. I didn't know you two were together," Niko said, rising to his feet. "I'd better take off before I get my ass kicked."

Damn right. Jake tossed him a friendly, "See ya, Niko," without taking his eyes off Addy.

"I didn't know you two were together, either," Sally said, glancing at Gage.

Gage shook his head. "Don't look at me."

Addy was busy peeling Jake's hand off her shoulder. "We are *not* together."

Gage laughed. Sally blushed. But Addy continued glaring at Jake like she couldn't believe what he was insinuating. He couldn't believe it either, but hell, he might as well go with it. Filling another shot glass, he pushed it in front of her.

"Drink up, sexy girl."

Her jaw gaped, and just as quickly, she schooled her expression. Her eyes narrowed with defiance. "You only have to drink when you lie." She set the drink in front of him. "You should be drunk all the time."

He moved the glass in front of her again, leaning in so close it took every shred of his restraint not to claim that sexy mouth of hers and show her just how much she was missing out on. He was vaguely aware of Gage and Sally saying they were taking off, and waved a hand in their direction, unwilling to look away from the woman before him. His eyes dropped to the frantic pulse beating at the base of her neck. He'd like to suck that throbbing vein between his teeth and feel her fingernails dig into him as he did it.

Meeting her gaze, he said, "I don't lie."

Her eyes darkened, and the tip of her tongue slid across her lower lip. She raised a perfectly manicured brow. "Oh no?"

"I never said you were with me. That was their assumption. *Your* assumption. Or maybe your *wish*."

She searched his eyes. The lights from above reflected in hers. "Really? You don't lie?"

"Really."

"You didn't lie three months ago when we were all at NightCaps and you told Blue it'd been weeks since you'd gotten laid?"

He cringed. "You heard that?" When he'd answered Blue, it had been four weeks since he'd had sex. The stubborn, sexy girl sitting beside him now had refused another of his propositions two weeks and six days prior to that night. He remembered it well, because that was the night he'd cornered her by the bathroom and she'd hesitated for so long before denying him, he'd thought she was finally going to give in. He hadn't been able to think of anyone but her ever since.

"Everyone at the table heard it." She smirked. "Truth or lie?"

Fuck. He'd sound like a pussy if he answered honestly.

She rolled her eyes and handed him the shot. "Drink it, liar."

"That's kind of harsh, don't you think?"

She crossed her arms and pursed her lips.

"Wait a minute. Why do you even remember that?" Man, did he like knowing she'd been thinking about him just as he'd been thinking about her. Well, maybe not in the same naked, kinky ways he had, but he'd at least been on her mind.

She shifted her eyes away. "Drink, jackoff."

"That's quite a mouth you have there, sexy girl."

"Like that bothers you." She knocked back a shot, closing her eyes as she swallowed. She set the glass down hard on the table, licked her lips, and arched a brow again.

His girl loved a challenge. He pressed his leg against hers, testing the waters. When she didn't move away, he added a hand on her thigh. "Actually, I like your dirty mouth very much."

"Jake..." Her eyes dropped to his mouth, lingering there long enough for him to think about all the things he wanted to do with hers.

"Yes, sexy girl?" He squeezed her thigh, feeling her muscles flex beneath his hand. He inched his fingers higher, to the hem of her dress, and squeezed again.

"Does this usually work for you?" she asked with a sarcastic lilt to her voice. "All that 'sexy girl' stuff, and talking about dirty mouths?"

He grinned, ignoring her question, because hell, it was ridiculous. They both knew how to get what they wanted, and he wasn't about to admit that he'd never called another woman *sexy girl* in his life.

"What do you want me to do with *my* mouth, Addison?" He let that question hang between them, his fingertips grazing her inner thigh. "Do you want me to drop to my knees and pleasure you? Make you come on my tongue while you claw at my shoulders?"

She let out a long, slow breath, as if she was thinking about it.

"Oh, you like that idea, don't you?" They'd teased each other for so long it should feel normal, but he'd never taken it this far as to spell out exactly what he wanted to do to her. But he was done pussyfooting around. He used to be able to flirt at the drop of a dime with any woman who caught his eye. Now no one but Addy ever caught his eye. She'd ruined his ability to flirt with other women.

She placed her hand on top of his, squeezing his fingers into her flesh. "Probably about as much as you like the idea of me on *my* knees pleasuring you."

"You are a dirty, dirty girl." He took a strand of her hair and wound it around his fingers.

Her eyes sparked with a *dark* challenge. "Have I ever alluded to being anything else?"

No, you sure as hell haven't, but you've denied me every time I made a move.

Tonight she appeared to be dipping her toe in the *Jake and Addy* water. *About damn time.* They said weddings made women want in ways they never had, but he knew Addy had wanted him long before the wedding, even if she refused to let herself go there. It was in *his* mind that he was seeing more than a one-night stand in their future, and it had nothing to do with the wedding and everything to do with the sensual, witty, challenging woman before him.

He tugged that luxurious dark strand of hair until it was taut. Her hand tightened around his, but she didn't lean forward to ease the sting he knew he was causing, telling him more than that sassy mouth of hers ever could. The daring gaze never faltered, exuding confidence like no woman he'd ever met. The vibe she emitted was fierce, determined, and one hundred percent sexual, reeling Jake in like a fish to water.

He leaned closer.

She didn't budge.

He pushed his hand beneath her hair, holding tightly to that strand as he grasped the back of her neck and tugged her toward him. Her eyes widened just a little. If he hadn't been looking for it he might have missed it. But he was *this close* to making Addy *his*, and he refused to miss a thing.

"Jake." The warning came across loud and clear.

He nudged his knee between her legs, and with a hand around her waist, tugged her forward, so their legs were intertwined, their faces so close he could smell her shampoo. Jesus, he was breathing hard. How many months had he wanted to do this? To feel her body trembling, hear her breath hitch, for *him*?

"Gabby and Duke," she said breathlessly.

"Will never know," he answered, pausing long enough to give her time to protest.

"We can't screw this up."

"I never screw up sex." He brushed his thumb along her jaw. "Scared, sexy girl?"

Her eyes narrowed. "Never."

"What, then?"

She pressed her lips together, then opened them as if to speak, but no words came. Vulnerability flashed in her eyes, and in the next breath that innocence was gone, replaced with ferocity she couldn't feign. She wanted this just as badly as he did. *Thank fucking God* she'd finally hit her breaking point.

But he'd seen that moment of hesitation.

He'd felt it in the way her body tensed, and not the good kind of tense. The oh-fuck-what-am-I-doing kind. Jake was a lot of things, and cocky asshole was probably near the top of the list as far as women were concerned. But he'd never take a woman against her will. He slowed down long enough to gaze into her beautiful eyes and make sure he wasn't misreading her approval. Was she simply meeting a challenge? Would she do that? Give herself over rather than back away simply to prove she could?

She was looking at him like she wanted to devour him, licking her lips like she couldn't wait. All the right signals were staring back at him. But that moment of hesitation, no matter how short-lived, held him back. His body pushed him to take, take, *take*. It was what he did, what he excelled at, what he *knew*.

But this was Addison.

The woman he'd fantasized about for months on end.

His brother's wife's best friend.

A friend *he* cared about.

Shit. He hadn't really picked *that* apart before. He'd always thought of Addy as Gabriella's friend. Once removed. But she was his friend, too. Hadn't she called him when she wanted to surprise Gabriella for her birthday and asked him to help by keeping Duke busy while they set up the surprise? She could have asked Trish, or Cash, or Blue. But she'd called him. *Jake, I need you.* He'd actually thought it was a booty call, and he'd told her it was about time she realized she needed a real man in her life. He'd been thinking, *in her bed*, but he'd bitten his tongue. She'd set him straight then, too. *Wishful thinking, big guy. I don't want or need a man like you in my life.* They'd argued that point. And he'd hung up wondering why the hell they'd argued. He hadn't been looking to be any woman's man. And then he'd helped keep Duke busy, as she'd asked, and they'd gone right back to being friends who toyed with each other's emotions.

This was totally fucked up.

She was watching him with that bold look in her eyes, waiting for his next move. For the first time in his life, he wasn't sure what that move should be.

"Addy," he pretty much growled. "Do you *want* me to kiss you?" Where the hell did that come from? He couldn't remember *ever* asking a woman's permission before kissing her.

She blinked several times, as if he were speaking another language, and then she was kissing him. Her hands were in his hair, and she was moaning into their kiss. She was so fucking hot, he didn't hesitate to devour her eager mouth. She moved even more sensually than he'd imagined, hard and hungry, arching against him like she couldn't get enough. And *damn*, he definitely wanted more. His arm circled her waist, and he lifted her onto his lap, taking the kiss deeper. She was so petite his hand nearly covered the width of her back, and he had the strange, intrusive thought that if he wasn't careful, he might break her. She rocked against him, her sweet ass creating mind-blowing friction.

The lights strewn above them suddenly went out, and they both pulled away, breathless and panting. Instinct sent his arms protectively around her as he scanned the area. They were alone beneath the starry sky, the sounds of distant waves breaking through the darkness. It took Jake's lust-addled brain a minute to remember the lights were on a timer. Breathing a little easier, he ran his hands over her soft curves. A salty breeze swept up the hill, blowing a lock of Addy's long brown hair across her face. He tucked it behind her ear, feeling the softness of her cheek against his fingers. Addy had that vulnerable look about her again. Her cheeks were flushed, her lips swollen from their kisses. Gone was the take-charge vixen he knew her to be, causing his chest to feel full.

"Jesus, you're beautiful." The words came easily, taking him—and by the shock in her widening eyes, Addy—by surprise. He'd thought it many times, but man, those words sure felt powerful coming out of his mouth. Jake loved the soft, feminine feel of women. But in his mind, he had always lumped them into a group. *Women.* Realization hit him like a kick in the gut. He was noticing *her*, not the gender she was born into. He ran his hands along the length of her arms, soaking in the feel of her warm skin and trying to chase away the *Addiness* in her and fit her back into the general category with which he was comfortable.

As if she realized this lowering of the veil, she drew her shoulders back, and a cavalier laugh sailed from her lips. She glanced down at their bodies. Her dress was bunched around her thighs, her legs straddling his lap. "A little late to be buttering me up, don't you think?"

To cover up his momentary lapse in emotional control, he scoffed and tugged her in for another passionate kiss.

CHAPTER THREE

ADDY'S MIND SAID, *Slow down. Think, think, think.* But her body had completely disconnected. It had hung up the phone, thrown out the memo, and was sprinting toward the finish line. The lust that had coiled deep in her belly at the first touch of Jake's lips had swelled, flooding her veins, her limbs, and seeping out her pores. His big, hungry mouth consumed her as his hands roved and teased. And her hands followed suit, exploring his incredibly hard chest, while her very lonely girly parts enjoyed another deliciously hard part of his anatomy.

He fisted his hand in her hair and bit down on her lower lip, hard enough to sting. She cried out and he stopped cold.

"Too hard?"

"Never."

She barely got the word out before he was kissing her again, ravishing every crevice of her mouth, then moving on to her jaw, her neck, her shoulder, nibbling and sucking, abrading her skin with his whiskers, while hanging on tight to her hair. She closed her eyes, enjoying each and every sensation: the exquisite sting on her scalp, the wetness of his tongue, sharpness of his teeth, and most of all, the low, appreciative groans he made as he took his fill. He clutched her hip, still gripping her hair, holding her as she ground against him and rocking up to meet her efforts. *This* was what she craved and what no man had been able to give. Raw, untethered passion. Manliness, and not the whip-me-baby kind. No, Addy wasn't about to be anyone's submissive, but she liked strength and virility, the feel of a man's rough hands on her skin, the repositioning of her body exactly where he wanted it, the hard pounding between her legs. When he'd asked her if she wanted him to kiss her, she'd wondered if she'd made the wrong decision teasing him as she had. If there was one thing she'd had enough of, it was men who pretended to be one thing when in reality they were the exact opposite. She was thrilled to find that Jake knew how to take control, and she was surprised to realize that she was also strangely touched that he'd sought her approval.

He released her hair, and she grabbed both of his hands. She soaked in the look of surprise in his dark, hungry eyes as she captured his mouth. A torrent of excitement swept through her. Taking rather than giving was her second favorite thing. And *take* she did, claiming him in another scorching kiss, nipping at his scruffy jaw. Releasing his hands, she worked open the buttons on his shirt, and he watched, those deep-set eyes drinking her in as his hips created a perfect rhythm beneath her. God, she loved that.

She tore open his shirt, sending the last few buttons flying across the lawn and baring his glorious muscles, hidden only by a dusting of dark chest hair. Her eyes slid to the Superman tattoo on his left arm. She'd seen it before, and she was dying to know what it meant to him, but there was no way she was slowing down to ask. Not when there were lickable abs in reach. Another flick of her eyes to his intense stare brought a resurgence of desire. She lowered her mouth to his nipple and bit down.

"Fuck, Addy." His hips bolted off the chair, sending her

hands to his biceps to steady herself.

His arms were as hard as steel, just like in her fantasies, only a million times better.

"Again," he growled.

Oh yeah, Jake definitely wasn't all talk, no action. She repeated her assault on the other side, and he hissed out a curse. She laved her tongue over the bite, then sucked that tight peak. A long, low groan rumbled up his chest, vibrating against her mouth.

He clutched her hips, forcing his words through gritted teeth. "Why did we wait so long to do this?"

Her eyes snapped up to his, her heart stuttering at the answer she was trying not to think about. "Why do you have to talk?"

He flashed an arrogant grin.

Her mind reeled back to all the times he'd propositioned her, cornering her in bars when they were out with friends, whispering in her ear as they left clubs. One thing had been constant, and it had been enough to hold her back from accepting his offers. Gabriella had always been present, an important reminder that she shouldn't have a one-night stand with someone who was soon to be—now was—her best friend's *family*. But now that she'd tasted his kisses, felt his power, she was past the point of no return. She wanted him. *All* of him. And there was only one way she could get through this without guilt stopping her at every turn.

"No talking."

He arched a brow. "Seriously?"

"Yes. Unless you'd rather I stopped."

He swept a hand toward his body, offering himself up. She lowered her mouth to his chest again, but damn it, her mind was stuck on the reason she'd always held back.

She breathed him in, loving his potent musky scent, and closed her eyes, trying to get back into the moment. She concentrated on the feel of his hot skin, the way his heart beat hard and steady against her lips. But with every kiss, every touch, she worried about the ramifications of their hookup. She sat up again, needing guidelines, rules, expectations, and earning another arched brow from the incredibly sexy man beneath her.

"This isn't going anywhere," she said flatly.

"Seemed like we were on the right track." He sat up straighter and placed a kiss to the exposed skin between her breasts.

She melted a little at the tenderness of the kiss, which further rattled her. Addy didn't *melt*.

"I mean *us*, Jake. This is just one night to get it out of our systems. Nothing more."

His jaw clenched for only a second. She might have imagined it.

"Works for me." Gripping her hips harder, he lowered his mouth to her neck.

"Your brother is married to my best friend. We..." Good Lord, he knew just how hard to suck. "We can't let this get awkward." He continued his oral assault while he untied her halter from behind her neck. The royal-blue material slid down her breasts, and he grazed his teeth along the overly sensitive tip of the taut peak.

She clung to his head, holding him to her as she struggled to remain coherent enough to speak. "I mean it, Jake," she panted out. "If we do this..." *If?*

His hand pushed up her thigh, and his thumb brushed over her panties. She was breathing too hard. Her mind flitted away with every stroke of his thumb, every slick of his tongue.

"They can't know." She closed her eyes as his thumb snuck beneath her panties. "Jake." He continued teasing, moving to the other breast as he stroked her most sensitive nerves, thrusting his fingers deep inside her. She gasped at the exquisite intrusion, but lingering in the recesses of her mind was the need to know he'd heard her.

"Jake!" She grabbed his wrist and he leaned back, looking annoyed. "Do you even hear me?"

"I'm busy, not deaf," he said sternly.

"This is important. I need to know you won't let things get awkward, or brag about this."

"I assure you," he said, his fingers moving adeptly inside of her, stroking the spot that made her toes curl under, "there will be no awkward naked moments or bragging."

She squeezed his wrist, a smile curving her lips despite herself. She couldn't help it. She loved that he was as much of a smart-ass as she was. "I mean *tomorrow*." She tried not to think too hard, because after the way the thought of tomorrow had stolen her concentration just now, she didn't want to chance getting sidetracked again. She wanted this with Jake. Hell, she'd wanted it for so long she was surprised she had enough rational thought left to think about the consequences at all. She just needed this assurance. Then she could go back to having her way with Mr. Sinful Pleasures.

He withdrew his hand from between her legs and gripped her thighs again. "I thought we were both on the same page. That this is a hookup."

Why did that sting? "We are. I was just making sure."

"No second thoughts?" His expression turned serious.

"No. As long as you're not going to get all weird and jealous, like you did with Niko." She was not new to one-night stands, and she wasn't worried about feeling regretful tomorrow, because this was *her* decision, and she was going in with her eyes wide open. *Aren't I?* She hoped she really *could* keep this to a one-night stand. But one thing was certain. She couldn't risk making things uncomfortable for Gabriella and her family.

JAKE CLENCHED HIS jaw. He'd been as shocked as she was over his jealousy. It had been a momentary lapse in judgment, that was all, but he had trouble making that feel true. Thinking fast to cover his tracks, he said, "That wasn't jealousy. I was protecting you."

She crossed her arms, looking hotter than hell with her breasts perched high and a scowl on her magnificent mouth. "Protecting me?"

"From making a mistake. A guy like Niko is looking for a wife, and you've made it clear that relationships aren't your thing."

She seemed to think about that, her expression serious. He hoped like hell she believed it, because it was partially true. Niko had said he hoped to find the right woman to marry soon, and she'd made no bones about the fact that she'd never been a relationship girl.

She huffed out a breath and her arms dropped to her sides. "How kind of you." Each word dripped with sarcasm. "But I don't need protecting."

"Every woman needs protecting," he said sharply.

"Jake! I'm not arguing this ridiculous point with you *again*. I have no idea what I'll do ten minutes from now, much less tomorrow. I might meet a guy I'm interested in, and I don't want to worry about you getting all weird about it."

"I promise you, sexy girl. Once we do this, the only thing you'll want tomorrow is a rerun of tonight. You'll feel me with every move you make. And flirting with any other guy won't even enter that bright mind of yours, because every single thought will bring you back to me." Holy fuck, he wanted that. He wanted that so badly he vowed to make it happen.

She laughed. "You're an ass, you know that?"

That laugh, that smile… "So I've been told."

He eyed her breasts and realized she had absolutely no embarrassment sitting there half naked in front of him. He liked that a whole hell of a lot. Until he thought about it a little more, bringing all her sassy attitude into focus, and realized she must have been naked with a lot of other guys. Another unfamiliar wave of jealousy hit him, and it took all his focus to push past it.

"I will *not* think of you in that way after tonight," she said firmly. "Just reassure me you won't get weird."

"No worries in that department, sexy girl." Okay, so *that* was an outright lie. There was no way he could rein in his jealousy after this. He had no idea what was going on in his fucked-up head, but there was no way he was turning back when everything he wanted was right there in front of him.

"Okay," she said, her voice a little less confident. "Because after tonight you'll be safely in the friend-I've-done zone. No repeats. No weirdness."

He nearly choked on the urge to ask her how many friends she'd *done*. But he wasn't about to go there and screw up his one chance with her.

"Any other questions?" He moved lower and flicked his tongue over her nipple.

"No. Stop talking and get busy." She closed her eyes as he chuckled, and he drew her nipple against the roof of his mouth.

"God I love that," she said breathlessly.

Grinding her ass against him, arching her back, she held on to his biceps, making his entire body throb. A flurry of thoughts raced through his mind. He wanted her naked, beneath him in his bed, on all fours, in the shower. He wanted her every which way he could have her, but they were outside, and he had only two condoms in his wallet. He never left the house unprepared, but *nothing* could have prepared him for the onslaught of emotions bowling him over at the thought of a single night with Addy.

He had to break free from whatever craziness was taking over his mind, and treat her as if she were any other one-night stand and not the woman he'd dreamed of sinking deep inside every damn night of the week. Wrapping his hands around her ribs, he lifted her from his lap and set her on the table. She grabbed his open shirt and tore it the rest of the way down his arms.

"Off," she said in one long breath.

He looked around the property again. Save for the distant sounds of the ocean and the rustling of the leaves, there were no signs of life. The bluff was high above the rest of the town, and the enormous villa was used only for celebrations. They were definitely alone. Still, he felt compelled to make sure she was still cool with where they were. "Are you okay right here?"

She was reaching for the button on his pants and stopped, giving him a deadpan stare. "I'm sitting on a table with my boobs hanging out and *now* you ask me?"

"Hey, we've been a little sidetracked."

She tugged at his button. "Stop worrying about me. I'm a

big girl. I want this, so hurry up before I change my mind."

He pushed her legs apart and stepped between them, drawing her against him. A hot ache grew in his throat as unexpected emotions piled up inside him. He slanted his mouth over hers, kissing her hard to chase them away, but they burrowed deeper inside him. She wrapped her legs around his waist with a needy moan. Cupping her face between his hands, he drew back just far enough to gaze into her beautiful eyes, taking his time to really *see* her. The longing look in her eyes, her parted, glistening lips, and the flush of heat on her cheeks brought another tidal wave of unfamiliar emotions. He rode the wave this time, battling the need to push it away and reveling in the way they made him feel. He expected this to be a fast, reckless fuck, not a lesson in being careful what he wished for.

"Don't change your mind, Addy. Not about this." He wanted to say about *us* but chickened out. He was no longer sure why he thought he'd ever be able to walk away from her after this.

Heat pulsed in the silence, and something in her eyes told him she was feeling their overwhelming connection, too.

"I won't. I want you, Jake."

He helped her off with her dress, spreading it out behind her, over the tablecloth, his mind fully absorbed in the intimacy of the moment. She was gorgeous, looking up at him with those big hazel eyes, watching his every move as he withdrew his wallet and the condoms from within and set them beside her. His eyes raked down her body to a small tattoo between her left hip and the juncture of her thighs. She inhaled a jagged breath, looking vulnerable again, and his heart took notice, slowing him down.

"What's this?" He ran his fingers over the inked image of something tangled up in chains. It was too dark to make out the details of the design.

She swept his fingers away, a look of discomfort in her eyes. "Nothing. Hurry up."

Making a mental note of the nerve he'd struck, he stepped from his clothes. Keeping one hand on her knee, unwilling to completely break their connection, he took her in his arms. He was surprised to feel her trembling.

"Cold?" he whispered in her ear.

She shook her head.

He touched his lips to hers, kissing her slow and deep, and enjoying it immensely. *Slow* and *Jake* had never gone hand in hand, but the unexpected vulnerability Addy had revealed made him want to be careful with her.

"I really dig kissing you, sexy girl," he murmured, and felt her smile as he kissed her again, harder this time, more possessive.

But kissing her wasn't enough, and before long he was kissing a trail down her neck and between her breasts, over her taut belly, to the tender skin below her belly button. He lingered there, loving the way her stomach quivered beneath his touch. He wanted to touch and taste every inch of her gorgeous body, but he was too impatient. His body pulsed with greed, wanting all of her at once, and he splayed his hands over her thighs, spreading them farther apart, enjoying the hitching of her breath as he brought his mouth to her sweet center.

"Oh, God, *Jake*." She writhed against him, grabbing at his shoulders.

When he brought his fingers into play, she made a long, low, pleasure-filled sound that was so erotic he wanted more. He ate at her, teasing and searching for the magical spots that would send her spiraling into oblivion. Her legs flexed, her hips rose off the table, and she curled her fingers into his skin, giving in to the passion between them.

"Jake—"

Her body quivered and quaked, shuddering through her climax. He stayed with her, riding the wave with her, until she fell back limp and breathless. He held her close, wishing they were in his bed, in a room where he could close the rest of the world away. For once, the confinement would be welcome. He rose, and she sat up with him, clinging to his biceps with shaky hands as he rolled on a condom. He kissed her again, aligning their bodies. She held him so tight, kissed him so hard, he couldn't hold back, and he drove into her in one hard thrust. Her fingernails dug into his skin, and a sound somewhere between a mew and a plea escaped her lungs. They both stilled.

"Sweet Jesus." She was clamped around his shaft so tight it blew his mind. Their mouths were still touching, their breath comingling. He pushed his hands beneath her hair and cradled the back of her head, drawing her face away so he could look into her eyes, but they were closed. She had to feel what he felt, like they were lock and key, made for each other. "Addy," he said, at a loss for any more words.

She opened her eyes and he saw something bigger than lust staring back at him, but in the next second it was gone, replaced with that seductive glimmer she wore like a shield. "Didn't I tell you to stop talking ages ago?" She pulled him in for a kiss, and this time he listened.

He didn't say another word. All she got were grunts and groans as he struggled to hold in his emotions. Until her third orgasm, when lights exploded inside his head and his emotions roared to life, sending *careful* and *cool* out with the tide. He followed her into oblivion, chanting her name like a prayer.

"*Addy, Addy, Addy…*"

CHAPTER FOUR

ADDISON AWOKE TO the sound of women's voices as the sun snuck over the horizon. Her fuzzy mind tried to make sense of why she was lying within the circle of Jake's arms on a blanket by the edge of the bluff. She glanced at the empty bottle of tequila on the grass a few feet away, which explained her throbbing headache. Her pulse quickened as memories of the night before tumbled in. She very clearly remembered having sex on the table and then again on the ground. Memories of a desperate search for condoms in the big house rolled in. They'd found two stowed away in a nightstand, and she might have done a naked hula dance. She didn't want to think about whose condoms they'd stolen or how that hula dance must have looked. It was all coming back to her now, the way she'd ridden him hard and then he'd taken her harder. She vaguely remembered the sting of a spank on her ass, and cringed. She remembered listening to him talking, and drinking tequila, although her memories of their conversations were broken at best. She closed her eyes against the pounding in her head.

The sound of women laughing brought them open again. She lifted her head and peered over the slope of the ground to see who was going to have the lovely surprise of finding them.

"What the—"

"Shh!" She slapped a hand over Jake's mouth and whispered, "Gabriella's aunts are over there! Why are they here at the butt crack of dawn?"

He pushed up on one elbow and squinted toward the group of women who were about half a football field away and heading for the villa. Luckily, they didn't seem to notice Jake and Addy's clothes, which were on the grass by the bar on the opposite side of the lawn.

"Breakfast," he grumbled.

She smacked him on the arm, whispering harshly, "You're such a man. Stop thinking about food. In case you haven't noticed, our clothes are out there."

"Aw, hell. I meant they're here to make breakfast. Don't you remember? Gabriella's family is throwing a big family breakfast this morning. I'm surprised she's not with them."

He rubbed his eyes as she processed the idea of Gabriella finding them. His sleepy eyes came to life as they coasted down the length of her body, leaving a trail of heat.

"Jake!"

"What? You're naked. I'm naked. Things could be worse."

She rolled her eyes. "No condoms, remember? And besides, it's the day *after* our one-night stand. We're done." Her stomach twisted at that.

She might be a little fuzzy about some of the details of last night, but there were a few things she knew she'd never forget. Like the way he looked at her the first time their bodies came together and how her whole body came alive when he was buried deep inside her. Not just from the way they fit perfectly together, but *everything*. His incredible strength as he touched her in ways she'd only dreamed of and the sound of her name coming off his tongue. Goose bumps raced up her arms with the memory. A hint of fear trickled in with another memory she was trying hard *not* to acknowledge—the most momentous thing about their torrid night of debauchery. But no matter how hard she fought to ignore it, there was no escaping the thudding of her heart and tingling in her belly last night when they were close, or now, as his leg brushed over hers. She wasn't ready to pick apart the new, distinct sensations. She wasn't even sure they were real and not an effect of the thrill of finally sleeping with the man she'd wanted for so long, or the result of too much tequila. Although too much tequila was not a new pre-sex activity. When she met his gaze again, her insides did that tingly thing, and she held her breath to try to quell the rising sensations.

"You're on the pill, sexy girl." He reached up to stroke her cheek. "And we're both clean, remember? We've already crossed that bridge. *Twice.*"

"How do you…?" She covered her face as their conversation came back in bits and pieces. She *had* admitted to being on the pill right after she *challenged* him to make love to her again. She was never going to live this down. At least they'd had the presence of mind to cover the most important aspects. He was clean; she was clean.

She'd broken all of her rules.

With *Jake.*

Her fantasy.

The one man I shouldn't have done this with.

Lowering her hands, she took in his handsome face, seeing him for the first time not as the player she knew him to be but as the man who had slowed down enough to ask permission to kiss her. Forget living this down. How would she ever go back to the way she was before she knew what it felt like to be in his arms? She'd done this to herself, stepped into the land of temptation. She was worse than Eve, because she'd not only eaten the forbidden fruit, but she'd fooled herself into thinking she could survive without it afterward.

"We've already crossed that bridge. Twice." Remembering what he said made her angry. She didn't need the reminder. The reminder brought lascivious thoughts of being close with him again, and this was supposed to be one night to get him *out* of her head, not make her want him even more.

She jabbed a finger toward him. "You promised that what happened last night would stay there."

"What is this, Vegas?"

She poked him in the chest.

"Ow! Fine, whatever. Jesus. You must need coffee."

"Clothes, Jake. I need clothes!" She tried to yank the blanket out from under him, and he swept an arm around her, pulling her on top of him. Holy moly did he feel good. "Jake." She went for a warning, but it came out with a soft laugh, because she'd expected him to be totally on board with the one-night-and-done thing, and this playful side of him was *almost* too attractive to resist.

His rough hands slid down her back to her butt, and he rocked his formidable erection against her. "Let's negotiate."

"You are such a *man.*" *A very delicious, enticing man.*

"You were into my manliness last night. In fact, if I remember correctly, which there's no way in hell I'm not, because the images are burned into my brain, you liked my manliness between your legs, in your mouth—"

She clamped her hand over his mouth and glared at him. He pushed her hand away and flashed the cocky grin that had gotten her into trouble last night, pushing all her sensual buttons again and sending warning signals blaring through her mind.

"*No* negotiating," she said firmly. She needed space to figure out why he made her stomach dip and her heart skip. Space to get last night out of her mind. She needed space to breathe like a regular person instead of a girl whose body was totally on board with Jake being tucked deep inside her, making her forget why breathing was important at all.

"You promised me things wouldn't be awkward," she reminded him. "And if I have to go over there *naked* and get my clothes, things are going to get more than awkward real fast."

"I think I liked you better when you were flirting with me." He flashed another devilish grin, and her stomach somersaulted.

In his next breath he rolled them both over and she was beneath him, his big body pressing down on her, his hips cradled between her thighs, and her hands trapped above her head. And *oh my*, did he feel good. Maybe he could just slip it in for a quickie. Nothing more.

He touched his cheek to hers, and in a husky voice that made her skin catch fire, he said, "Nothing beats morning sex, Addy."

Her pulse went crazy, and his hands drifted down her sides, which felt really, *really* nice. She closed her eyes, willing herself to be strong.

"You know you want me, sexy girl," he whispered, brushing his scruff against her cheek and sending shivers down her spine. "No one will ever know. Just you and me." He angled his hips back, pressing the head of his cock against her entrance.

"Jake," she said halfheartedly, already wet and ready.

"Tell me *no*. One word. Two letters. And I won't ask again."

No, no, no, no, no. I don't want to tell you no. She shook off the ridiculous faltering and said, "I already did, and they'll *see* us."

"They went inside. And no, you didn't. You said 'no negotiating,' and admittedly, I pushed that envelope." He kissed the corner of her mouth and dragged his tongue along her lower lip, reminding her of all the pleasure he'd given her with that tongue last night. "But if you look me in the eyes and tell me you don't want me, I promise not to ask again."

She could barely think as more memories of their incredible night rushed in. Her body hummed with desire, her hands pressed into his skin, urging him to make the decision for the two of them so she would not be to blame if she didn't stick to her guns about one single night. She could still taste his addicting kisses, and now he was looking at her differently than he always had. The predatory look was still there, but there was more than just wanton desire. He wasn't just looking *at* her. He was looking through her, inside her body, viewing the darkest crevices of her mind, invading every ounce of her, like she was the only thing that existed.

The words *kiss me, Jake* were on the tip of her tongue, and she knew he wouldn't hesitate, because he'd been right about one thing last night. Every single thought led back to him. To their sinful night. To that look in his eyes.

"Be mine one last time, sexy girl."

Sighing inwardly, she dug deep, forcing herself to think of her bestie. That *almost* gave her the kick in the butt she needed to refuse him, but gazing into Jake's eyes, his seductive words, *Be mine*, still lingering in her ears were tough to dismiss. And the idea that this would be their last time also made her long for more. She'd been worried about him being jealous, but already his words were wreaking havoc with her impulses—making them stronger than she'd ever experienced before. How would she skate through the minefield of seeing him flirt with other girls after the night they'd shared? How could she have thought she could ever look at him after that and *not* want him? Why, oh why, did she let herself fall asleep with him? Now she couldn't imagine anything more wonderful than being wrapped up in him for a few more hours, despite the group of relatives who had almost discovered them.

All of it—the unfamiliar emotions, the memories, that heated stare, the feel of him nestled so intimately against her—picked at her nerves, making her edgy and nervous. Addy was big on talk and equally big on research, which was how she knew exactly what to say to a man, how to *touch* and *take* and *tease*. She had perfected her verbal sparring and seduction techniques, and it had been easy, because she was never in danger of feeling a damn thing beyond physical excitement. But being with Jake was different, and no matter how many times she tried to write it off as something else, her *heart* had taken notice. And now, being *naked* with him in the light of day *without* tequila on board, after all the dirty things they'd done last night, she struggled to find her voice. She had to escape before she got in deeper with a guy who probably couldn't spell the word *faithful—Holy cow. Since when do I worry about that?* She wiggled out from beneath him.

She met his disappointed gaze, trying to hide her own faltering resolve, and said, "Clothes, Jake. Now."

LATER THAT MORNING Jake worked alongside Blue and Gage fixing the leg of the table inside the big house on the bluff.

Actually, he was talking shit and trying not to dwell on thoughts of Addy, pacing while Blue fixed the table and Gage ate breakfast. Jake couldn't eat a damn thing. His stomach had been squirrelly since earlier that morning, when, after sprinting naked to retrieve his and Addy's clothes, she'd argued all the way to her door about not needing a bodyguard. She was as stubborn as a mule, and just to prove her point, she'd been pointedly looking away every time he caught sight of her since she'd arrived for breakfast.

"You're helping us set up the beach for Trish's wedding tomorrow morning, right?" Gage asked Jake.

"Sure. Whatever she needs." They were in the kitchen, which opened up to the grounds, giving him a clear view of Addy sitting with the girls, pushing food around on her plate. He wondered if she had the same weird shit going on in her head as he did, or if she was blowing him off because she really was done with him.

"Did Boone tell you his family is arriving a day early?" Blue asked.

Jake stopped pacing and glanced at Gage, who looked as clueless as he was.

"I forgot you were both late for breakfast this morning. They rearranged their schedules to arrive a day early," Blue explained. "We're all meeting up at Niko and Dimitri's tavern tonight for his bachelor party."

He'd rather meet up with Addy. Maybe another night with her could fix the crap going on in his head.

The sound of laughter drew his attention outside, just in time to see Niko twirling Addy, as if they were dancing. Every muscle in Jake's body tensed as the green-eyed monster clawed at his gut. She looked sexier than sin in a pair of cutoffs barely long enough to cover her fine ass and a T-shirt the color of red clay. How she managed to make a loose-fitting shirt look hotter than hell was beyond him. Several sparkly bracelets slid up her arm as she spun back into Niko's arms. Jake's fingers curled into fists as he fought the urge to storm outside and claim the woman who didn't want to be claimed.

"Jake?" Blue called out sharply, as if he'd already said it a few times. "You in for the bachelor party?"

"What?" He turned his attention back to his brothers. "Tonight? Yeah, sure."

"Sounds good," Gage agreed.

"Good," Blue said. "The girls are having their bachelorette party at the beach."

When Jake thought of bachelorette parties, male strippers came to mind. Not that they'd find any of those here on the island.

That he knew of.

He glanced out the doors again, seeking the woman he had finally connected with, and was relieved to see her sitting with Gabriella again. She lifted her eyes, meeting his gaze for only half of a second before looking away, but in that short moment, heat blazed between them. He *really* needed to pull his shit together. It was only one night. *One incredible, intense night.* One of the best fucking nights of his life, and it had left him wanting more. Not just sexually, although he wanted so much more his cock was at half-mast just thinking about her. But the other things he wanted made him feel like a pussy, because they had nothing to do with sex. He wanted to *talk* to her, alone and stone-cold sober. She was so tough, so bold and challenging, and yet devastatingly feminine at the same time. Had she always been that way? She never talked about her family, and he was so close to his, it made him curious about what hers was like. Had she always been full of rebellion, or was stubbornness a family trait? And why was she taking that damn hiking trip alone? Other questions peppered his mind, too. Annoying shit, like why the hell did it take her so long to hook up with him?

"You and Sally were both late for breakfast," Blue said to Gage, drawing Jake's attention again. "Did you two finally get together?"

Gage rubbed the back of his neck with a pained expression. "What do *you* think?"

"Seriously? Dude, just make your move already." Blue tightened a screw beneath the table.

Gage shook his head. "It's not that simple."

"Sure it is," Jake said, thinking of Addy. "If you want her, tell her. If she doesn't blow you off completely, then keep telling her until she either gives in or sends you packing."

"That's how you operate, Jake. That's not my MO." Gage set his coffee mug down and paced. All the Ryder men paced when they were faced with something they'd rather not talk about. "You've always moved from one woman to the next without ever looking back. I've never been that guy, and where Sally's concerned, I never will be."

I was that guy until Addy, apparently. "So…What? You're just going to walk around with a hard-on for the woman you've been bat-shit crazy about since you moved to Colorado until some other guy gets through to her and takes the decision away from you?"

Gage's jaw tightened. "What do you suggest? I mean, short of asking her to jump in my bed every night of the week. Because that hasn't worked out so well for you with Addy, has it?"

If he'd said that yesterday, Jake would have wanted to slug him out of sheer frustration because it hadn't worked for him. But after last night, Jake fought to keep the grin tugging at him from making its way across his face. And when memories of Addy in his arms came crashing in, there wasn't a damn thing he could do to stifle the revealing emotion.

Blue rose to his feet and set the screwdriver on the table with a knowing look in his eyes. "You gonna clue us in or just flash that cocky-ass grin all day?"

Jake scrubbed a hand down his face to try to get a handle on his emotions, but for the first time in as long as he could remember, he *wanted* to talk about what it felt like to have a woman in his arms. More specifically, he *needed* to talk about what it felt like to be with Addy, because she was seriously messing with his head.

He stole a glance outside, catching Addy staring at him, and hell if his pulse didn't ratchet up again. He lifted his chin and smiled, but she'd already turned away. That erased the frigging smile from his face.

"It paid off," he said gruffly. "It paid off better than anything ever has, or at least I thought it did."

His brothers exchanged a look he couldn't read.

"You two finally hooked up?" Blue asked.

Jake nodded.

"So what's the issue?" Gage asked. "Why do you look like a bug crawled up your ass?"

"Because she's blown me off ever since."

Blue chuckled. "Maybe you're not as good in bed as you thought you were."

Gage laughed, and Jake took a step toward him. Gage held up his hands in surrender. "Calm down. We're kidding."

Jake paced, even more frustrated having admitted to being with her, because he suddenly remembered she'd asked him not to brag. He wasn't bragging, but it equated to the same thing. *Chalk it up to being an accidental asshole.*

"Was she on the same page?" Gage asked. "Or did you push so hard she had no choice?"

"Do you really think I'm that much of a douche?" The truth was, Jake had asked himself the same question a hundred times since they'd argued about him walking her to her room this morning. He'd come up with the same answer every damn time. *No way.* He'd given her plenty of chances to back out.

His brothers shared another annoying look.

"Christ," Jake grumbled. "It wasn't like that. We were totally in sync. One hundred percent."

He wrung his hands together, shocking himself with the need to bare his soul. He trusted his brothers with his life, and if anyone would tell him he had his head up his ass or was barking up the wrong tree, it would be Gage or Blue. Duke would chastise him for hooking up with Gabriella's best friend, and Trish would start planning their wedding. He had no fucking clue what Cash would say or do. Probably lecture him for not treating her like a lady. Cash was big on being a gentleman, whereas Jake was admittedly a player. He chewed on that thought for a minute, mulling over what it said about him and not liking the answer. He knew how to be a fucking gentleman. But if Addy wanted a gentleman, she sure as hell didn't act like it. She was as much a one-night-stand person as he was.

If his mixed-up head was any indication, she was more of a one-night-stand person than he was. *It's the day after our one-night stand. We're done.* He was playing by her rules. Jake didn't play by anyone's rules. And based on his current state of mind, not even his own.

"Do you want to talk about it?" Blue asked.

He cleared his throat to try to bring his mind back to their conversation, but he no longer wanted to talk to his brothers about this. Not only because Addy had asked him not to—although that was enough to stop him from divulging anything more—but also because they weren't the ones he needed to talk this out with. There was only one person who could help him get his head on straight. He needed to clear the air with Addy and find out why she was treating him like…like…

A freaking one-night stand.

"Hell no," he snapped.

Gage patted him on the back. "She's been all you could think about for months. It's not surprising that she's got you tied in knots. But you should be used to moving on, Jake. As I said, it's how you operate."

Jake scoffed to cover up the truth he wasn't ready to admit. It was how he operated. *Was* being the key word. "Don't go blabbing this to anyone. Especially not Sally or Lizzie. The last thing I need is Addy giving me hell because I told you two."

He headed for the yard, intent on playing by his own rules and mentally preparing as if he were going on a search and rescue mission. Assessing his time in the field, or in this case, how long it would take to clear up this misperception of hers, that they were going to play by her rules. He gave it half an hour. But this was Addy. Stubborn, sexy, out-to-prove-something Addy. Okay, maybe it would take *days*, but he didn't have days. He looked up at the sky, thinking about his next assessment, weather and resources. There was a storm brewing inside his gut, and a quick glance to his left placed his eyes on the bar. *Plenty of resources.*

Jake had yet to fail a mission. He had this.

As he scanned the grounds, he began putting together a game plan for getting Addy on board with playing by *his* rules, the first of which was that she was going to talk to him, like it or not.

But first he'd have to find her.

Chapter Five

ADDY AND GABRIELLA followed Lizzie, Siena, and a mob of Gabriella's female relatives down the dirt road toward the dress shop in the center of town for Trish's wedding dress fitting. Trish and her mother led the chatty procession. Prewedding excitement electrified the air. Addy felt like she was in a scene from *Mamma Mia!*, where the entire town fell into step as women joined the group along the way. Addy was glad to be invited. If she had to sit around on the bluff trying not to look at Jake for another minute, her mind would have exploded. She'd thought he was going to rip Niko's head off when they were goofing around. As much as she liked and respected Niko and would never want anything to happen to him, she'd been unexpectedly flattered to know Jake was jealous. A little thrill ran through her with the realization that Jake was still thinking about her just as much as she was thinking about him. One night together was supposed to get him out of her head, not embed him in her every thought.

When they reached Main Street, Addy realized Gabriella's relatives hadn't said two words to her all morning. Usually they pestered her nonstop about meeting Mr. Right. Maybe she was just being paranoid…or maybe they'd seen her and Jake on the bluff this morning after all.

Her stomach sank, and she tried to concentrate on her surroundings to settle her nerves. She'd always loved the unique mix of Greek and Southern cultures the island was known for, as evident in the diverse architecture in town. Niko and Dimitri's tavern was built in richly Mediterranean style with a tile roof and stucco walls, while the enormous white bank was true four-columned Georgian-style. A market boasting a typical small-town brick storefront was situated between an old-fashioned pharmacy, complete with a green awning, and an empty villa-style building that looked like it had been plunked down from the streets of Greece. Duke's company had begun making strides toward beautifying the area, as evidenced by the scaffolding in front of the shops and the telltale noises of men working. But even that wasn't enough to distract Addy from her worries. Looking for a better distraction, she turned her thoughts to Gabriella, who was emitting I-found-my-happily-ever-after vibes from her sparkling dark eyes to the gleaming diamonds on her finger.

"How was your first night of wedded bliss?" Addy asked quietly.

Gabriella sighed. "Amazing. Truly, wonderfully incredible. I didn't want to get out of bed this morning."

If she'd been Gabriella, she wouldn't have gotten out of bed. But she knew Gabriella would never blow off her family's breakfast for sex—even with her new husband.

"Funny, I didn't want to get *into* mine." Yeah, Addy went there despite her demand that Jake not tell a soul. But Gabriella was her best friend, her sister from another mother, and the *only* person Addy trusted to give it to her straight. *And the one person who could get hurt by my actions.*

"You...?" Gabriella's brow wrinkled, and a second later, her jaw dropped. She lowered her voice and said, "Ohmygod.

Addison! You slept with Jake, didn't you?"

"I'm sorry!" Addy said, although she was only sorry that it might bother Gabriella. She wasn't sorry she had experienced being in Jake's arms. "I didn't mean for it to happen. I mean, not at first, but then..." She was selfish. That was the bottom line, and she needed to own up to it. "Then he was *all* I wanted. But I promise things aren't going to be awkward or weird."

"I think they already are," Gabriella said. "Now this morning makes sense. You were acting so weird, looking away every time he was near you. I thought you'd just grown tired of him always trying to sleep with you."

She ached at how far from the truth that was. "I'm sorry. I don't know what happened, but somewhere between last night and waking up in his arms, I...I got confused about it all. I promise you, Gab. I will fix this. I will act absolutely normal around him from now on. I won't let this come between anyone, especially you and Duke's family. I'm such an idiot." Addy hated herself right then. She couldn't even look at Jake. Every time she did she got all revved up again.

"Was he a jerk to you?" Gabriella asked. "Because if he was, Duke will set him straight."

Addy shook her head. "No. Not at all. He was..." *Great? Perfect? Amazing?* Every word she came up with sounded sexual, and what they'd shared felt like so much more. She settled on, "He wasn't at all jerky."

"What does that mean?" Gabriella eyed her skeptically. "You usually describe guys as 'sex machines' or 'orally challenged.' What am I supposed to make of 'wasn't at all jerky?'"

"He's your brother-in-law, Gab. What do you want me to say? I can't go into juicy details about him without making things even weirder. It was a mistake. That's all it was. And it was just one night. We agreed to that. I'm sorry for crossing that line. I know better, and it was totally selfish of me."

They stopped in front of the quaint dress shop, Pretty Things, housed in a small brick building with enormous windows and a cute pink and white awning. Gabriella touched Addy's arm, indicating for her to let the others go inside first.

"You guys okay?" Siena asked.

"Yeah. I just want to talk to Addy for a sec. We'll be right in," Gabriella answered.

"Take your time," Siena told them. "I've got a few hours without the babies. I'm not in a rush to get back."

Once all the others were out of earshot, Addy apologized again. "I will make this right. I promise."

"Addy, *please*. What am I, a child? I don't care that you hooked up with Jake. I mean, I *care*, but it's your life, your decisions. You know that." Gabriella hugged her. "I'm actually kind of relieved. You two have been dancing around each other for so long, Duke and I wanted to lock you in a room until you finally did it just to get it out of your systems."

"Oh Lord. You *and* Duke? He must think I'm a slut."

Gabriella laughed. "The girl who talks about vibrators the way other people talk about pencils, like they're a staple of every woman's daily supply list, is worried about what someone thinks of her?"

Addy laughed. "I do not talk about them around *him*."

"No? I seem to remember at dinner last week when Jake made a comment about helping you deal with your stress and you said you had plenty of batteries on hand to deal with it."

Oh, shit.

"Face it, Ad. You don't exactly hide your thoughts on sex."

"*Fine*, whatever, but sleeping with his brother is different."

"Only because Duke cares about you and he'll beat the shit out of Jake if he hurt you or forced himself on you."

"First, I think Jake could take Duke. Just sayin'. But really, Gab? Jake, forcing himself on me? I think you know us both better than that. Besides, Duke doesn't need to know. Okay? Please don't tell him. I'm leaving right after Trish's wedding tomorrow to go back to the city, and the next day I'm leaving for my trip. This will all blow over by the time I return. And you'll be on your honeymoon, so there's no need to say anything." Trish and Boone were having a small afternoon beach wedding. There would be absolutely no opportunity for drunken sex with Jake afterward. Addy tried to convince herself that was a good thing.

"If that's what you want," Gabriella said, looking intently at her. "But you seem…I don't know. Nervous? Something's different. I'm so used to you going on and on about how you're better off watching porn, and you're not saying that."

"I'm exhausted," she said as they walked up the steps to the dress shop. "We pretty much stayed up all night screwing like bunnies. I think there was an ass slap involved. It was a million times better than porn and battery-powered boyfriends combined."

"Ohmygod. Do *not* tell me anything else." Gabriella whispered as they walked inside, "Ass slap? Really?"

"Shh. I never said that."

The dress shop was bustling with activity. Trish came out of a dressing room in the back looking stunning in her mother's wedding gown. The shop owner, a busty brunette who looked to be in her late forties, and a handful of Gabriella's relatives converged, guiding Trish onto a platform in front of several tall mirrors. Gabriella's other relatives stood at the ready, sewing gear in hand, prepared to nip, tuck, and perfect the fit of Andrea Ryder's wedding gown for her daughter. Addy had been to Elpitha often enough to know that every event was a community affair, but that didn't dull the astonishment of witnessing the women coming together to help Trish. They treated the preparation of daily meals with as much love and attention as they did weddings and birthdays. It was no wonder Gabriella missed the island so much. If she'd had her wedding in New York City, the venue would have been cleaned up within hours of its end and they'd be on to the next party in no time, Gabriella's big day forgotten. Here on Elpitha, the lights and decorations Duke had arranged around the bluff were left up, and the plants he'd brought in were cared for and would be replanted after the weekend. The women had gotten up at dawn to prepare a feast for relatives and friends, then moved seamlessly to the next task of graciously giving Trish her own perfect wedding.

The coming together of extended family—some of whom weren't even blood related—made Addy think of her own family. She couldn't imagine her mother ever being involved in this type of camaraderie, and that realization made her sad. She often wondered if her mother liked having all of her needs taken care of and hired help to handle things to the nth degree. Did she enjoy having only to show up and look pretty? Or did she secretly long to be more involved as an equal partner in her marriage, hiding her disappointment beneath an expertly practiced, refined facade? The thought spurred another, more troublesome one. Had her mother simply resigned herself to accepting a role as the silent, adoring wife, as she knew her grandmother had?

Addy couldn't get caught up in analyzing her parents' marriage. She firmly believed that people determined their own happiness, and if her mother had chosen to forgo happiness out of loyalty or something else, that wasn't Addy's issue to fix. She had enough on her very full plate, with thoughts of Jake taking up residence in her head. She was bombarded by memories of the hungry look in his eyes as he went down on her and the way he took and demanded in equal measure. Her body shuddered with the memory.

"I still can't believe Boone arranged all of this without you knowing," Siena said to Trish as the ladies untangled the web of gold ribbons on the back of Trish's wedding gown and fluffed the layered skirt.

Addy drew in an unsteady breath and shook her head to try to clear the dirty thoughts from her mind.

"I can't believe I fit in my mother's wedding gown." Trish smiled at her mother. "I also can't believe you thought to bring it with you, Mom. Thank you."

"Honey, the minute Boone asked us for your hand, we knew we were looking at an immediate wedding." Andrea stepped closer, but there were too many women for her to get too close to her daughter. "That man is so in love with you he can't see straight."

"I still remember the day Marilynn gave me that dress. I was in Oak Falls, Virginia, for Marilynn's wedding." Andrea glanced at the other women. "She was Marilynn Calhoon at that point, but Montgomery now. She was my college roommate's younger sister, and she is such a doll. Anyway, Marilynn made all sorts of clothes back then, and this was one of her designs. People used to come around from all over just to see the things she made. Her daughter Morgyn inherited her talent for fashion and opened her own shop, but Marilynn sewed for fun. She had other passions—"

"Mom," Trish said gently. "They don't need Aunt Marilynn's life story."

Not for the first time, Addy longed for moments like these with her own mother. Despite growing up in the same house, Addy had always felt distance between them. Her mother wasn't nearly as confident or capable as any of the women in this room; nor was she open with her opinions. She'd never once shared a story about her past with Addy. Not the way her grandmother had when she'd told Addy about her marriage to her first husband, who had died when Addy's mother was a little girl. Or the way her grandmother had shared her true feelings about her second marriage, which was the same kind of marriage her mother had fallen into. Addy was definitely wired more like her grandmother than her mother. The idea of *not worrying her pretty little head* about anything made her want to give her parents a lesson in nineteenth-century womanhood. Her father was a philanthropist who could—and tried to—give Addy anything she desired. But what she wanted couldn't be bought. Her parents loved her to the ends of the earth, and she couldn't fault them for having different ideals than she did. But deep down she'd have given anything for her parents to encourage her to do more, be more, step outside their pampered world and excel. To place value on her ability to succeed in her own career and create her own path and to recognize her achievements instead of seeing them as *unnecessary wastes of energy* or rebellion. They'd like nothing more than for her to come to her senses, find a man within their social circles, and settle down.

The trouble was, Addy wasn't rebelling. She loved being intellectually stimulated and challenging herself. And she wasn't looking to get married. She couldn't imagine settling down with one man. Heck, last night was the first time she'd felt anything beyond turned on by a guy, and she was still struggling with that realization.

Andrea pushed her stylish amber frames up to the bridge of her nose and began straightening the layers of lace on Trish's dress. Her serious expression reminded Addy of Jake, the way his mouth pulled tight at the corners and his brows drew together. His voice whispered through her mind. *Be mine one last time, sexy girl.* For the hundredth time, Addy pushed thoughts of Jake aside and tried to figure out how to make it through the rest of the weekend with her sanity intact.

"Anyway, Marilynn said I should try the dress on, and when I did, it was love at first sight. And these gold ribbons"—Andrea looked fondly at the thick satin ribbons that crisscrossed over Trish's waist and back, where they attached to delicate white spaghetti straps—"were an afterthought."

"Really?" Gabriella said. "I think they add so much."

"I agree." Trish ran her fingers lightly over the beaded bodice. "With all these embellishments, the gold, and the plunging neckline, it's perfect for the red carpet or the beach."

"Or your favorite camping spot," Andrea said with a smile that lit up her eyes.

"My mom and dad got married at their favorite camping spot, by a river," Trish explained. "They were both barefoot. But she wasn't pregnant."

"It wouldn't matter if she was." Gabriella's mother's thick Southern drawl contrasted with Andrea's New York accent, though both were warm and friendly. Peggy Ann was in her late fifties, with the boundless energy and confidence of a woman in her thirties, ready to take on the world.

In Peggy Ann, Addy found the mother she felt she should have been born to, from her say-it-like-it-is attitude to her dark hair, they were more alike than Addy and her mother were.

"True," Andrea said. "Babies are always welcome in my book."

"Ours, too. We all know how love gets the best of us." Peggy Ann's eyes drifted to Addy, lingering just long enough to make Addy's heart skip a beat. "Sometimes we just can't help ourselves. And if we're blessed with a young 'un, then it's meant to be."

Addy stood frozen in place. Was Peggy Ann with Gabriella's aunts at the crack of dawn? Had she seen her and Jake out on the bluff? Addy wished she could close her eyes and go back in time. She thought about that for a beat and realized the only thing she would have changed was to make sure they'd gone back to one of their rooms. She had no interest in taking back their night together. But she'd known Peggy Ann and most of Gabriella's relatives for more than four years. They'd welcomed her into their family with open arms, treating her like a daughter. And what did she do? Have sex on one of their tables and steal their condoms. Maybe she didn't deserve a surrogate mother like Peggy Ann after all.

"Mama," Gabriella said. "You're so in love with love."

"You bet your sweet bottom I am." Peggy Ann cinched the waist of Trish's dress a little tighter. "Nothing will make your head spin as quickly as the man who was meant to set your world on fire. And Boone is going to go up in flames when he sees you in this dress, little miss Trish."

That sparked a flurry of activity as Gabriella's aunts began lifting, smoothing, measuring, and pinning Trish's dress, while commenting on how handsome Boone was and what gorgeous babies they'd have together.

"Trish, we don't have bridesmaids dresses," Siena said. "Should we buy some here?"

"No. I want you guys to wear your own dresses. It's more fun and natural. I have enough fancy-schmancy in my daily life," Trish assured them. "I want this to be low-key and I want you all to just be comfortable and have fun."

They discussed the details of her small family wedding, which included only immediate family and closest friends. Gabriella's extended family seemed to be as used to that as they were to big community-style weddings and didn't appear to be bothered by not being included. They nipped and tucked for what seemed like hours, providing the perfect distraction for Addy to slip away unnoticed. She hurried into the ladies' room to try to collect her thoughts.

A few minutes later the bathroom door opened and Gabriella poked her head in. "I thought I saw you escaping."

"Hey. Come in."

Gabriella walked in with Sally, Siena, and Lizzie on her heels, each one wearing a bigger smile than the last.

Addy crossed her arms. "You *told* them?"

"No!" Gabriella insisted.

"She didn't have to. I saw you this morning," Sally said sweetly. "But I swear I didn't mean to rat you out. I heard the twins crying and went out on my balcony to see if Siena was taking them for a walk, and I saw you and Jake walking toward your room." She cringed a little, hiding behind her straight blond hair. "Wearing the same clothes you had on last night."

Oh God. Addy leaned back against the sink.

"In her defense, she did hear our twins. So it's kind of our fault." Siena peered into the mirror and fixed a smudge of eye makeup, then ran her fingers through her long brown hair.

"And you assumed…Of course. Why wouldn't you?" Addy wasn't new to owning up to her trysts, but this felt different, because everyone in this room was part of Jake's family. Including Sally, even though she technically wasn't. She and Gage did everything together.

"This is the part where you might want to kill me," Sally added. "At breakfast I made the mistake of mentioning that I saw you two together."

"It didn't take much for us to figure it out." Lizzie smiled, bringing out her dimples. "We're happy for you!"

"Great. Why don't we hire a skywriter in case anyone missed the announcement," Addy said sarcastically. She couldn't even enjoy that Lizzie said they were happy for her. She was too worried about being so hard on Jake about keeping his mouth shut, and not only did she tell Gabriella, but now all the girls knew. *Which means his brothers do, too.*

"Should I tell you the worst part?" Gabriella asked. "And I swear to you, I had no idea about any of this until two minutes ago."

"There's a *worst* part?" Her stomach sank.

"It's not so bad. We did great damage control," Siena said.

"The worst part needed damage control?" Addy reached for Gabriella's hand.

"My aunts caught wind of it," Gabriella said softly.

"Ohmygod. Everyone knows?" Addy closed her eyes, wishing she was a crier, because it would feel a lot better to shed tears than it would to bang her head against the wall.

"Don't worry," Siena assured her. "We cornered them before word spread too far. I *think.*"

"What does *that* mean? That maybe if I'm lucky Gabriella's

grandfather doesn't know? No wonder they haven't spoken to me today."

"They're trying to behave," Lizzie explained. "Gabby's mother threatened that if they said anything about it she would tell their husbands what they really do when they get their hair done."

Addy looked to Gabriella for an explanation.

"When my cousin Eva moved back to take over the salon, apparently she brought her knowledge of Pinterest with her. They sit around with spotty Internet connections gawking at silver foxes."

Addy laughed. "Seriously? That was enough to keep them quiet?"

"Only on Elpitha." Gabriella shook her head. "Eva said she makes sure to only show them PG-rated boards, but still."

"Hope they don't catch wind of my Cocks I Want to Rock Tumblr page."

They all laughed.

"Wait." Siena grabbed Addy's arm. "Do you really have *that*?"

"I can't go on Tumblr," Lizzie said. "Everything you search ends up being naked people and sex, sex, sex."

"Why do you think Addy likes it?" Gabby teased.

"Maybe you should distribute that site address," Sally said shyly. All eyes turned toward her. "What? It's no secret that I haven't been with a guy since I lost my husband." Her husband had been killed in a skiing accident several years earlier, leaving her to raise Rusty, her teenage son, alone.

Lizzie hugged her. "Blue told me about everything you and your son have been through. I'm so sorry."

"Thank you. It was a long time ago. I can hardly believe

how many years have passed." Sally smiled, but Addy could see it was forced. "I'm okay, really. But I wasn't kidding about that site address. You know, until I'm ready to climb back on that horse."

"I think Gage's saddle is ready and waiting," Siena said, and immediately clamped her mouth closed. "I'm sorry. I didn't mean—"

"It's okay. I know..." Sally nibbled on her lower lip. "That situation is complicated. He and Rusty are close, and there's a lot to consider."

"You could try stalking, like Addy did. That seems to have paid off for her," Gabriella teased.

"Stalking?" Addy snapped.

"When I first met Duke, remember? You were checking out Duke and you got sidetracked. I think you said you spent *twelve* hours checking out his 'hot brother Jake' on Facebook."

"Oh God, Gab! I *did*!" She'd spent hours looking through pictures of Jake caught midclimb as he scaled a mountain, or with an arm slung over one of his brother's shoulders, or tending to a campfire, or a hundred other outdoor activities. In every picture he was paying attention to something or someone else, as if the actual photographs meant little compared to the task or person he was with.

"But I'm not a creepy stalker or anything. You know that," she insisted.

"We know," the girls said in unison.

"You two have been flirting for months," Siena said. "I was surprised you two didn't catch flames that first time we all met for drinks. Remember, Gabriella? I was afraid we'd have to call in Cash's fire department to break out their hoses."

"I remember Jake wanting to break out his hose," Addy

mumbled, and they all laughed. "Now that my sex life is out on the table, can we forget about it, please?"

"Do you *want* to forget it?" Lizzie asked. "Because it took me and Blue a year to get together and when I finally gave myself permission to go out with him, that was it. I was a total goner, and there was no turning back."

"That's a good point," Sally said. "There are some things that aren't meant to be taken back."

"I'm not wired to be a *goner* over anyone," Addy insisted, although as she said it, she was no longer sure how she was wired.

"Everyone's wired for love." Lizzie tucked her dark hair behind her ear, and her eyes turned serious. "I didn't think I had a chance at love since I hosted the Naked Baker webcast. I mean, what guy wants a girl that prances around nearly naked on the Internet to earn money to put her little sister through college?"

"Blue," they all said in unison.

Lizzie smiled. "Yeah. I'm so freaking lucky. That man...*God*, my man is so..."

"Did you have a point?" Siena teased.

"Oh, right. Yes." Lizzie looked at Addy. "I don't know why you think you're not wired for love, but I've known you a few months now, and you're one of the most sensual, kindest people I know. You're smart, funny, you don't take crap from anyone, and you're obviously gorgeous." She wrinkled her nose. "Sensual? I don't know if that's the right word, but you're *it*. The total package. You're obviously wired for everything, but love won't come until you let it."

"It's not like I don't want love," Addy said. "I mean, I've never found a man who made me want to see him more than once, but it's not like I don't *want* love. I'm not purposefully keeping myself closed off from it. I just don't experience the same feelings that other people do."

"So, you felt nothing when you were with Jake?" Siena asked.

"No. I mean, *yes*, I felt something." Addy didn't want to have this conversation. She was still struggling with what she felt and whether it was real or imagined.

A knock sounded at the bathroom door and they all turned. Gabriella opened it and her mother peeked her head inside.

"Addy, sweetheart, you have a visitor."

CHAPTER SIX

JAKE KNEW HE was taking a big risk by showing up at the dress shop where Addy and the girls were doing whatever girls did before a wedding, but he was bound and determined to set the record straight and let Addy know he was done playing by her rules. He stood in the front of the shop feeling like a cross between an animal in the zoo and a game show contestant. A group of Gabriella's relatives were watching him from the other side of the shop, whispering and waving and giving him the thumbs-up. He smiled, waved, crossed his arms. Their eyes dropped to his biceps, and he uncrossed his arms, feeling oddly self-conscious.

He heard Addy's determined footsteps fast approaching and his pulse kicked up. She looked beyond gorgeous in her tight little shorts, with her hair fluffing out behind her, but her squinty eyes and tense posture had him seriously questioning why he'd thought this was a good idea.

"Jake?" she said with hushed urgency. "What are you doing here?" She settled a hand on her hip and glared at him.

"Can we talk for a minute?" He hiked a thumb over his shoulder toward the door. "Alone?"

She glanced at the women, who turned away in mass, acting as if they weren't hanging on their every word.

"Fine." She walked past Jake and right out the door—and

she kept on walking.

"Hey," he said, falling into step beside her. "Sorry to interrupt. I just wanted to talk."

"I asked you to do me *one* favor." She stared straight ahead as she crossed the dirt road. "One simple thing, Jake. All I asked was that you not make this awkward. And you show up at the dress shop?" She stalked down a path behind a row of shops and stormed up a grassy hill.

Jake followed, getting more annoyed by the second. "I'm done playing by your rules, Addy."

She laughed. "My *rules*?"

"Yes, your rules. What did you expect me to do? You wouldn't even look at me this morning." At the top of the hill she stomped across the meadow. He kept pace with her. The sounds of the ocean faded, replaced with the sounds of her heavy breathing and their feet tromping through the long grass.

"Doesn't that tell you something?" They were in the middle of the meadow, surrounded by tall trees on either side, the town too far behind them to see. "They know, okay?" Her eyes slung daggers with each venomous word. "Every woman in that shop knows that we were out all night going at it."

He cursed under his breath, a surge of protective urges exploding in his chest. He was going to wring his brothers' necks.

"Don't even act like you care." She turned and stormed away again.

"Goddamn it, Addy. Slow down and talk to me." When she didn't, he grabbed her arm. So much for treating her like a lady, but she was not making it easy. He looked down at her, annoyed and beyond attracted to her despite her angry scowl. "Is that what you think? That I don't care if you're embarrassed? Because I do fucking care. I care a whole hell of a lot more than

I'm comfortable with."

She stared up at him and wrenched her arm free. "I'm *not* embarrassed."

Addy never lied, at least not that Jake could remember, which was why the unfamiliar tone of her voice stopped him cold. "You're a sucky liar."

She rolled her eyes, her go-to move when she had no response. Jesus, now he was reading her mannerisms? She really had gotten under his skin.

"It's my fault," he reluctantly admitted. "I told Blue and Gage, but I didn't think they'd tell anyone."

"You *told* them?"

"They kind of guessed, but...*Fuck.* Yes, okay? I'm sorry. But they swore they wouldn't tell anyone." Guilt sat like lead in his gut. "I'm sorry."

She turned away, breathing so hard her shoulders visibly rose and fell.

"Look, Addy," he said in a softer tone. "You're right. Normally I wouldn't give a damn who found out, but with you I do."

She huffed out a pithy laugh.

"What the hell? Do you really think I wanted all those women to find out?"

She shook her head, still not facing him, and said, "It wasn't your fault. Sally saw us walking back to my room this morning, and she said something, and someone caught wind of it. And then I told Gabriella." She turned, arms crossed, with an apologetic smile.

He blew out a breath of relief. "If you told Gabriella, then you're just as floored by whatever this is between us as I am. Talk to me, Addy. You're so pissed off. How could I have fucked this up already?"

She squared her shoulders. "There's nothing to fuck up."

That was a hard pill to swallow, because it meant last night had affected him far more than it had her. But when he stepped closer, heat blazed between them. Her eyes darkened, and her breathing shallowed. This was *not* one-sided. She stared at his chest as if she wasn't ready to face the truth.

"We're playing by my rules this time, Addison." He tucked a finger under her chin, lifting her face so she had no choice but to meet his gaze. "There may not be anything to fuck up yet, sexy girl, but we both know there could be. Be my date for Trish's wedding."

"Be your *date*? You don't date, Jake, and I think we both know that I don't either."

Needing a barrier between thoughts of her with other men, he crossed his arms. Her eyes went to his biceps. Damn he liked that. He flexed his muscles, earning a soft laugh that sounded a hell of a lot sexier than the snappy attitude she'd been giving him. He stepped closer, settling his hands on her hips. She was so petite he wanted to protect her, though as she'd flatly pointed out, she didn't think she needed protecting. Another hard pill for him to swallow.

"Go out with me, Addy. Let me take you to the wedding like a real date."

"Why? As some sort of one-upmanship with Niko? He's a really nice guy, by the way. You shouldn't look at him like you want to throttle him."

He took a step back and paced. "So now you're into him?"

"No, I'm not into him. I'm just saying he's a nice guy." Her eyes traveled along his torso, hitching at his chest. "*Too nice* for me."

That brought him to a stop. "How can a guy be *too nice* for you?"

"Nice is predictable. It's pretense. I want real."

Her eyes sparked with a challenge he didn't hesitate to accept. He tugged her against him, brushing his whiskers over her cheek. Her body shuddered against him as it had last night. "You want *me*, Addy," he said in a low voice beside her ear. "I'm as real as a man can get. And I want you. Don't fight it."

She pressed her hands flat against his chest but didn't push away. It wasn't much, but he'd take it.

"That's just a twisted girl hangover."

He laughed. "I think I've had enough women to know if I was prone to girl hangovers or not."

Her scowl returned. "Not helping."

"Come on, sexy girl. What's wrong? Did I ruin you for all mankind? Because I'm totally down with that idea."

"You wish, and don't call me that." She pushed from his arms.

"Oh, I'm calling you that." When she didn't respond, he said, "You're trying your damnedest to treat me like you don't want me, but I hear what your body is telling me far louder than the words you're saying. So if I've pissed you off, you'd better speak up."

She looked away.

"This is bullshit, Addy. You don't hide behind silence. You take shit by the balls and fling it against the wall. I have no idea why you're so mad. You wanted me last night. Didn't you?" His gut twisted. He couldn't imagine he'd misread her desires.

"Yes, okay?" She strode toward him and poked him in the chest—hard. "But I didn't know it would open goddamn Pandora's box. *Thankfully*, I'm leaving for the mountains, where

I'll completely forget about whatever this is. And you're going back to your life of a different woman every night."

He grabbed her finger and pulled her against him again, ignoring her struggle to be set free. "You want me, Addy. Admit it."

She lifted her chin, eyes narrow. "So what? You were a good fuck."

"You feisty little minx. You're so small, and so beautiful, and you've got a mouth on you that could make a trucker blush." He framed her face in his hands as he had last night, and that all-consuming heat swallowed him again. "I happen to really dig that filthy mouth of yours." He cocked a grin. "You were a good fuck, too."

She fisted her hands in his shirt. "Jake." She probably meant it as a warning, but it came out like a plea.

"Go out with me, Addy."

"Why?"

"Because you've gotten under my skin and messed with my head. Whatever this is, it's not going away, and we both know it. I want to get to know you better."

She looked at him skeptically.

"And then I want to fuck you again, the same way *you* want to fuck *me*. Only this time we're doing it in private, and you're not going to scramble away first thing in the morning."

He lowered his mouth to hers, kissing her gently at first, giving her a chance to pull away. When she tightened her grip on his shirt, he took the kiss deeper, sliding his hands to her ass and holding her against him. She went up on her toes, grabbing his chest so hard she snagged a few chest hairs, but he didn't care. He'd take whatever she had to give.

"I love your filthy mouth," he said between kisses.

She panted as he kissed her neck and sealed his teeth over the pulse point that had been taunting him for the last twenty-four hours.

"*God, Jake...*"

"You're mine this weekend, Addy."

"We're not a *thing*."

He sank his teeth into her skin and she cried out. When he didn't relent, she moaned, pressing her body against him.

"*God*, what you do to me," she whispered.

He wanted to lay her down in the grass, strip her bare, and take her every which way until the sun fell from the sky and the stars came out. And then he wanted to start all over again, until she lay spent in his arms. But he wanted something even more than he wanted another hot fuck. He lifted his face and looked deeply into her eyes. Pure, unadulterated lust stared back at him.

"Say yes, Addison. Go with me tomorrow to the wedding."

"Fine, but we're not a *thing*."

"Mark my words, sexy girl. We will be."

ADDY LAID HER black minidress on the bed and set her cute black strappy sandals beside it. Her sandals would be easy to kick off once they hit the beach for Trish's bachelorette party. She chose her favorite silver dangling earrings and silver knot necklace and set them on the dresser. She had just over half an hour to get ready before Gabriella got there to walk down to the party with her.

She went into the bathroom and undressed as she peered out the open window, inhaling the salty sea air and taking in the beauty of the ocean waves rolling along the sandy shore. The sun was just beginning to set, leaving ribbons of orange and gold in its wake. As much as she hated that she was leaving tomorrow, it was probably for the best. Not only did she have a full night of packing and preparing for her trip ahead of her, but she'd been so close to scaling Jake like a mountain today, she needed to get to the bottom of what she was really feeling for him.

She turned on the shower, glad the guys were having their own bachelor party. She didn't trust herself to behave around Jake. He'd thrown her for a loop when he'd shown up at the dress shop, and even more so when he'd asked her out. Other than their sexy banter and relentless flirting, it wasn't like they had a *deep* relationship. It had always been cursory. Hadn't it? She stepped into the shower thinking that over and remembering the intensity in his eyes when he'd asked her to be his date. Was he *that* jealous of Niko? Needing to bang his chest like a Neanderthal? Or did he really feel something more, as he'd claimed?

Closing her eyes, she tipped her head back, letting the warm shower wet her hair and slide along the length of her body. She remembered the feel of Jake's legs rubbing against hers as they made love on the bluff and the strength in his grip when he clutched her hips. Memories of his strong fingers teasing her nipples made them rise to taut peaks. She opened her eyes and turned, allowing the water to rain down her face and breasts, trying to quell the ache between her legs that always followed thoughts of him. But the water felt like his mouth, warm and wet. Closing her eyes again, she drew memories of his passionate whispers she'd been purposefully suppressing. *You feel so good, sexy girl. So good I want to fuck you all night.* She loved his dirty talk, his raw passion, and his forceful nature. Her fingers slid between her wet lips, dipping inside as she recalled more of their torrid night. The memory of his mouth between her legs, licking and sucking, made her fingers quicken, stroking the magical spot that brought her up on her toes. Remembering the sharp graze of his teeth over her clit, her other hand moved over the same sensitive nerves. Lust pooled and pulsed between her legs, her orgasm stirring just out of reach. She bit her lower lip, squeezing her eyes shut with the memory of his cock buried so deep inside her she felt every thrust in her chest. She could still feel his arms holding her so tight she could barely breathe as he found his release, chanting her name—*Addy, Addy, Addy.*

"*Jake*!" she cried out as her orgasm crashed over her. She rode the long peak, pretending her fingers were his shaft, the water, his tongue. Until finally, she melted blissfully against the shower wall, panting for air, eyes closed.

"Addy?"

She pushed from the wall, slipped, and caught herself on the shower door. What the hell was Jake doing in her room? Why, oh why, didn't the resort have doors that locked automatically? The whole Mediterranean charm thing had its pitfalls. Or maybe this was Southern hospitality at its best. *Why, yes, feel free to saunter into my room when I'm pleasuring myself.* She scrambled out of the shower and grabbed a towel, wrapping it quickly around herself.

"Addy!" he called more urgently.

She ran out of the bathroom and smacked into his chest, yelping as her towel fell to her feet. Then his hands were on her arms, holding her tight, with a pissed-off look in his eyes as his gaze ran over her face.

"Are you oka—" His eyes darted to the steamy bathroom,

his expression morphing to amusement.

"Why are you in my room?" she demanded, grabbing her towel and trying to cover up.

"I was..." His eyes sailed down her body, making her insides flame again.

Damn him.

He flashed a wicked smile full of sinful promises, reawakening her primed and ready body. "I was coming to see if I could walk you down to your beach party and I heard you call my name. You sounded desperate, like something was wrong."

She tucked the end of her towel between her breasts and put her hands on her hips, pulling it free again. "Damn it." She reached for it and he beat her to it, carefully wrapping the towel around her body and holding the two ends together.

"I didn't say your name. I said..." *You wanted to walk me down to the party?*

He arched a brow, that cocky grin making her stupid stomach flip again.

"Gah!" She stepped away. It was bad enough she couldn't get him out of her mind, but to have him know just how bad off she was mortified her.

He hauled her against him, his piercing stare boring into her. "I like the idea of you getting off to thoughts of me in the shower, but I could help you with that, you know." He pushed a hand up her thigh and under the edge of her towel. "It doesn't have to be a solo endeavor."

"I wasn't *getting off* to thoughts of you."

"No?" His other hand slid down her arm, then slowly back up the length of it.

She had no hopes of hiding the goose bumps he caused, which made her even more annoyed. Men did *not* cause her to react like that. But Jake wasn't like any man she'd ever known.

"It's really cute how your voice hits a different pitch when you lie," he said with a smirk.

"My voice does not do any such thing."

"No? Because your cheeks are flushed and your skin is hot." The hand beneath her towel snaked higher, moving around her thigh and cupping the back of it. His long fingers brushed between her legs as he squeezed the back of her leg.

"Jake," she said, breathing harder. He knew just how to touch her. Most men would have gone in from the front, but where was the seduction in that? He was a master at teasing and making her *want* him, *want* more. Want *everything*.

"Sexy girl." He brushed his mouth lightly over hers, and she felt his arousal grow against her belly. "You're wet for me."

She closed her eyes against the truth, and his mouth grazed hers again. She tipped her head up, meeting those warm, soft lips, but he didn't take the invitation. He skimmed over them, inhaling deeply. His fingertips brushed over her sex, and she opened her eyes to find him gazing at her with so many emotions warring in his eyes it made her dizzy.

"I didn't come here to seduce you." The honesty in his voice competed with the torrent of desire in his eyes.

"You came here to walk me to the party." Her voice came out quiet and shaky, with a touch of disbelief. Where was her quippy, smart-ass response? She didn't need to be escorted anywhere. And the Jake she knew was all about casual hookups, not walking girls to parties like a 1950s boyfriend. Then again, this was the same guy who had shown up at the dress shop demanding they clear the air. The same guy who insisted on sharing a cab with her after a night of drinking in the city with Gabriella, Duke, and a few of their friends because he wanted to make sure she got home okay, and helped her backtrack when she lost her keys that same night. The guy who called to make sure she was okay the night of a horrible winter storm when he was away on a search and rescue mission and heard the electricity had gone out in her part of the city. He'd told her he was *making the rounds*, calling *everyone. And the guy who refused to leave my side this morning at dawn, when you walked me home despite my incessant arguments.* Some long-forgotten part of her quivered at that. They hadn't had a cursory relationship after all, had they?

"Yes, I did want to walk you to the party," he said gruffly. "But now all I want to do is get my mouth on you."

She made a mewing sound in the back of her throat. At an utter loss for words, she let her towel drop to the floor.

Chapter Seven

JAKE WOULD SURELY go straight to hell for the sinful thoughts racing through his mind as he claimed Addy in a desperate kiss, crushing her to him and backing her up against the wall. He really had come to walk her down to the beach. To *treat her like a lady*. But all hopes of keeping their time together PG went out the door when he realized what she'd been doing in the shower.

He nudged her legs open with his knee, refusing to release her incredible, silky, hot mouth. He couldn't wait to feel it around his cock again, but his turn would come. The need to taste her was overwhelming. He drew back from the kiss, taking in the rosy flush on her skin, her swollen lips and long, fluttering lashes. A low growl bubbled up from deep within him. He was powerless to refrain from taking her in another demanding kiss. His hands roved over her hips, clutching her ass—God he loved her ass. It was made for his hands, filling his palms perfectly. She rubbed her body against him, all those lush, naked curves begging to be touched. It was the sexiest move he'd ever felt. His temptress couldn't get enough, and that made him hard as steel.

She opened her eyes, watching as he dragged his fingertips down her breasts, along her ribs, to the sweet indentation of her waist as he settled on his knees, eye level with her soft tuft of damp curls. He kissed her inner thighs, inhaling the intoxicating scent of her desire and enjoying the way she quivered against him. She watched him boldly as he took her hands in his, running his tongue over her fingers. He'd conjured up the image of her pleasuring herself in the shower. Now he was going to get a front-row seat.

Guiding her fingers between her legs, she didn't hesitate to slide them between her slick lips and over her swollen clit, eyes still locked on him.

"You're so fucking sexy." He slicked his tongue over her fingers, tasting her essence. "*Mine*, Addy."

"We're not..." Her words were lost as he brought his mouth between her legs, thrusting his tongue deep inside her. "A *thing*," she whispered.

He pushed her hand away and bit down on her clit just hard enough to sting. Her hips bucked off the wall, and she gasped.

"We're a *thing*," he growled. "A damn good thing."

He sucked her slick fingers and brought them back to play alongside his tongue.

"So good. *Ah, yes.* Right there." She grabbed his shoulder with her free hand, and the hand on her sex stilled.

"Touch yourself, Addy. Touch yourself like you did in the shower." Her eyes narrowed and he pressed a kiss to her inner thigh. "Come on, sexy girl. Get dirty with me."

She closed her eyes and moved her fingers again.

"Eyes open."

As she opened her eyes, a flash of wicked appreciation brimmed in them. She grabbed his hair and pulled his mouth to her sex.

Damn. That's the girl I know. She rocked against his tongue as he teased and tasted, pushing two of his fingers deep inside her and earning another greedy moan. He glanced up, catching her staring as he feasted on her, taking her expertly up to the edge of release, then slowing his efforts to keep her orgasm just out of reach.

"Jake," she pleaded, moving her fingers faster. "Please."

The feel of her thighs on his cheeks and the sexy little murmurs coming from his girl nearly made him lose it. He grabbed her hips, devouring her sex, and gave her what she craved. A stream of erotic sounds sailed from her lungs at the same time he realized in his mind that she was already *his girl*, despite what she admitted. Emotions bubbled up inside him as she lost control, making it that much sweeter.

He rose to his feet and gathered her in his arms. "We're a thing, Addy. A very *good* thing."

She let out a long, dreamy sigh. "We're something, but I think it's more like really good sex partners."

"Like hell," he growled. "You're pesty. Has anyone ever told you that before?"

She tipped her face up toward him and smiled. "Usually they say I'm a pain in the ass. But I like your word better." She shifted her eyes over his shoulder and gasped. "Oh no. Gabby's coming over and now I have to shower again."

He chuckled, watching her sweet ass as she ran into the bathroom and turned the shower on.

"You smell like me," she called out to him. "You can wash up in here."

He heard the shower door close as he stripped off his shirt and headed for the bathroom, closing the door behind him.

"I don't mean to leave you hanging, but I'm supposed to meet Gab—"

He opened the shower door, and her eyes dropped to his

very hungry python.

"What are you doing?"

He stepped into the shower. "You said I could wash up in here."

She crossed her arms over her chest, but her giggle and the way her eyes darkened told him he wasn't overstepping his bounds as much as he was turning her on. "I meant in the *sink*."

"My bad." He grabbed a bottle of body wash and poured it into his palm.

"Jake," she said, eyeing his junk as he lowered her hands to her sides. "We're not a *thing*."

"A gentleman always takes care of his girl." He began washing her neck, rubbing the knots from her shoulders and massaging each arm as he washed them.

"I'm not your girl." That dreamy voice came out to play again.

"Yeah, yeah. I know." He washed her breasts, and her breathing quickened. As he washed her ribs, she placed her soft hand on his hip. "Don't even think about getting dirty with me, sexy girl. You have a party to get to."

He took his time, washing her hips, her thighs, running his hands all the way down to her slender ankles. As he made his way back up her body, washing as he went, it took all his restraint not to back her up against the tile wall and bury himself deep inside her. His hands moved over her tattoo, seeing it clearly for the first time. Heavy chains encased a weathered box with thickly stitched seams that looked like sewn-up gashes. He glanced up at her and she covered it with her hand.

"Why chains, baby?"

"Please don't," she said in such a vulnerable voice it killed him.

He pressed his lips to the tattoo, growing more possessive of her by the second. All sorts of meanings for the tattoo plagued him as he circled her body, washing her back and shoulders. None of them were good or happy or even moderately acceptable. He gathered her close from behind and kissed her cheek, wanting desperately for her to let him in.

She sighed.

"You okay?"

"No," she said softly, but it was a confused answer, not distraught. "What are we doing, Jake?"

He turned her in his arms, needing to see her face. Her sweet, perplexed smile brought another rush of emotions. "I don't know, but I like it. It feels right."

She held on to his hips and touched her forehead to the center of his chest. "I don't do this."

"Shower? Because I'm pretty sure you were showering when I heard you call out my name."

She lifted her eyes to his. He smiled down at her and touched his lips to hers in a kiss so tender it struck him that he'd never kissed anyone like that before.

"*This*, Jake. You and me. You probably don't even want this to be that serious either, but if you do, you're looking for something I can't give you. I'm not the kind of girl you need."

"You don't have to hide your past, Addy," he said seriously. "I get it, and I can deal with it."

"Not *that*. *This*. *Us*. I don't know how to be whatever it is you want me to be." She lifted serious eyes to him, but he thought they looked a bit sad, too.

"Just be yourself. I *like* who you are. Sassy mouth and all." He shifted their positions so she was beneath the water and washed the soap from her skin.

"Addy?" Gabriella called from outside the bathroom door.

"Shit. Shh." She put her finger over his mouth and called out, "I'll meet you at the beach. I'm running a little late."

There was no response. Addy closed her eyes, hands fisted, and mouthed, *Please go away. Please go away.* "Okay, Gab?"

"I'm going," Gabriella said through the door. "Duke said if I saw Jake to tell him to hurry up. I assume seeing his clothes counts."

If looks could kill, he'd be lying dead on a very beautiful woman's shower floor. But her actions had betrayed her true feelings just as they had earlier, her fingers curling around his wrist as she rested her cheek against his chest, telling him he was exactly where she wanted him after all.

"I'M SO GLAD the paparazzi are gone." Trish gazed out at the water with one hand on her hip, the other holding a wineglass, complete with a tiny plastic man in a speedo hanging off the rim—one of her bachelorette party decorations.

"Boone and Duke's plan was genius," Gabriella said, topping off her glass. "I'm just glad it worked. I had serious doubts." Like horses chasing carrots, the story-hungry reporters had followed the models disguised as Trish and Boone away from the island.

"They were making Boone crazy," Trish admitted. "He gets so protective."

Maggie, Boone's sister, laughed and shook her head. She'd arrived earlier in the afternoon with the rest of Boone's family. She was outgoing and friendly, and had immediately clicked with the girls. "That sounds like my brother. He's spent his life watching over everyone."

"That's one of the reasons I love him so much," Trish admitted. "I love how protective he is."

"Did I ever tell you about when I first met Cash? I thought he was pushy, overprotective, and…" The reflection of the bonfire danced in Siena's mischievous eyes. "So frigging hot, it made him even more annoying."

"To hot, overprotective men," Lizzie said, lifting her glass.

Addy sipped her wine as they toasted, unsure how she felt about the whole overprotective thing. The chilly evening breeze sent their hair whipping across their faces and their dresses swishing around their legs. But Addy barely noticed the inconvenience. After nearly two hours, and two glasses of wine, she was still trying to untangle the web of emotions clouding her thoughts. She felt guilty for not revealing the meaning of her tattoo to Jake, but she sort of already had. *Pandora's box.* Her grandmother's words were always with her, like the tattoo. *Pride, lust, and anger aren't deadly sins, Addison. They're your saviors. Own them. They'll empower you with the ability to take what you want and always be in control. Harness the power to speak your mind, or you'll fall into the same loveless marriage your mother and I did.* Obviously harnessing the power of those things wasn't a problem.

Her grandmother had been married prior to marrying the man Addy had known as her grandfather. Her grandmother had described her first husband as *wild and passionate as a winter storm.* She'd said they'd fought—and loved—like their lives depended on it, and he'd respected her need for independence in a time when women were taught to cater to their men. They'd been married for only a few years when he was killed in the war, leaving her grandmother with a new baby girl to raise alone. She'd married her second husband with the hopes of finding true love again, but like Addy's father, he had negated her need to speak her mind at every turn. He treated her like a precious jewel, which would be nice for someone who didn't care about making decisions or doing what she wanted when she wanted to. Addy's grandmother wasn't that type of woman, and it was no secret that she had resigned herself to the role women of her time were taught to abide, citing her need for a stable home to raise Addy's mother.

Addy placed her hand over her tattoo, thinking of the warning her grandmother had given her in her last hours of life, when she'd pushed Addy to find someone like her first husband. Her true love. *You're a winter storm, Addison. Any man short of a stormy night will suck the life right out of you. Don't let anyone take your passion away. Lock it up tight and find your stormy night. True love comes only once, and only a love of that magnitude can survive the combined power of a winter storm and a stormy night.*

She'd gotten her tattoo shortly after her grandmother had passed away.

"I mean, really," Siena said, bringing Addy's attention back to the party. "Sure, Cash saved me when my car had careened off the highway in the middle of a snowstorm, but he was so serious!" Lizzie grabbed Siena's wrist and concentrated on writing something on the inside of it with a gold Sharpie as Siena finished telling her story. "He ushered me up to his truck to wait for the rescue crew and got mad when I didn't want to stay put."

Lizzie moved from Siena to Trish, turned her wrist over, and scrawled something on it.

"What are you doing?" Trish held her wrist down by the fire and gasped with delight. "Lizzie! I love that!"

"Bridal tattoos!" Lizzie grabbed Gabriella's arm next. They all gathered around to check out her artwork. "Well, not really tattoos, but gold sparkly ink. Ours say 'Bride Tribe,' and Trish's says 'Bride'!"

Everyone cheered as Lizzie worked her way around the group.

"Cash obviously didn't know you," Sally said to Siena. The girls all murmured in agreement.

"Obviously not," Siena agreed. "But he was relentless in his pursuit of me, and he was such a gentleman. It was as refreshing as it was frustrating. Because I'm a model, I was constantly bombarded with guys who saw me as nothing but a pretty face and hot body. You can imagine how well that went over with me. I wasn't exactly a pretty little flower there for the taking. And Cash got the harsh end of my bad experiences. I wasn't used to letting anyone take care of me the way he wanted to."

At least I'm not alone in my need for independence.

"Poor Cash. Sounds like he and Boone both had their hands full. I was so pissed at Boone when we finally met face-to-face, I think I was sporting fangs and claws." Trish turned toward the wind so her hair flew out behind her instead of whipping across her face. "But boy did I misjudge him. He is everything I could ever hope for and more. Passionate, thoughtful, and as loyal as the men I grew up with, which is a big deal, because you all know how the Ryder men are."

A day ago Addy thought she could tell the difference between a smooth-talking guy and an honest one, but now she wasn't so sure. She had Jake in a mental box marked OFF-LIMITS PLAYER, and now he wasn't just trying to climb out of it, but he wanted to crash down the sides and obliterate the damn box in one fell swoop.

"What changed that made you get past your claws and fangs?" Addy asked Trish.

Gabriella turned an inquisitive look to Addy.

"Stop it, Gab. Just because you caught us in the shower together doesn't mean I'm looking for more. He's just a friend with benefits, tiding me over for my long, lonely weeks in the mountains." Addy tried to drown the acidic taste of that fib with wine.

"Caught you in the shower together?" Lizzie and Trish said in unison.

She'd spoken so fast, her reveal hadn't registered. She mumbled a curse for feeding the grapevine and guzzled more wine.

"Uh-huh. I sure did." Gabriella laughed. "If there are two people alive who can stockpile sex to tide them over, it would be you and Jake."

"I'd say. Shower sex is hot," Siena said.

"We didn't have shower sex," Addy snapped a little too harshly.

"Well, why not?" Siena asked.

Trish held her hands up. "Wait. This is my brother. Please don't answer that."

"If Jake's set his sights on you"—Lizzie leaned closer to Addy, wobbling a little—"there's no way he'll ever let go. Nope. Ryder guys aren't made that way. Blue asked me out for a year. *A year*!" She waved the pen at Addy and Addy took it from her hand so she didn't end up with gold ink on her face. "I fell so hard I'm surprised I didn't break."

Lizzie laughed so much she snorted, sending them all into fits of laughter. Except Addy, who couldn't imagine any man pursuing a woman for a year without giving up. *But Jake propositioned me for months.* Months. Not days. Not weeks. *Months.* Their feelings didn't come out of nowhere. They'd been simmering for a long time. She thought about Blue and Lizzie. Could she ever love and be loved like that? Would it be smothering? She looked at her friends, who were busy chatting about their adoring men. None of them appeared to feel smothered. They seemed truly happy. Not for the first time, she wondered what held Sally back from getting involved with Gage. Did she have trouble feeling something for him because she'd lost her husband? Or maybe because she'd loved him so deeply? Addy's thoughts turned inward. She didn't have an excuse as to why she'd never connected emotionally with a man before Jake, and she found that frustrating. She'd wanted to feel more, hoped for it, but it had never happened. She'd always remained totally in control. But Jake obliterated that hold over her emotions. How did he manage to make her feel so flustered?

"Jake didn't set his sights on me." The words came unbidden, and all the girls looked at her with confusion in their eyes that mirrored the confusion inside her. "I want to clear that up. We just have a healthy sexual appetite. Jake and I click in that department. Let's not make it into something it's not." Addy refilled her drink and downed a mouthful, wondering who she was trying to convince—them or herself.

"Speaking of healthy sexual appetites." Sally's cheeks flushed. "I might have spent some time on your Tumblr page."

"And then with her battery-powered friend," Lizzie chimed in.

Addy was glad for the change of subject and took another gulp of wine.

"No, I most certainly did not!" Sally took a drink, then said, just above a whisper, "I took a *long*, hot bath."

"Same, same," Lizzie said.

"Tumblr page?" Maggie asked. "What am I missing out on?"

Siena jumped in and told Maggie about Addy's Cocks I Want to Rock social media habit, while Lizzie appeased Sally.

"There's no shame in it, Sal," Lizzie said. "Heck, I peeked at Addy's Tumblr page and attacked Blue afterward. Of course, I can never do that again, because the man is about as jealous as a green-eyed lizard."

"So is Cash, although he'd never admit it." Siena went on to share a story about a lingerie magazine shoot she'd done and how Cash had hidden all the magazines from the guys at his firehouse. That sparked a long line of jealousy tales and seductive remedies.

Jealousy had no place where hookups were concerned, so Addy didn't have much experience to add her two cents. Instead, she joined their discussion, offering her forte. "Distracting your man from jealousy with seduction. I like it! Especially since seducing a man is easy as one, two, three."

The girls leaned in a little closer.

"Do share," Siena begged. "Since having the twins, I feel like I'm losing my ability to go from mom to seductress."

"Cash can't keep his hands off of you," Trish refuted.

"Still," Siena said. "I need a refresher, and Gab said Addy's got all the moves."

"She did?"

Gabriella turned her hands palms to the sky.

Addy laughed. "Well, she's right. There are so many ways to turn your man into a sex machine, and you can do most of them in *public*. The payoff will definitely come later."

"Pun intended, I assume," Maggie added.

"Always." This was where Addy shined. She might not know much about deep-seated emotions, but she was a master at seduction. "Okay, so, you know how you take great care in picking out just the right lingerie before you go out? Like at Gab's wedding. I bet you guys all wore sexy, lacy thongs or matching bras and panties."

They all nodded.

"But what good did it do you?"

"Hey, speak for yourself," Gabriella said. "I definitely got plenty of my man last night."

"You were the *bride*. It's expected. But that doesn't even matter. It's not about the sex. It's about the buildup. The anticipation, breaking the rules."

"Not that I have a boyfriend, but I'm not much of a rule breaker," Sally admitted.

"Me either," Lizzie said.

"Not real rules. Socially appropriate flirting rules. But no one will know you're breaking them except you and your man. At Trish's wedding, instead of dressing sexy and then hoping your man will notice, let him know, but *don't* show him. Dress in a different room, and then throughout the day sidle up to him like this." She rose to her feet and pulled Gabriella up with her. Gabriella swayed and Addy steadied her. "No more wine for you, Gabs. Watch, girls."

Addy stepped behind Gabriella and brushed the front of her shoulder against the back of Gabriella's arm while stroking her hand up Gabriella's chest. She put her hand around Gabriella's neck and whispered, "I'm wearing new lace panties." Her hand slid down Gabriella's chest, and she sauntered away slowly, swaying her hips and tossing one seductive glance over her shoulder.

"She's good," Lizzie whispered.

"Told you," Gabriella said proudly.

An hour—along with a few more glasses of wine and enough seduction techniques to make Addy want to use that side of herself on Jake—later they were practicing their newfound skills on each other, when they noticed Eva, the woman who ran the salon in town, walking along the shore. They waved, and Eva lifted the hem of her long, flowing skirt and headed up the beach toward them. Her dark hair was secured on the top of her head in a messy nest, with wispy tendrils whipping around her face. Several long necklaces hung around her neck, pooling in her cleavage.

Gabriella handed her a wineglass. "Join us?"

Eva wrinkled her brow. "Can I have the whole bottle?"

"That bad of a night, huh?" Trish asked.

"That bad of a decision. I'm not sure I'm cut out for Elpitha," Eva admitted tentatively. "I really wanted to come back and make a go of it since my mother left me the salon, but all the signs were there telling me not to, and I think I made a huge mistake."

"Where did you move from?" Addy asked.

"Chicago, and my life there was amazing." Eva sank down to the sand, and they all followed suit around the bonfire. "The island is a bit limited for me. I forgot how serene and *small* it really is."

"But everyone loves you and your knowledge of Pinterest," Gabriella said.

"Somehow I don't think she's talking about showing the ladies in town hot guys on Pinterest," Addy added. "I admit, I couldn't live here. I love visiting, but I'm not cut out for a quiet life. I get too restless."

"She means bored with the men." Gabriella giggled and leaned in to Addy, clearly more than tipsy. "But Jake's trying his best to fill those sexy, shmexy needs."

"You've hooked that man mighty hard," Eva said.

"Is nothing sacred on Elpitha?" Addy glared at Gabriella, who shrugged.

"It wasn't gossip that revealed your secret," Eva explained. "Hasn't Gabriella told you? I'm a seer. I knew when I met you two at the wedding you were destined to fall for each other."

"You are?" Trish asked with wide eyes. "Can you see our futures?"

Gabriella nodded. "She can."

"Sorry, Eva," Addy said. "But I think your seeing abilities are out of whack, because I'm not falling for anyone."

Eva patted Addy's thigh. "Okay, honey. You keep believing that, but those questions ricocheting in your mind should tip you off. Don't fight so hard against them. You're no stranger to exploration."

The glimmer of understanding in her eyes was so vivid, Addy felt exposed, like Eva could see her past and the way she owned her sexuality.

"This is just a different type of exploration." Eva winked, finished her wine, and pushed to her feet. "I think you've helped me make my decision."

"How could I possibly have helped?" Addy asked.

"Being a seer is a part of me that I can't turn off, and seeing too much isn't always a gift. I already know more about my relatives than I'd like. But that shocked look on your face? That's when I know I've hit the nail on the head. I think I need to start thinking about going back to Chicago, where lots of strangers need guidance and I don't have to worry about being the bearer of news they're not ready to accept. Once they leave my center for spirituality I never see them again. But here, every time I reveal something like I just have, the recipient will have that look on his or her face. And then they'll start to avoid me. Until they see that I was right. But those uncomfortable weeks in between? No thanks."

"Sorry to rain on your parade, Eva," Addy said. "But I'm not going to look at you in any way, because I'm not into all that mystical stuff."

"That's okay," Eva said. "You don't have to be. The universe knows what it knows." She set her wineglass down on the table and shifted her gaze to Maggie. Her brows knitted, and she reached for her hand. "You lost your father," she said carefully.

"Yes," Maggie said. "Many years ago."

Eva nodded. Then her expression softened and she said, "But you still speak to him."

Maggie blushed. "Not literally, but I think of him often, and I hope he hears me."

"He hears you, honey." Eva embraced her. "And that other thing?" She winked, causing Maggie to blush again. "There's a special someone waiting to meet you."

"Please draw me a map to his front door," Maggie said with a laugh.

"You won't need it." Eva moved to embrace Trish. "Congratulations on your impending marriage. It will be a happy one with lots of babies to keep you busy."

"Really?" Trish squealed.

Eva glanced at Sally. "I'm getting *lots* of baby vibes from this group." She waved. "Have an uplifting night, girls."

As Eva walked away, Sally sidled up to Addy. "You're right. She doesn't know what she's talking about. *Babies*? You need to have sex for that to happen."

But as Addy's mind drifted back to Jake, she was no longer so sure it was all a hoax.

CHAPTER EIGHT

"ONE THING I can tell you about my brother is that he's a sappy bastard." Boone's younger brother, Cage, patted him on the shoulder. Cage was a professional fighter, as evident in the way he carried his massive body, like he could plow down anything in his path.

Boone faked a punch, which Cage dodged. "Sappy my ass."

"Seriously, dude?" Lucky said. "You adopted a *kitten*."

Boone had rescued a kitten when he and Trish first met. He reminded Jake of Blue, who used to bring home stray or injured animals they'd find in the woods behind their parents' house. He glanced at Blue, who would also soon be walking down the matrimonial aisle. It struck him that only he and Gage were still single, and Gage might as well not be. *Do I want to be?*

"That's how Boone won our sister's heart." Duke winked at Boone, as if to say he had his back. He always had everyone's back. Hell, they all did.

"Hey, you could use that ploy with Addy," Cash said to Jake.

They'd gone out for a long, hard, enjoyable run up the coastline earlier and had spent the first part of their run talking about how proud they were of Trish and Boone for the Oscar buzz they'd earned. The conversation had turned to the twins and Siena—as per usual—and Jake had tried to keep up, though his mind had been stuck on a certain petite brunette who had woken up in his arms and slithered around naked in the shower with him just a short while ago. Cash stopped talking about his family only long enough to give Jake one bit of sage advice. *What you're feeling and not talking about? There is no rescue from it. That's the real thing. And the only thing you'll think about day and night until you get your girl.* Jake had laughed it off, but now, as he sat in the tavern for Boone's bachelor party thinking about Addy, he had a feeling his brother's wisdom wasn't so far off base after all.

Lucky reached for a beer and Boone pushed it away from him. "Eighteen is eighteen. Not on my watch, little brother."

Lucky scoffed. "At least I don't need a kitten to get laid."

That brought a round of laughter to the table, and a few curious looks from nearby customers. Nearly every table on the patio of Liakos Taverna was full and loaded up with bottles of wine, plates of grilled meats and vegetables, baskets of fresh-baked bread, and casserole dishes.

Niko and Dimitri came out of the kitchen with two large platters stacked high with skewers of meat and set them down on a neighboring table. As the owners of the tavern, they explained that they never really took time off. Jake couldn't imagine working in the same place every day, which was why he volunteered with search and rescue in several states. He could be on the West Coast one day, the East Coast the next, and in middle of the States a week later. But for the next two weeks, he wasn't traveling outside of New York. As soon as he heard about Addy's ten-day stint in the mountains, he made sure he'd be nearby in case she ran into trouble. Although he was still holding out hope that she'd let him go with her.

Niko said something in Greek, which caused an eruption of

laughter from the family they were serving, and then he returned to their table, taking the seat beside Jake. "Sorry I pissed you off last night."

"No worries." *Just keep your hands off my girl.*

"Get used to it, brother. We're family now. I'm sure I'll piss you off more than a few times, but not over a woman. I didn't realize you two were together, and it was just harmless flirting. I've known Addy for years. I'll steer clear." Niko lifted his beer. "To family."

Jake toasted, wishing he'd known Addy for years. He looked around the table. He'd never understood the point of bachelor parties with strippers and lap dancing. If a guy was committed to getting married, why would he *want* a lap dance from someone other than his fiancée? Hell, before he'd even spent one night with Addy the thought of being with another woman was so far gone he needed a GPS to find it.

He wondered what she was doing with the girls. One look at Niko brought back the memory of Addy in his newfound "brother's" arms. That little nugget sat in his gut like a bowling ball. His leg bounced nervously beneath the table, his fingers itching to hold her again. *We're not a thing.* Her comment about *Pandora's box* told a different story. Did she really want no strings attached? Everything had changed, and he knew she felt it, too.

Pushing to his feet, he leaned his palms on the table, his eyes skating around it. "Who's up for crashing the bachelorette party?"

"Hell, yes." Boone high-fived him. "Man, I love you guys, but I sure as hell would rather have your sister in my arms than sit around drinking and talking shit."

"Are there any single women at this party?" Cage asked.

"No," Jake answered without hesitation.

Gage shot him a curious look. "Technically there are." He turned an intense stare on Cage. "But you don't want to go there."

Cage held up his hands. "No worries. Lucky and I'll go hang out at the bar." He snickered. "Oh, wait. You're too young." He ruffled his younger brother's hair and bumped fists with Boone.

"Seriously? Y'all are going to ditch me?" Lucky spotted a group of girls walking by the patio. "I'll catch you losers later. I see a few ladies who are in need of my company. They just don't know it yet."

"Behave," Boone called after him.

Cash said something, but Jake was already too far away to hear him. He jogged across the street and down the road toward the beach. The flames of the girls' bonfire came into view before his eyes adjusted enough to make them out. As he ran down the beach, he zeroed in on Addy's slim figure, with curves so perfect she could grace the cover of any magazine and a beautiful face that made him smile and ache at once. She stood at the edge of the water, her dress flapping around her thighs, her hair whipping like a wild mane.

"Jake? Is everything okay?" Trish called out as he jogged by.

"It's about to be."

Addy turned at the sound of his voice, and he swept her into his arms and kept on running.

"Jake!" she shrieked. "What are you doing?" She laughed as she tried to push free. Something dug into his chest.

The other girls cheered him on as he slowed to a jog, carrying Addy toward a secluded spot he'd found during his run with Cash. He snagged the pen that was digging into his chest from her hands and shoved it in his pocket.

"I should throw you in this water for denying we're a *thing.*" He rocked her in his arms as if he were about to toss her into the waves, and she threw them around his neck, shrieking at the top of her lungs. "What's the matter? Afraid of a little water, sexy girl?"

"Do it!" Gabriella hollered, and so began a chant from all the other women. "Do it! Do it! Do it!"

"Don't, don't, don't. *Please* don't," she begged.

Jake inhaled the sweet lavender lotion he'd helped her apply to her beautiful naked body just a few hours ago. He could still feel her smooth skin against his hands, could still hear her sweet noises of restraint as she kicked him out the door before she could *give in to skipping the party and letting him devour her.* Because of that, he hadn't gotten to walk her to the party, but the time they'd shared had been even better.

"I should toss you in just to show you how much your rules suck."

"You wouldn't dare." She tightened her grip around his neck.

He swung her again, and she shrieked, clinging to him like a monkey to a tree. *Perfect.* "Are we a *thing*?"

"Jake!" She buried her face in his neck. "Please don't. *Please*?"

He should demand she give in and tell him what he knew was true, but she looked up at him with wide, pleading eyes, sparking the need to take care of her again. The feel of her body against him, her hot little hands on the back of his neck, and her beautiful face within kissing distance had him quickening his pace to get her alone.

"Jake! Put me down! Where are you taking me?" She poked

him in the chest. "Hello? Do you hear me? Put me down!"

He shifted her over his shoulder like a sack of potatoes and slapped her on her ass.

"Hey!" she protested with the sexiest laugh he'd ever heard.

"You need a man who can put up with your shit *and* slap your ass."

A trail of claps and whistles from his brothers, who had finally made it to the beach, sounded out behind them.

She laughed, and it was music to his ears. He repositioned her, cradling her in his arms, and brushed his lips over hers, laughing when she pressed hers into a defiant line.

He was *done*.

He was *hers*.

He debated tossing her in the water just to prove they were playing by his rules this time, but he finally had her back in his arms again. The last thing he wanted to do was let her go.

CHAPTER NINE

JAKE HADN'T SAID a word in the last ten minutes as he carried Addy down the beach. He'd walked so far the bonfire was a mere spark in the distance, and he showed no signs of stopping. "Do you really think being a Neanderthal is the way to win me over?" Addy asked.

He didn't answer, just continued walking, staring straight ahead. His pecs danced against her side as he tightened his grip.

"This big, tough, silent thing you have going on is really annoying. You can't just abscond with me and think I'll be okay with it."

He shifted a narrow-eyed stare her way, then looked straight ahead again, his thick brows hooding his vigilante gaze.

"Jake, seriously. At least let me walk." Not that she *wanted* to walk, but despite how incredible it felt to be snuggled against him, being carried made her feel ridiculous. She suppressed a smile, watching his body tense up, and she took a moment to study him. There was nothing pretty-boy about Jake. His skin was slightly weathered, as if he spent his days facing harsh winds and blazing sun, which she knew he often did when he was on rescue missions. His features were symmetrical, his jawline chiseled and squared, with an ever-present tan and a coarse dusting of whiskers. Her stomach dipped at the memory of his coarse whiskers against her inner thighs.

He turned up the beach toward a long ridge of large rocks. The lighthouse blinked slowly in the distance, and the languid pace of the fading beam made her realize how fast and hard her heart was pounding. He scaled the boulders without missing a step, expertly cradling her against him.

"Jake?" she asked softly.

He stopped atop a large rock, his gaze dialing down to concern, the wind making his thick hair stand up.

"Where are we going?"

He ground his teeth together again and continued traversing the rocks to a patch of sand and grass just beyond. He knelt, setting her carefully on the ground, and sank down beside her. He pulled his knees up, leaned his forearms on them, and gazed out at the water as if he hadn't just kidnapped her.

She looked around, digging her toes into the pebbly sand beneath her bare feet. She'd left her sandals with the girls, but she didn't care. The rocks formed a barrier from the wind sweeping up the sand, blowing only the tips of long tufts of grass. She followed Jake's gaze to the dim golden haze of the lighthouse reaching into the darkness and reflecting off the inky water. The starless sky was tinted a dusky shade of blue. Sitting there in the dark beside the only man who had ever challenged her, who understood that she needed a man to put up with her shit *and* spank her ass—*and God, did she ever*—felt *romantic*. Even the way he'd kidnapped her was romantic. Either she was losing her mind, or she really was falling for him.

"It's beautiful here," she finally said.

He dropped his gaze to the sand, tilting his face toward her. The moon caught his eyes, bringing out a thin ring of green around the edges. She'd never noticed it before. All this time, she'd been too swept up in his alpha hotness to notice. What else had she missed?

"*You're* beautiful, Addy."

She lost her breath at the unexpected compliment spoken so tenderly it sounded strange coming from such a big man. She swallowed hard and couldn't help studying him again, searching for signs that he was kidding or this was just another wicked flirtation. But what she saw wasn't either of those things. It was honesty.

He smiled. "Expecting to see someone else?"

"Kinda. Yeah," she said, glad to have found her voice. "I don't…"

"You don't get it? Or…?" He leaned closer and ran his hand up her calf, his gaze turning hungry.

There was the man she knew. The sexually driven, demanding one she expected.

"You are beautiful, Addy, but that's not why I'm into you." He cupped her cheek, his eyes moving slowly over her face, the demand in them fading away, throwing her for another loop.

She felt shy as he studied her, causing an avalanche of emotions she was nowhere near prepared for. Her breathing quickened, and her skin prickled with awareness of everything—the chilly air sailing over her skin, his faint musky cologne mixing with the salty scents of the sea, the feel of his rough hand caressing her leg, and the way he was looking at her, which felt far more intimate than anything they'd done to each other in the last twenty-four hours.

The minutes ticked by in interminable silence, amping up her anticipation as she waited for him to say more.

"Do you not get it, Addy, or was there something else you were going to say?"

She looked away to break the spell he'd cast, but a soft press of his fingers on her chin brought her eyes back to him. She couldn't even begin to remember what she was going to say, and that rattled her, too. He'd kidnapped her. Carried her off like he owned her. She should be livid. The woman she knew herself to be would never put up with that. *That* woman would push to her feet and stomp away, refusing to be manhandled or manipulated in any way. But her eyes found his again, and her resolve to prove her independence lessened, and that brought another rush of emotions. Fear? Discomfort? Excitement? She wasn't sure, but it was unsettling. She curled her fingers into the sand, willing herself to push through her confusion.

"I'm not going to fall at your feet because you made a grand romantic gesture." *Grand romantic gesture?* Geez, she was really going for that *goner* status.

His jaw went tight again. Did he have to look so hot when he was angry?

"Why are you so stubborn? I didn't bring you out here to be romantic. Jesus, Addy. That's not me. *Romantic.*" He uttered the last word under his breath, like a curse.

"Why, then?" She didn't mean to raise her voice, but the roller coaster of emotions had taken its toll, and there was no stopping the words flying from her lungs. She pushed to her feet. "I'll never be a mindless woman you can tell what to do, or fawn over for that matter. You're barking up the wrong tree. I take what I want and move on. I've never hidden that about myself. I've got things to do, and no one is going to stop me from doing them."

Tears of frustration burned in her eyes as he rose beside her, towering over her, and placed his hands on her upper arms, holding her just tight enough to make it clear that he wasn't going to let go.

"I swear you're deaf as a doorknob." The words flew harshly from her lungs, but inside she crumbled a little with each one as she struggled against her lifelong need for independence and her desire to be all in with him.

He stared down at her without saying a word.

"Are you going to say anything, or just hold me hostage?"

"I'm waiting until you're done ranting."

"Ranting? That's an asshole thing to say."

"Is it?" His stare was brutal. "Because I think an asshole thing to say is more like, 'Get off your fucking high horse. I have no interest in *fawning* over you or any other woman.'" He loosened his grip on her arms. "I'd like to see the guy who believes he can tell you what you can and cannot do."

"You want *something*, Jake," she spat. "Maybe it's not to fawn over me, but it's something."

"Yeah. *You*, Addy. I want *you*."

Crumble, crumble, crumble... Crash!

"I told you this earlier and you're too stubborn to even consider it. I like your pushy, smart-ass ways. God knows I might regret admitting this, but you're the only woman I've felt anything for. *Ever*. We're not kids, Addison, and you're not clueless. We click. We're good together. I *get* you. So what is really going on? Why are you fighting it?"

She dropped her eyes, unwilling to allow him to see the emotions he was unearthing inside her, each one stacking up on top of the last, building pressure like a shaken-up soda bottle ready to burst. She closed her eyes for a beat, trying to sort through a response, to figure out how to describe what she felt, when his words finally sank in. *You're the only woman I've felt anything for. Ever.*

Lifting her chin to meet his gaze, she felt like she was looking at him through new eyes. Gone was the pissed-off alpha who wanted to get his way, replaced with a guy who was pouring out his soul. Guilt pressed in on her along with something far more weighty. If what he'd said was true, then he really did get her.

"What do you mean, I'm the only woman you've ever *felt* anything for?"

"Exactly that," he said sternly. "I *fuck*. I *take*. I get rid of my stress through sex. But never in my life have I wanted more, or cared where the women I'd been with went next—or who they'd been with before me. But I can't get you out of my frigging mind. When I think of another man's hands on you I want to tear them apart limb by fucking limb. But it's more than that. Ever since the day I met you, I've thought about you every fricking day, and not just about sex. Although my mind's an ocean of dirty thoughts where you're concerned. I tried to lose myself in other women, which I shouldn't admit, because you can totally use it against me, but it's true. It didn't work. You were right there, front and center in my mind. And then you finally take me up on my offer and we *connect*, Addy. We connect on every level. You joke, you push, you..." He raked a hand through his hair and sighed. "You're just like me, Addy. You talk dirty. You like it rough *and* tender. You push boundaries. I get turned on just thinking about kissing you. *Kissing* you."

I do, too. She clenched her teeth, disbelief holding her words in.

"And tonight? I *wanted* to walk you to that party, but not to fawn over you. I wanted to spend that time with you. To walk to the beach and talk like normal people. To get to know you—beyond the sex, beyond the flirting. I wanted to treat you like you deserve to be treated. Like a *lady*."

"I'm hardly a lady," she said too sharply.

"Bullshit. And I fucked that up big time in too many ways to count. But my intentions were solid, Addy. You drive me out of my mind, and that's..." He released her arms, turned away, and said, "It's scary as shit."

Scary? The man who faced the most harrowing rescue missions a person could imagine and refused to acknowledge the meaning of the word *danger* where his own safety was concerned was *scared*? Hearing his confession was like being pummeled by waves and sent tumbling over the ocean floor. She was drowning in it, unable to swim to the surface. She sank down to the sand, staring blankly out to sea.

He moved into her line of sight and crouched before her. With the dark sky at his back, he looked even more powerful, more confident and alluring, than ever. His penetrating gaze challenged and enticed her. She'd never looked for her equal in a man, but Jake was just that. Unyielding. Dirty talking. Boundary pushing. He was the epitome of *alpha*—the leader of the pack. *The one to mate with every female*. Her stomach twisted at that, but wasn't that who she was, in the female version? What he'd just said made her believe he didn't want that anymore. The question was, did she?

The sounds of the sea fell away, and all that was left was the sound of his deep, confident voice. "You know that moment when you hook up with someone and you experience those first few seconds of *what the fuck am I doing*?"

Swallowing the unexpected shame that came with her answer, she nodded.

"That what-the-hell moment?" he clarified. "It didn't happen with you."

They both fell silent. Jake was breathing hard, as if he needed a moment to wrap his mind around what he'd admitted, just as she did.

"So, what *did* happen?" she asked in a shaky voice.

Jake shook his head, and when he spoke it was low and gravelly, like it was hard for him to admit. "The instant our bodies came together…Damn, Addison, just thinking about it makes my chest—" He banged his fist over his heart with a pained expression. "I remember the warmth of your skin, the way your face fit so perfectly in my hand, like the rest of our bodies. As if we were the only two people on earth who could fit so well together. Everything was different—every thought, every urge." Taking her hand in his, he said, "I know we're right for each other, Addy, and I'll spend every minute we have proving that to you."

"I'm leaving tomorrow." *I'm leaving tomorrow?* That didn't even come close to a worthy or appropriate response to all he'd revealed, but her head was spinning. And her heart—an organ she'd spent no time considering in the past—was beating so hard she could feel it pulsing in the space between them.

"I know. I wanted to talk to you about that, too."

"I'm going, Jake." The knee-jerk response came out too fast for her to stop it.

"I'm not asking you not to go. *Jesus*, Addy. Give me a chance. I just want to be sure you're safe when you're up there. Why is that so frigging bad?"

The frustration in his voice brought a thread of guilt. Another emotion she didn't have a lot of experience with. She took a moment to gather her I'm-not-changing-for-any-man rebellion and focused on the one thing she had to know.

"Was all that stuff you said true?" The heart she'd never

paid any mind to suddenly morphed to glass, fragile and vulnerable, terrifying her even more as she awaited his answer.

His eyes never left hers. "Have you ever known me to lie?"

She shook her head, and an image of him cradling her glass heart formed in her mind. Her own confession vied to be set free, but fear trapped it in her throat.

He lifted her hand and pressed a kiss to the back of it. "We're a *thing*, Addy. Even if you say we're not, you can't escape us any more than I can. When you leave here, you're going to think of me. Of *us*. As often as you breathe."

A lump rose in her throat with the truth. He sat back on his heels and placed his palms on his thighs. His riveting gaze willed her to break through her fears and meet him halfway. Did he know how scared she was? How much she hated being scared? Could he see it? Feel it? She'd gone forever refusing to acknowledge fear, but Jake brought it to the forefront, like other emotions she'd long ago buried, and he refused to let her hide behind them.

"You make me feel, too," she admitted. "And that terrifies me."

JAKE LET OUT a breath he hadn't realized he was holding. She was scared. *Well, join the fucking club.*

"Don't look so relieved," she said sharply. "It's not like I'm going to give in to your cavemanlike demands just because I admitted that what I'm feeling scares me."

He laughed because she was so…*Addy.*

She scowled. "I reveal something like that to you and you laugh at me? I think I liked this better when we were trying to ignore the desire to rip each other's clothes off."

He pulled her toward him. When she resisted, he tugged harder, purposely tumbling backward and bringing her down on top of him. He wrapped her in his arms and rolled her onto her back, trapping her beneath him.

Her scowl twitched as she stifled a smile. "You're so…"

He felt that cocky grin she teased him about spreading across his face. "Hot? Hard? Relentless? I'll take all three, thank you very much."

"Frustrating." Laughter broke through her steely resolve.

He pressed his hips against her sweet, soft body. "I can ease that tension for you."

She laughed again.

"I love your laugh, sexy girl."

"You don't love anything, except maybe sex."

"I do love sex, and sex with you is beyond incredible, but your laugh? I hear it when you're not even around."

She rolled her eyes. "Don't use silly lines on me. I'd much rather you say what you meant. You're glad I'm past my rant so you can get down and dirty with me."

"I'm glad you're past your rant, yes. And I *do* want to get down and dirty with you." He reached beneath her and grabbed her ass. "And I love your ass." Her smile widened and he kissed her neck, earning a giggle that made him want to hear more of it. "I cannot wait to feel your plump, sexy lips around my cock again." He slicked his tongue over her mouth and she leaned up, but he drew away.

She grabbed his shirt and yanked him back down. "If I were a guy, I'd call you a cock tease."

"Would you?" He pushed his hand beneath her dress, loving that they could still play this game even though everything had changed, and stopped at the feel of lace on his fingertips. "I do love you in lace."

He kissed her softly, but she grabbed his head, deepening the kiss. He fought to ignore the seductive grinding of her hips. He'd messed up once today when he'd wanted to treat her right, even if she'd seemed to enjoy it as much as he had, and he wasn't about to mess up again. He needed her to know she was more than a good fuck. Hell, the word *fuck* felt wrong as it rumbled around in his mind.

Dominating was what he did best. Easing off? Not so much. But he forced himself to do just that. Telling himself he'd make it up to her later, he removed his hand from her thigh and pushed up on his palms. Her eyes brimmed with desire, tempting him to the edge of reason. Struggling to do the right thing, he said, "But I'm not taking you here, and I don't use lines. I fucking love your laugh. Deal with it." He pushed up to a sitting position, the air between them sparking so hot he was sure the dune grass would ignite.

"Fine," she snapped. The underlying breathiness of her response told him it was sexual frustration driving it, not anger. "You like my laugh."

He rose to his feet, bringing her up beside him, and he noticed glittery ink on her wrist. "Bride Tribe?" He remembered the pen she was holding and withdrew it from his pocket. She cocked her head to the side, watching him curiously as he uncapped it and turned her wrist over, scrawling *Taken* over the other words.

"Possessive much?"

"Only as much as you'll allow." He shoved the pen in his pocket, watching her brush sand from her legs. He turned her by the shoulders so she was facing away from him, and moved her hand. "I've got you. Get used to it. Pretend it's your idea if that helps." He brushed the sand from the backs of her legs, and when he brushed it from her ass, she wiggled her butt.

"Having a *hard* time?" she teased.

"*Christ.*" He smacked her ass.

"Hey!" She spun around with a fierce and seductive look in her eyes, and he dragged her across the rocks again. "Where are you taking me?"

"Right here if you're not careful." He draped an arm over her shoulder, tugging her against his side so hard she squeaked, and her hand flew to his stomach. Her fingers slid off and he put them back, flattening them against his abs. "This is what you do when you're a *thing*."

"I never said we were a *th—*"

He silenced her with a hard kiss. She leaned against him, her hands circling his neck, yielding to his demand. He didn't know what the hell was in *her* Pandora's box, but he was pretty sure it had nothing on the typhoon of emotions she'd released in him.

He pushed abruptly from the kiss.

"What?" She smiled as innocently as a tigress licking its chops, and he led her down the beach. "Where are we going?"

"For a walk before I decide that treating you like a lady blows and bend you over one of these boulders."

Chapter Ten

A LONG WHILE after Addy and Jake set out for their cool-down walk along the shore, her hormones had calmed, and she was enjoying listening to stories about his childhood. He'd told her about trips to the beach with his family, how his father had taught him and his siblings about preparedness and how to live off the land. That was another thing she really admired about Jake and his family. It was no secret that Jake and his siblings had inherited family money. She wondered how they'd all turned out so down-to-earth. The more they talked, the clearer the answers became. Their parents had pushed them to better themselves and pursue their dreams and given them the knowledge and tools to survive on more than money and circumstance. He'd endured broken bones, failed projects, and had to fight his way through figuring out his problems.

"My father used to tell us, if we wanted something bad enough, we wouldn't stop until we had it. If we didn't, then..." He shrugged.

"That explains a lot."

"Whatever, Addy. *Yes*, I wanted you. *Yes*, I pursued you. You can be sarcastic, but at least I own my feelings."

That stung, and her thoughts stumbled, but he was right. "I'm sorry. Please tell me more. I like to hear about you and your brothers."

"What was your childhood like?"

"Totally boring compared to yours. Private schools, traveling with private tutors when my father had to attend fashion shows. Pretty dresses, fancy dinners, and absolutely no pushing from my parents about anything other than primping and etiquette." She leaned her head against his arm as they walked. "Tell me more, please. It's nice to get a feel for how you became the person you are."

"What do you want to know?"

"I don't know. Who did you explore the world with when you were younger?"

"Anyone who would go," he said with a smile. "Cash and I spent one whole summer honing our tracking skills. We stayed out in the woods from dawn to dusk. I was only seven or eight, but we considered ourselves *mountain men*. We had skills to perfect and animals to track."

He lowered his voice an octave as he said the last two sentences, and Addy laughed. "Do you want to bang your chest now?"

He pulled her tighter against him. "Ha-ha. And yeah, maybe I do. So what?"

"So, it's cute." It was cute, but she understood the need to prove himself. She'd spent many hours poring over his pictures on social media, and besides getting a good sense of who Jake was, she'd realized how little she'd pushed herself outside of her comfort zone. That had been the impetus for her upcoming camping trip.

"Yeah? Well, don't say that in front of my brothers. I'll never live down being *cute*."

"Making a mental note—say 'cute' often around Jake's brothers."

He grabbed her ribs and she shrieked and bolted ahead. In seconds she was in his arms, being twirled like one of those ridiculous couples on a Hallmark card. Only she didn't feel ridiculous at all. She felt happy, though still unsure about how to navigate this new territory. When he set her on her feet, she smiled up at him.

"Still scared?" he asked.

"Shitless." She grabbed the waist of his shorts and stepped forward, surprised she admitted that so readily to him. But something had changed during their walk. He wasn't pushing her to talk about why she was scared or trying to fix it for her. As minuscule as that might sound, to Addy they were the most important things he could have done. And in doing so, Jake had unknowingly torn a fissure in the protective armor she kept around herself. It felt good not to be trying to seduce him or fight *his* seduction. It felt right, and nice, to allow herself to enjoy him without secondary motives or worries about what it all meant.

He took her hand and they walked in silence. After a few minutes he said, "I get it. Being scared shitless, I mean."

"Are *you* still scared?" She looked away, realizing his answer mattered more than she'd anticipated.

"Only that you'll go away and I won't have done all I could have to convince you we're right together."

"Jake..." She paused, swallowing a multitude of knee-jerk responses that came so easily. He deserved more than that.

Before she could get another word out he said, "Tell me about your trip. Why are you so dead set on trekking through the Silver Mountains alone?"

"Why not?" *So much for refraining from flippant responses.*

His deadpan stare was well deserved. He'd been blatantly

honest with her and deserved to hear the truth. Her legs stopped moving, refusing to carry her as she tried to muster the courage to reveal such a big part of herself. She drew in a lungful of air, along with whatever strength of his she could borrow, and said, "I'm not sure."

"Come on, Addy. I thought we were past toying with each other."

"It's the truth," she said evenly, although her insides were weaving themselves into knots.

"You're not sure? Then why insist on doing it alone? Let me come with you to—"

"No," she interrupted. "I'm definitely doing this alone. I have to, and I have big plans to clear my head and see what I'm really made of. I'm going to set up camp at Riser's Ridge, hike five to six miles in a different direction each day to see as much as I possibly can, and spend one night on Pirate's Peak."

He exhaled loudly. "You're climbing Pirate's Peak alone?"

"I sure am. People do it all the time. I'm sorry, but this is something I need to do on my own."

"Why ten days alone on a mountain? It's dangerous."

"You're going to think my reasons are stupid, but I'll tell you anyway, because I don't think they're stupid. First of all, I'm going for ten days because that's how long it'll take to see all the places I want to explore. And what would I be proving to myself if I went for two or three days? That's nothing. *Anyone* could do that. Besides, *you're* the inspiration behind the trip. You should think it's a good thing."

"Oh no, don't you blame me for this."

"Chill out, okay? Not you specifically. When Gabby met Duke, I was doing some research on him and his business. You know, to see what Gabby was up against, and I saw all those pictures of everything you'd accomplished and the places you'd been on your Facebook page—"

"*My* Facebook page?"

"Duke didn't have one. It was *research.* Don't get so hung up on that. It's not like I even knew you existed at that point, but…then I did, so I *lingered.*" She'd been immediately taken with his rugged good looks. The deeper she dug—*okay, snooped*—the more appealing she'd found him. Her favorite picture was of Jake and his mother standing on a grassy lawn. His hands hung loosely by his sides, his head slightly bent, a small smile on his face, and his mother's hand was resting on his cheek. It was as if he were caught in the most unguarded, meaningful moment. Addy had spent endless nights wondering about the man behind the image, who relinquished his rugged facade for the woman who had brought him into the world. And when she finally met him, she couldn't reconcile that tender image with the über-alpha, slick-talking player. Now, after catching glimpses of his softer side, she found herself thinking of that picture once again.

"Uh-huh," he said. "And how long were you on my page?"

"I don't know." There was no way she'd tell him she was on there half the day. He had a *lot* of half-naked pictures in all sorts of interesting places, like mountains and forests, which she'd studied, feeding her late-night-fantasies mental camera roll until it was nice and plump for cold winter nights. But her search had also turned up something she'd never anticipated.

"Looking at your pictures made me realize that I haven't pushed myself to do anything out of my comfort zone since college. Sure, I refused my parents' money and built a life for myself, but it's a comfortable life. While I was traveling in first class to international fashion shows, pampered to the hilt, you were roughing it in the heart of nature. I wanted to experience that so badly I could taste it. I've never even gone camping."

"We'll get back to the Facebook stalking thing, but you've never camped and you're going to spend time alone in the mountains?" An incredulous laugh escaped. "That puts a new spin on things. Are you out of your mind? It's iffy for an experienced person to go hiking alone in the mountains for a long stretch of time, but an inexperienced hiker? That's dangerous, Addy. I wish you'd rethink this."

"Says the man who puts his life on the line with every unfamiliar terrain when you do search and rescue." She gazed down the beach at the lights of the resort shining against the evening sky. So much had changed over the past two days. For months she'd fought the urge to give in to the heat between them, and now that they'd crossed that bridge, they were crossing another. How did they get to the point where he felt like he was allowed to question her decisions? And why did she *want* to explain them instead of telling him it was none of his business?

She'd thought they had only one thing in common: the desire for hot, aggressive sex. But it didn't end there. Not even close. He was just as stubborn as she was. When she met his gaze, frustration and desire stared back at her, and it was the combination of the two that stopped her in her tracks.

He reached for her hand. She needed *space* to give him the honesty he deserved, but she inhaled an unsteady breath, focusing on the tingling in her chest, the way his hand swallowed hers, and how much she liked those things, rather than focusing on the vulnerability swimming inside her.

He tightened his grip and must have thought better of it, because he dropped her hand and moved closer, putting a possessive—*protective?*—arm around her shoulder. And *God,* that felt even better than holding his hand. How did he know exactly what she needed to get through this conversation, when it was the absolute opposite of what *she* thought she needed?

He didn't say a word, letting the silence settle in the sounds of the waves breaking against the shore, and pressed a kiss to the side of her head, unraveling the knots inside her.

Addy mentally picked apart all the reasons she wanted to take the solo trip in the mountains and decided the only way to explain it was to start at the beginning, which meant revealing a part of herself she'd only partially shared with Gabriella. Drawing every ounce of courage she could muster, she said, "You know how you have all those great memories of exploring and fishing and learning cool things with your family?"

"Sure."

"All those rites of childhood that you enjoyed were things I was sheltered from. My parents adore me—don't get me wrong. I'm not a broken, unloved girl who rebels as a way to get attention. I'm the girl who was loved and cherished like a fine diamond, when all I wanted was to be allowed to get dulled and scratched and chipped up by life."

"It's not that uncommon for parents as well off as yours to protect the kids, is it?" he asked. "I mean, look at Paris Hilton."

"You did *not* just compare me to Paris Hilton."

He laughed, squeezing her a little tighter. "Not you. Just the idea of being pampered by well-to-do parents."

She weighed that answer and smiled. "Okay, you can live."

Leaning down with a devilish grin on his handsome face, he cupped the nape of her neck and kissed her. He tasted so good, felt so right, she turned to him, giving herself over to the slow, scrumptious kiss. He kissed her as he never had before, with a tenderness and possessiveness that melted her heart.

"I know you're not a pampered princess." He looked at her with such genuine affection, she had the urge to crawl beneath his skin and pour out her soul. Those feelings might be new, but they were becoming more familiar by the second, and any doubts she'd had about whether they were real or imagined drifted away like smoke in the wind.

"Thank you."

He looked at her for a long, silent moment before pulling back. She had the sense that he was giving her space to recover from the heat simmering between them. She was surprised by how much she appreciated the gesture, no matter how much she disliked the space between them.

As if he sensed her displeasure with his gentlemanly move, he crushed her against his side again, gave her a chaste kiss, and began walking. Recovering from Jake's inherent knowledge of what she needed wasn't as immediate as she'd hoped. The emotions were too powerful to simply push aside. *No wonder Gabriella fell so fast for Duke.* It was as exhilarating as it was frightening, and trying to make sense of it without her entire world catching fire was like walking through a minefield.

"So this trip is your way of doing what you wished you could have done when you were younger?"

"I guess so, in a general sense. But that's not really why I'm doing it. I like pushing my boundaries to see what I'm capable of. It's hard to explain, because it's not only that. I know I can do anything I set my mind to, but I want to experience more of life. And it's not that I blame my parents for how they raised me, or even that I feel like I missed out. I adore them and I had a great childhood, even though it probably doesn't look that way since I turned away their trust fund and—"

"Wait," he said, eyes wide with a tease. "You have a trust fund? Hell, baby. That changes everything. Let's get married!"

"Like *you* need money."

"Money is the last thing I need."

He stared at her so long she began to wonder if he was implying something else. Just when she was convinced he was going to say he needed her, he said, "I could live completely off the grid and I'd be happier than if I lived in a castle. My whole family's like that. Well, maybe not Duke. He likes creature comforts. But look at the house Trish and Boone bought in West Virginia. It's small, run-down, and in a town as big as my thumb. They make enough money to buy the *state*, but Trish isn't pretentious. She's as tough as nails, and if she had to, she could live off the land, too." He shook his head and laughed softly. "She's as stubborn as you are. When we were kids she always tried to beat us in everything we did. It's one of the things I respect most about her."

Hearing Jake talk about how tough Trish was struck another appealing chord. She loved that he placed value on intelligence and drive, regardless of whether a woman or a man possessed those traits, so unlike what she'd grown up with.

"*That's* what I'm talking about. I want to do more. I want to beat myself, I guess. I don't want to look back when I'm seventy and wonder why I never went camping. You were encouraged to push yourself in everything you did. I never had that. Even going to college was a battle of wills. My father wanted me to go to one of the most prestigious schools, or study overseas. All I wanted was to be a normal kid and go to a school that didn't cater to only the wealthiest families. And I'm sure you're thinking I'm just trying to validate my own self-worth, or rebelling against overprotective parents, or some other psych crap, and maybe I am. Who knows?"

"You don't know me at all, sexy girl. I was thinking about how admirable it is."

"I'm sorry. I shouldn't have assumed that, but I'm sure lots of other people see it that way. All I know is that I enjoy pushing myself, and if that means leaving safety behind, then that's what it means. I've proven I can make it on my own. But now that I've done that, I want to do *more*. It still feels like something is…I don't know. *Missing*?"

She paused, uncomfortable with how she sounded. "Saying this out loud makes me sound rebellious or foolish, and probably spoiled rotten, because how can something be missing when I was born into a family that wants for nothing? I can't explain it. My mom is perfectly happy living a jet-setting life, in Paris one day and who knows where the next, letting my father make all the decisions for the two of them. But I'm wired differently. I need *more*. I get restless if my mind isn't stimulated."

He raised his brows.

"You have such a dirty mind." *And I love it.*

"I told you we're perfect for each other."

He leaned down for another kiss, and when their mouths met, he was in complete control. With the ocean breeze at her back and Jake's hard frame pressing against her from chest to thighs, fire sparked beneath her skin, and she let him take, and take, and *take*. The fact that she craved his dominance wasn't lost on her. Neither was the realization that she was in no hurry to reclaim the upper hand.

"I get you, sexy girl," he said in a sensual tone. "You're smart and capable and you don't want to be told what to do or when to do it. But…"

He kissed her neck and then gazed deeply into her eyes. The emotions staring back made it hard to breathe, and she could see that he was drowning in them. *But…?*

As he lowered his lips to hers again, she put her palm against his chest, holding the next delicious kiss at bay. She couldn't get swept away just yet. Not with whatever he was going to say left unsaid.

"Wait, Jake. Now that Gabby and Duke are trying to start a family and Gabby's cutting back on her practice, this is my chance to set out and experience more of the world on my terms. You're not going to hold me back."

JAKE WASN'T BIG on keeping his thoughts to himself, but in Addy he'd found not only a woman he wanted, but also someone he related to on every level. She was a strong-minded, intelligent, risk-taking beauty with a penchant for pushing her boundaries—in and out of the bedroom. But he knew what happened when someone tried to forbid him to do something. He not only defied them, but he went above and beyond, proving just how wrong they were. He had no doubt Addy's reaction would be pretty close to his own, and he wasn't willing to risk their last night together to prove a point. There was more than one way to scale a mountain.

Tamping down the protector in him was akin to taming a bear, but his feelings for Addy were more powerful than his need for her to yield to his demands.

"I'm not trying to hold you back," he promised, although he sure as hell wanted to talk some sense into her about going on her trip. When he gazed into Addy's determined eyes, he knew he'd do whatever it took to be with her, including waiting until morning to talk about her trip. His brothers would call this "relationship compromise." He may not know much about relationships, but he didn't think that mattered. He only needed to know what *Addy* needed. And right now she didn't need to be pushed. She needed to be loved and cherished and shown that how he felt had nothing to do with controlling her decisions and everything to do with keeping her safe.

"I want tonight," he said softly, drawing a long, sensual sigh from her. "And tomorrow." His mouth brushed over hers. "I want you in my bed, Addy. I want to wake up with you in my arms tomorrow."

She trapped her lower lip between her beautiful white teeth, looking so different from the bold woman he was used to, he wanted to protect her from the cause of her vulnerable reaction. But there was no protecting her from what was meant to be. Every time they were close it became harder for her to erect those walls she wore like armor, just as it did for him.

Lowering his face beside her ear, he said, "Want me to take you right here on the sand? Or do you want me to strip you bare in the safety of my bedroom, blindfold those pretty little eyes, and make you feel more than you've ever felt in your entire life?"

Her lip sprang free, and all that vulnerability went up in flames. She went up on her toes and he met her halfway in a feverish kiss. They stumbled up the beach, kissing as they hurried across the dirt road toward the path that led to the resort, stopping only for more kissing and groping. By the time they reached his room they were both breathless. He pushed the door open and swept her inside, kicking the door closed behind them.

"Lock it," she said as he tore her dress over her head and tossed it to the floor.

Done.

He turned back, stilling at the sight of her wearing nothing but a black lace bra and matching panties. "You are an incredible sight." And she was all his. He tugged his shirt off, holding on to it as he stripped out of the rest of his clothes.

She eyed his shirt. "Security blanket?"

"Baby, I made a promise, and I never back down on my promises." He lifted her into his arms, reveling in her smallness. Her legs wound around his waist, and her mouth met his as he carried her into the bedroom.

He flung the blanket back and laid her down in the center of the bed, coming down over her. "I've dreamed of seeing you in my bed for so long I could give you a play-by-play of what I'm going to do to you." Her eyes widened just a hair, immediately narrowing again in pure seduction. "But that would ruin the surprise, wouldn't it?"

She licked her lips, the pulse in the base of her neck throbbing frantically.

Holding his shirt by a scrap, he dragged it over her chest. "Say hello to your blindfold, sexy girl."

Her lips curved up. "My new best friend."

As he covered her beautiful eyes with his shirt and tied it in place, he told himself it didn't matter that she seemed *too* comfortable with being blindfolded. He lowered her head gently to the mattress and touched her cheek, wrestling to keep his jealousy in check.

She covered his hand with hers. "Jake?"

Her voice was unexpectedly shaky. "You okay, sexy girl?"

Her fingers curled around his hand, and she nibbled on her

lower lip again. "I didn't expect to miss seeing your face."

He let out a sigh of relief and kissed her softly. "Want me to take it off?"

She shook her head. "No. I just wanted you to know. I didn't expect to feel so much for you."

"Neither did I," he said honestly, noticing how much easier it was for her to reveal her true feelings when she couldn't see him. That made him want to earn her trust even more.

Kissing her again, he brushed his thumb along her cheek, and her fingers loosened, falling limply beside her head. He laced their hands together, drinking in the sight of her surrendering to him completely. Her lips were slightly parted, glistening wet from their kisses. Her chest rose with each quick breath. He wanted to take his time, to explore all of her, find every pleasure point, until she was liquid heat beneath him. Lifting her hand to his mouth, he kissed each delicate finger, then placed it palm up beside her head, and continued kissing a path along her slender wrist, to the crook of her elbow. His cock brushed over her lace panties as he kissed her shoulder, then dragged her bra strap down her arm. Sinking his teeth into the curve of her shoulder he sucked hard, testing the waters. She arched up to greet him, moaning with pleasure.

"My girl likes pain and pleasure." He laved his tongue over the tender spot.

"Sometimes," she said breathily.

He kissed and licked the swell of her breast, traced the edge of her bra with his finger. His thumb brushed over her taut nipple through the lace, and she bit her lower lip again. She was so sexy, so beautiful, writhing beneath him as he learned the curves of her body, discovering what made her squirm and what brought out the shy girl he'd only yet caught a glimpse of. He tasted the soft skin between her breasts, earning a stream of sexy murmurs. He sucked the swell of one breast while unhooking the front clasp and moved the cups to the side. Using the tip of his tongue, he teased one rosy peak.

"More," she pleaded, arching off the bed.

"Not so fast, beautiful." He took his time, slowly moving the straps of her bra down each arm, then lifting her off the mattress just enough to remove it completely.

"You're gorgeous, Addy." Lowering his chest over her abdomen, he pushed her breasts together, slicking his tongue over both peaks.

She fisted her hands in the sheets, and he sucked one nipple hard. A low moan escaped her lips. Damn, he liked knowing he was giving her such pleasure, and he'd only just begun. Tasting every inch of her warm, soft skin as he went, he kissed from her nipples to the undersides of her breasts, down her rib cage, loving the whimpers and sexy noises he incited. When he reached the juncture of her thighs, he reached up and squeezed her nipples between his fingers and thumbs, just hard enough to earn another stream of thrilling pleas. Licking her through the damp material between her legs, tasting her desire, was heaven and hell.

"*Jake*," she begged, rocking her hips.

"I'll never tire of hearing that plea in your voice." Needing more of her, he claimed her in another scorching kiss. Her arms circled him, her knees opened wider, and she rubbed her wetness against his eager cock.

"*Fuck*," he ground out, tearing his mouth from hers. "I want to fuck you so bad." A sliver of regret spiked through him. He shouldn't have said he wanted to *fuck* her. What they were doing felt completely different from fucking. But the word didn't feel altogether wrong either, because this was who they were. Dirty-talking, boundary-pushing lovers.

"Then do it," she challenged.

He felt a grin tugging at his lips. "You haven't come on my mouth yet, sweetheart, and I want to taste you tomorrow at breakfast."

In his next breath, he grabbed her panties and dragged them off. "You're all mine, sexy girl."

She was breathing so hard, gripping the sheets with white knuckles, that he almost mistook it for fear, but she spread her legs wider and lifted her hips, giving him an open invitation. And he didn't hesitate. He buried his face between her legs, taking everything he wanted.

"*Oh God, Jake*," she cried out.

Loving her with his tongue and grazing her most sensitive nerves with his teeth, he took her right up to the edge of release. Her body trembled, and her back bowed off the mattress. He lowered his mouth to the tender skin between her sweet center and her ass. Testing her boundaries again, he slicked his tongue lower, over her tight puckered entrance. Her body went rigid.

Noting her boundaries, he felt like an asshole for the relief, and the immense pleasure, sweeping through him with the knowledge that there were some things they could explore together for the first time.

"Don't worry, sweet girl. I won't do anything you don't want me to."

Moving his mouth higher again, he slid two fingers inside her slick entrance, homing in on the pleasure point he'd discovered last night, and used his tongue to stroke her into a panting, clawing frenzy as she lost her last shred of control. Her hips bucked off the mattress and his name sailed from her lips—

"Jake—"

He loved her through the very last pulse of her climax, and then he took her up to heaven again. *Twice.*

Chapter Eleven

AS ADDY SLOWLY came back down from the clouds, Jake gathered her quivering body in his arms and kissed her. Every inch of her tingled and throbbed. The blindfold heightened her senses, making her acutely aware of the feel of his chest against hers, the roughness of his hands caressing her skin. The feel of his whiskers scratching her chin was erotically delicious. The scent of her arousal clung to him, the pungent taste transferring as their tongues tangled and he breathed air into her lungs. She pawed at his shoulders, his back, his arms, unable to touch enough, to feel enough, to *take* enough. He brought nerve endings she didn't know she possessed to life, and she wanted *more.* There were only a few sexual things she hadn't ever had the courage, or the trust in her partner, to explore. Being blindfolded was one of them and letting any man touch her second most private entrance was another. In a single night he'd unknowingly conquered one, discovered another, and made her crave the third like an addict. And she was about to get the hit she needed.

"Jake," she said, feeling encumbered by the blindfold now. As titillating as it had made his exploration of her body, it now felt like a barrier between them. "I want *you.*"

"Oh, you'll get me, sexy girl."

"*Now.*" She pulled off the blindfold, needing to see him as badly as she wanted to touch and taste him.

"Demanding, aren't we?" he teased.

Wiggling out from beneath him, suddenly overwhelmed by the urge to get her mouth on him, she tossed his shirt to the floor and raked her eyes down the length of his body. He was sitting up on his knees, his thick erection bobbing against his belly, all his glorious muscles there for the tasting. He truly was unfairly hot. Like put-her-Tumblr-dudes-to-shame hot.

"Eyes up here, sweetheart."

She shot him a sultry gaze. "I've already got that cocky grin memorized. I need the rest of you memorized, unless you want to give me a picture for my Cocks I Want to Rock Tumblr page." *Oh shit.* She hadn't meant to say it, but sometimes her words came out before she could stop them.

"What the fu—"

"Don't dwell on it," she said quickly. Hoping to sidetrack him, she motioned for him to lean back against the headboard. "My turn. No blindfolds required."

He moved stiffly. "You seriously have that Tumblr page?"

She knelt between his legs, meeting his very jealous gaze. "Something had to get me through night after night of thinking about this." She wrapped one hand around his cock, and he hissed out a breath. "You should take great pleasure in knowing I've never trusted any man enough to blindfold me."

She gave his cock one slow, tight stroke and leaned forward, taking him in a languid kiss that rivaled the one he'd given her on the beach, the one that had gotten her into his bedroom faster than the speed of light. When they parted, he still had that green-eyed monster hovering in his eyes. She could kick herself for saying what she had and for sounding so cavalier about it. There was no way that Tumblr page could hold a candle to him. She wished she could take the words back, because the truth was, if the tables were turned, she'd be just as jealous. The idea of Jake with other women made her want to claw someone's eyes out.

But she was about to let him do something she'd never allowed another man to do, and that, she knew, would make him forget about the stupid Tumblr page.

"You might want to hold my hair so you can watch as you conquer another Addison Dahl first."

"You blew me last ni—" Understanding flamed in his eyes.

The appreciative groan that accompanied the fisting of his hand in her hair brought a smile to her lips as she lowered them over his eager arousal, taking him directly to the back of her throat.

"Jesus, Addy." He tightened his grip, his hips rising off the bed.

She held his heated stare, feeling him swell impossibly thicker in her hand. Each time she took him to the back of her throat he made that groaning sound, and it sent streaks of heat between her legs. She brought her other hand to his balls, tugging just a little, and he made another heady noise. His desperate eyes bored into her. When he grabbed both sides of her head, she let him lead, wanting to bring him as much pleasure as possible.

He tried to yank her head back, but she fought his efforts, sucking harder, stroking tighter, and wanting every last drop he had to give her.

"Addy, I'm gonna come."

She smiled around his cock.

"Jesus, *fuck*. You're sure, baby?"

She answered by quickening her pace. He joined in, rocking

his hips and caressing her cheeks as they hollowed out. She expected him to grab her harder, to nearly choke her with his thrusts as he came. But he never stopped caressing her cheeks as his release shot down her throat. His tenderness belied his insurmountable power, sliding like a ghost into her heart.

He gathered her close again, cradling her in his arms, and he kissed her hard, possessing every piece of her mouth without a moment's hesitation—even after what she'd just done—making the kiss so freaking hot she could barely stand it. She wanted to stay right there, being devoured by him, safely enveloped within his arms, with a million sparks blazing inside her, forever. How had she gone her whole life without ever feeling this way? Without knowing she was missing something so decadent it should be illegal?

They kissed for a long time, moving down the bed so they were lying side by side. He pressed his hand flat against her back, and she was aware of every point where they touched, from her feet on his legs all the way up to their noses brushing as they kissed.

"I can't get enough of you," he said between kisses. "I want to kiss you until your mouth is too tired to kiss anymore."

"You're so different than I thought you would be."

He kissed her again, his brows knitting together. "You've messed with my head. I've never loved kissing before. I'm more of a 'catch, come, release' kind of guy."

A pain skittered through her chest, bringing with it another wave of guilt. "I'm sorry I brought up my Tumblr page."

"Yeah, that kind of sucked." The hurt in his voice made her ache.

"So did hearing about your 'catch, come, release' habit," she admitted. He brought one hand to her cheek, and she leaned in to it. How could she already crave his touch?

"I'm sorry. Neither of us are saints," he said honestly. "But whatever we've done has led us to each other. And I know you don't want a serious relationship—"

"But the thought of you and other women makes me sick to my stomach." She held her breath, unable to believe she'd admitted that.

"Good," he said with a grin, though his voice was dead serious.

"Good? Not good, Jake. Before this weekend it didn't make me feel sick to think about you and other women." As she said it, she realized she'd never allowed herself to think of such a scenario. She knew, and accepted, that he was a major player, but those were just words. She hadn't actually thought of him making out with other women.

He cocked a brow, like he wasn't buying it.

"Fine." A frustrated groan preceded her big, embarrassing confession. "I pretended that after we met for drinks you went home alone, like I did."

"Then we were both playing the same mind games. You want *us*, Addy. I see it in your eyes. I feel it when you touch me. And you're not looking at me like I'm a weekend hookup."

She opened her mouth to deny it, but the truth slipped out. "I do like you, Jake. More than a weekend hookup."

"Thank you," he said smugly.

She laughed. "But I'm not going to cancel my trip, and you're not coming with me."

"You've made that perfectly clear."

"Good. Can you please not talk about your…*habit*?"

"If you can refrain from talking about your…*page*."

"Fine."

"Or looking at it," he added.

"For this weekend? Fine. But then you'd better have a lot more energy left in you for the night, because I'm just getting started."

He rolled her onto her back and kissed her. "Addison Dahl, I will put the Energizer bunny to shame for more than just this weekend." He kissed her again, swallowing her laughter as he nudged her legs open wider. "Say you're mine."

"Kiss me again," she whispered seductively. She didn't know what was keeping her from saying she was his. Maybe it was that she was going away tomorrow afternoon and before last night she'd been dead set on clearing thoughts of him from her mind. Or maybe it was that taking that step, calling herself *his*, reminded her of ownership, and ownership reminded her of all the reasons she'd gotten out from under her father's thumb. Whatever it was that was stopping her from saying the words wasn't strong enough to stop the emotions behind them.

"You're going to push all my buttons, aren't you?" he whispered as he brushed the tip of his nose up her cheek.

"Only in the very best way." She rocked her hips, and he nestled his cock at her entrance.

"Say it, baby. Say you're mine. Admit we're a *thing*, and I'll make love to you like you've never been made love to before."

"That should be easy," she said softly. "I've never been made love to before."

He cradled her face in his hands, his eyes pleading with her to cross the next barrier. "Neither have I. Say you're mine and we'll cross this bridge together."

Her heart was too full, her throat too thick, to allow words to flow, so she nodded.

As their bodies came together, his arms enveloping her,

holding her as close as two people could be, he whispered, "You're mine, Addy. You may not be ready to admit it, but we're going to obliterate thoughts of there ever being another man in your life."

She had a feeling they already had.

CHAPTER TWELVE

THERE WERE TEN essential elements for survival in the wilderness, most of which Jake could survive without. A map and compass for navigation. No problem there. He was so in tune with nature, he could recognize a tree he passed a week before if he had to and find his way based on the position of the sun, moon, and stars. Sunglasses and sunscreen were important so he didn't burn, but he could make a visor out of elements found in the woods, and mud was a natural sunscreen. Extra clothing, a headlamp, first-aid supplies, those were pretty much no-brainers, but he could do without the headlamp and clothing. Firestarter and matches, a knife, and of course, extra food rounded out the list. He knew how to start fires without those essentials, and if need be, he could fashion a weapon from rocks and sticks. And he was an expert on living off the land. Jake knew survival like some people knew their ABCs. But when it came to matters of the heart, he was pretty damn clueless. He lay with Addy tucked safely within his arms, wondering how he'd survive giving her the space she needed without losing his mind.

Jake hadn't ever been a stay overnight kind of guy, but he wanted more of that with Addy. Her slender back nestled against his chest, her hips tucked against his, and even in her sleep, she clung tightly to his hand, as if she wanted more, too.

Was this how it happened to his brothers? One day they were fantasizing about a woman, and the next they couldn't imagine letting her walk out of their life? He and Addy had made love so many times last night he'd lost count, but it wasn't the physical act that he was thinking about now. It was the multitude of intimate moments they'd shared over the course of those fervent hours. The looks, the hand-holding, the laughter. He'd never had that before, and each instance had embedded in his mind like a bullet.

Addy stirred, and he pressed a kiss to her cheek, tightening his hold on her. Would she mind if he never let go? This time tomorrow she'd be gone, while he was remaining on the island for an evening fishing trip with his father and brothers and traveling back to New York the following day.

He kissed her again, and she turned in his arms, a sleepy smile on her face. "Hi," she said groggily.

He kissed her softly. "Hey, sexy girl. The look of a satisfied lover suits you."

She touched her forehead to his chest. "God, those lines sound so…"

"Real?"

She shook her head. "Where's my Neanderthal? This guy embarrasses me, and I hate being embarrassed."

He hauled her closer and kissed her again. "You called me *your* Neanderthal."

"Did I?" She brushed her fingers over his chest. "I guess I have a thing for Neanderthals."

"You have a thing for *me*."

Flashing a sweet and mischievous smile, she said, "There's a lot I don't know about you, so the verdict is still up in the air."

He gave her ass a light smack, and the giggle that followed

made his heart thump harder.

"What time is it?"

He glanced at the clock. "A little after four."

"I should go." She made no move to leave.

"Stay."

"Your family might see me."

How could five words cause a two-hundred-and-fifteen-pound man so much grief? "And if I want the world to know you're mine?" When she trapped her lower lip between her teeth, he scooted lower on the bed, so they were eye to eye. "*Why* are you toying with me?"

"I'm not. I mean, not on purpose."

"Well, sweet cheeks, you are, and it's pissing me off."

"It's sort of a knee-jerk reaction and sort of not." She paused, as if thinking about what to say next. "Everyone knows about us, but should we really throw this in their faces? I mean, it's not like we've been dating or anything. After this weekend, I'm going away and you're going back to…whatever it is you do all day. I really don't know anything about you beyond…"

"Beyond what you *do* know? Like that I'm an honest guy who's crazy about you. I spend my days doing search and rescue wherever I'm needed. Sometimes I'm on a rescue for a few hours, sometimes days. No two are ever alike. And now"—he kissed her again—"I want to spend my nights with you. What else do you want to know?"

"Hm…" She scrunched up her nose and tapped his chest, looking insanely adorable. She was so unguarded, so open and sweet and playful, he felt like he'd peeled back another layer, revealing another secret part of her.

"Gosh, there's so much, like, I don't know…what your favorite food is."

"You." He stole a kiss and she laughed.

"Seriously. I *need* to know these things."

"I doubt you seriously need to know my favorite foods."

She rolled her eyes. "If I don't know, then how can I smear it all over my body so you can lick it off?"

"Jesus. How am I supposed to think past that?" He took her in a long sensual kiss, wanting so much more. "In that case," he said, kissing her softly, "my mother's cream puffs. They're amazing, but eating them off of you would make them out-of-this-world delicious."

As he went in for another kiss, she stopped him with a hand on his chest. "Okay, next must-know item. What do you do when you're not saving people's lives or trying to get me in bed?"

"Lately I only have time for the latter, so…"

"Come on," she complained. "What do you do when you're not doing search and rescue? Gabby said you were a volunteer search and rescue guy, so what's your *real* job? How do you earn a living when you're flying all over the country at the drop of a hat?"

Jake's initial reaction was to tell her what he told everyone else, that he helped train search and rescue professionals. Usually that was enough to end the conversation, because most people didn't know the majority of the trainer positions were also unpaid. He had a feeling Addy was too wise for that off-the-cuff answer. His next thought was that he didn't want to sleep in a bed of lies with Addy, so he told her the truth.

"A few years ago a buddy and I developed a search and rescue app, and the income from that enabled me to quit my job as a park ranger and dedicate my time to search and rescue." He was pretty sure Addy knew there was family money that had been passed down for generations, but he didn't see a need to bring that up, since he never touched his trust fund.

"Wow, really? So, first you were a park ranger? Like, the guys who wear those cute little uniforms and tell people not to litter?"

He laughed. "Something like that."

"I bet lots of girls got lost in your park on purpose."

"It's probably safer if I don't comment about that."

She swatted at his arm and he caught her wrist and kissed her, loving the feel of her smile against his lips.

"We aren't saying things that might strike a chord, remember?" he said, holding her close. "Jesus, baby. Now I have to protect you from your own smart mouth." He kissed her again.

"Mm. I might have to make that mistake a few more times."

Slanting his mouth over hers, he took her in another delicious kiss. "My lips are at your disposal. Now hurry up and finish your deposition so I can move on to something way more fun."

"Okay, I'll be fast, if you promise to take a *very* long time with the fun stuff."

He swept her beneath him, letting her feel just how much *fun* he had in store for her. "You're allowed two more questions. After that no more talking."

That earned a wide, playful grin. "How did you go from park ranger to developing an app and don't you need technical skills for that? That counts as one question because I didn't pause between them."

"I sure do like you." He lowered his face to hers, and she held him at bay with one hand on his chest.

"Answer fast, because one more second of those lips on mine and my mind won't work."

"Good to know." He stole another quick kiss and spoke as fast as he could. "In addition to my *cute* little job as a park ranger, I have a degree in engineering. My buddy Chris Boyer, an aeronautical engineer and fellow SAR—search and rescue—guy and I had an idea and followed through with it."

"Jake, that's huge! How many people can say they've developed an app?"

"Yeah, it's pretty cool, but I don't go around telling people, so please keep it on the down low."

"Why? Aren't you proud of what you accomplished?"

"That's way more than two questions, but yes, I'm very proud of it. But I didn't do it for notoriety. I did it because it was a tool that could help with the thing I'm most passionate about. Search and rescue. It's actually a cool app. A few of the major SAR teams have recently begun integrating our newest updates, which simultaneously takes feeds from a color camera, thermal camera, and infrared camera and georectifies them over a map, allowing you to flip back and forth between the images on the live map. It's a live feed from drones and can be fed to phones, iPads, computers..." He realized he was rambling about details she probably didn't care about. "Sorry. I know it's boring. I get a little excited when I actually start talking about it."

"Boring? Not at all. You light up when you talk about it. I never knew you had a hot geeky side. It's like getting a peek at you in your element, instead of the flirty hotshot."

He grabbed her ribs, and she squealed with delight.

"Flirty hotshot?" Lacing his fingers with hers, he pinned them beside her head and nipped at her lower lip.

"It's pretty freaking hot, hearing you rattle off all those techy terms. Maybe even *hotter* than the flirty hotshot."

"Yeah?" He liked that a whole lot. "I never took you as a girl who got excited over tech talk."

"I like when *you* talk," she whispered. "And when your mouth is too *busy* to talk." She pulled one hand free and stroked his cheek.

"Mm." He closed his eyes, reveling in her touch. "I love when you touch me."

"Then you better enjoy it," she whispered. "Because if your parents end up hating me because they think I'm slutty for sleeping with their baby boy, this might be all the touching you'll get."

Did she really believe that? "Is that why you didn't want to chance someone seeing you leave my room?"

She lifted one shoulder in answer, revealing that vulnerable side again. Why hadn't he thought of that? She was so brazen about her sexuality, he hadn't given a thought to what his family might think.

"I'm sorry. I should have thought of that."

"No, you shouldn't have. It's just that I think you're right. The two of us together like this feels different. It feels private."

"It is private, baby. It's special. You're special." He rubbed his nose along her cheek, breathing her in. "Thank God you're finally able to admit it."

She pursed her lips together, her smile threatening to split her faux frown in two.

"Don't taunt me, Addison, or I swear I—" He realized there was only one way to get her to say what he so desperately wanted to hear. He rolled off of her and onto his back. "I guess we won't be having fun after all."

"What?" She leaned over him, her hair curtaining her beautiful face. "You're seriously going to withhold sex?"

"There was a time when I was easy, but now I'm a guy with stronger morals. I don't give it up to just anyone." He closed his eyes and draped an arm over them so he wouldn't be tempted to peek at her—she had the power to get him to do anything with a single sultry glance.

He felt her moving over him, straddling his hips, her warm, damp center settling over his erection. Uttering a curse, he ground his teeth together as she came down over him, her nipples brushing against his chest.

"I'm not above begging," she whispered, before gliding her tongue along the outer shell of his ear. She slid over the length of his arousal, applying just enough pressure to make him lose his mind.

He grabbed her thighs and held on tight.

"You know you want me," she whispered over his lips.

Glide, glide, torture, torture.

She ran her hand up his forearm and laced her fingers with his, settling both his hands beside his head, as he'd done to her moments earlier. He opened his eyes and was immediately swept up in her. Her hair was messy and wild, her eyes dark and alluring. He wasn't strong enough to deny her a damn thing.

He said, "I want you, baby," at the same time she said, "We're a *thing*." They both laughed, and as he folded his arms around her and swept her beneath him, she said it again and again.

"Was that so hard?" he teased.

"No, but this is." She lifted her hips and slid lower, aligning their bodies perfectly. "You promised me you'd take a *very* long time."

"Baby, if I have my way, we might never leave this room."

CHAPTER THIRTEEN

"YOU'RE LOSING YOUR alpha status," Addy teased as she and Jake walked out of his room and headed toward hers, a few doors down. After Jake made good on his promise several times over, she'd wanted to stay in bed for the entire day just to revel in the aftermath of their lovemaking. And what they'd done had *definitely* been making love and not wild monkey sex, as they'd been doing with reckless abandon these last two days. But Jake insisted they watch the sunrise from the beach. They'd tapped into their wild sides, having sex in the shower, conquering another first she'd forgotten to add to her list earlier.

"Do you need me to throw you over my shoulder and carry you back to my bed?" He carried a blanket in his free hand, and wore a confident, cocky grin on his face. "I want to watch the sunrise with my girlfriend. There's no shame in that."

"Girlfriend?" she whispered to herself. She liked the sound of that a lot more than she'd thought she might, although she hadn't put their being a "thing" and "girlfriend" together until just now.

"Don't get all weird about it. Multiple orgasms earn me the right to call you my girlfriend."

"How about 'better half'?" She pushed open the door to her room and found her flip-flops inside with a handwritten note from Gabriella. *That was so Tarzan of him! You belong together,*

Ad. He's as bullheaded as you are. Have fun! Xo, G. She turned the note over, feeling embarrassed by how much Jake carrying her off had affected her. It had been romantic, and sexy, and beyond alpha.

Jake grabbed her around her waist, hauling her against him again.

"How about I bend you over that couch and *take* your better half?"

"Promises, promises." She wriggled out of his grip. He was so big and broad he made her cozy room feel small. "I'll be right back. It'll only take a sec for me to change. Make yourself comfy."

All the rooms at the inn had a living space separate from the bedroom. As she left the room, she noticed sore muscles from their extracurricular activities. She changed into clean shorts and a T-shirt and slipped on a hoodie as she walked into the living room.

The blanket Jake had brought for the beach was lying on the coffee table. Jake sat on the couch, his long, jeans-clad legs spread wide, his bare feet flat on the floor. Oh, how she loved the look of frayed jeans over masculine bare feet. His arms were stretched out along the back of the couch, reaching nearly end to end, and his head was tipped back, eyes closed. He was...*stunning.* Her stomach fluttered, thinking about how much she liked waking up in his arms, snuggled up in his warmth.

He lifted his head, his eyes zeroing in on her like lasers, causing her pulse to spike. As he rose to his full height, his chin fell to his chest and he gave her a slow, deliberate appraisal. She felt self-conscious, wishing she'd chosen something sexier than a purple zip-up hoodie and a loose, comfy shirt. His mouth curved up in that wicked invitation she knew so well. *My wicked invitation.* A sense of power and warm appreciation accompanied the naughty thought.

He was beside her in two long strides, his hand circling her waist. "We're going to have a problem if you plan on looking this hot all day." His hands slid down her thighs, moved over her hips, and he grabbed her ass. *Tight.*

Enjoying every second of his attention, she rubbed against him, pleased to feel that even after all the sex they'd had he was still raring to go. "I never knew you were such an ass man."

Kissing her neck, he said, "With you I'm an everything man. We'd better go, sexy girl, or we'll be in here all day."

"That wouldn't be so bad." She wound her arms around his neck and went up on her toes. He brushed his mouth teasingly over hers.

"I promise you, it would be very, very good. But I only have one sunrise left to watch with you until you're back from your trip." He kissed a path across her neck to the sensitive pulse point at the base and laved his tongue over it.

Her knees weakened. He'd found *all* her pleasure points.

"Unless you're ready to let me come with you on your trip," he said seductively. "Then we can have ten days of sunrises and ten nights of sinful sex and sunsets."

Curling her fingers around his forearm, she forced her brain to push past the lust. "Jake." His name came out breathy and wanting. "I'm going on the trip alone."

He leaned back, his face a mask of sexual restraint—his eyes full of disappointment. It was *almost* enough to make her reconsider.

"Sorry," she whispered.

He shrugged it off and grabbed the blanket. When he took

her hand and leaned in for another kiss, she whispered, "Sorry," again.

"Like I said," he said. "I'm not missing my one chance at watching a sunrise with you before you go."

This time when she gazed into his eyes, she was met with acceptance, and something more. Understanding? He was surprising her at every turn, and it meant the world to her that he wasn't pushing her harder.

"You're a romantic," she said as they left her room. He pushed open the door to the resort and they were greeted by crisp ocean air.

"Whatever," he said, taking her hand in his. "Keep that to yourself."

"Making another mental note to tell your brothers." She'd never been romanced, and as they started down the dusty dirt road hand in hand, with morning dew on the grass and mist in the air, everything seemed more intimate. The fear she'd experienced about opening up and accepting that she had feelings for Jake no longer overrode the goodness of the emotions.

"It seems like a month ago when you carried me away from the bachelorette party," she said as they crossed Main Street.

He leaned down and kissed her, and she noticed he was doing that more often, too. Like he'd been stockpiling kisses until she opened the floodgates.

"Because every thought leads you back to me?" he asked.

"I'd never admit it if it were true. It's not like your ego needs a boost." She leaned in to him with the tease.

Addy glanced down the road, where gorgeous sprawling oak trees with long, thick branches draped in moss bordered a dense forest. Just beyond, the newly renovated docks looked as pretty as a postcard in the morning haze. Addy remembered when she'd first visited the island with Gabriella and they'd joked about how one day they'd jump from the boat to the old dock and it would crumble beneath them.

Jake held her a little tighter as their feet met the cool, soft sand. "What are you thinking about?"

"The work Duke's having done on the island. I'm glad he's doing it. It's funny, Gabriella had worried about an investor coming in and taking away all the cultural elements that were so important to her and her family. Did you know her family emigrated here from Greece? They were the original settlers. And then Southerners came from the mainland. It's surprising that the two strong cultures didn't clash."

He stopped to spread out the blanket in the sand. "Duke would never do that. He respects family too much."

"That seems to be a theme among the Ryder clan." She glanced back the way they'd come and startled at the sight of Jake's parents headed their way. Andrea carried a picnic basket, Ned carried a blanket, and both were watching them curiously.

"Um, Jake…?" she said nervously.

Jake put a proprietary arm around Addy's shoulder, and she froze, instantly hating herself for it.

"I didn't expect to see anyone else out here this early," Andrea called across the beach. "Mind if we join you?"

"Not at all." He tightened his grip on her.

"Hi, yes, of course. Please, join us," Addy said, shooting Jake her best way-to-ease-into-it glare, which he chose to ignore as he sank down to the blanket and pulled her down with him. She crossed her feet at the ankles and leaned back on her palms, leaving a few inches between them.

Jake repositioned her so she was leaning against the side of his chest, tucked beneath his arm. It was a mighty fine position, despite her worries.

"Someone needs a lesson in girlfriending," he said to his parents.

Lord, could he give her an inch? "I'm a little out of practice, and was unexpectedly thrust into coupledom."

She'd dated in college, but even then she'd never felt particularly close to anyone. She was kind of glad, though, because she might have missed out on noticing the little things that she found so overwhelming yesterday, and until a few minutes ago she'd found surprisingly exhilarating. Now she was as nervous as a high schooler on her first date, and no matter how hard she tried to calm her nerves, it wasn't happening. She'd known she'd need Gabby's approval, but she hadn't expected to want his parents' approval this badly.

"Girlfriending? Never thought I'd see the day." His father draped an equally as possessive arm around his wife and kissed her cheek. "You were right, doll face."

Caught off guard, Addy was still processing the *Never thought I'd see the day* comment when Jake's parents leaned in closer to each other. She watched with fascination as they gazed into each other's eyes with the same intense attraction as she and Jake had so many times in the last two days. She'd never seen any passion between her parents, and she felt a little like a voyeur.

"I know my boys." Andrea kissed Ned, then smiled at Addy. "It's all in the eyes. My boys think they can hide their emotions behind muscles and gruffness, but"—she pointed to her eyes—"it's all right here."

"Christ," Jake mumbled.

Addy tilted her head up, studying the softening of his face.

That's it. That's the look I saw in the picture of you and your mom. Her fight for space washed away like the rumbling tide.

He caught her staring and lowered his mouth beside her ear, whispering, "Even she knows we're a *thing*. Get used to it. The cat's so far out of the bag, it'll never find its way back in."

A thrill raced through her. She was in a relationship with the man she had hoped to forget. How could she have been so shortsighted? She could have missed out on all his goodness.

Ned opened the picnic basket and set out two plates and muffins. He split each muffin in half and handed one plate to Jake. Andrea poured two mugs of coffee from a thermos and gave one to them.

"Thank you," Addy said, accepting the mug and offering it to Jake.

"You first, sexy girl," he whispered in her ear, one arm still locked around her.

Sexy girl. Was he trying to make her even more nervous by pulling out all of his seductive techniques? It took two to tango, and she was always up for a good game of secret seduction.

Cupping the mug between both hands, she inhaled deeply and licked her lips.

"Mm. It smells heavenly." She sipped the coffee, closing her eyes as the warm liquid slid down her throat, emitting a pleasure-filled sound. Turning a sultry gaze up for Jake's eyes only, she licked her lips again, slowly and sensually, capturing his rapt attention. "Pure nirvana. Would you like some?" She batted her lashes innocently.

Jake repositioned his hips and took the mug. A quick glance south told her she'd had the desired effect on him. *Score one for me!*

The sunrise graced the sky with gorgeous golden and crimson hues. They made small talk as they ate breakfast. It was nice to be with Jake's parents without the jokes and chaos of the entire family. And having this relaxed time with Jake was even nicer.

"I'll never forget our first sunrise," Ned said to Andrea.

"We were camping," she said with a thoughtful expression. "Ned dragged me from the tent at the crack of dawn to climb to the highest point. Talk about waking up fast. The mountains are cold in the mornings, even in the summer."

"Speaking of," Ned said. "Tell us about this trip you're going on. Ten days of solo mountaineering?" He lifted serious eyes to Jake before returning a softer gaze to Addy. "Are you prepared for that? Have you had proper training?"

"Training?" *Hiking 101? Put one foot in front of another.* Addy pictured a circle of girls standing and mulling over directions for putting up a tent. She'd bought the easy-erecting type. Put the nylon flooring down, hammer in a few spikes to hold it down, pop open the tent, hook it to the spike heads, and *poof!* A tent. The guy at the outdoors store assured her it was perfect for her trip. "No, but I've read online about what to bring and what to expect. And I bought extra clothes, new hiking boots, a compass. All the things I need. I should be okay."

His father and Jake exchanged a worried look, but it was the heaviness of the vibe between them that made the hairs on the back of her neck stand on end.

"Addy," Ned said. "Nighttime in the mountains is no day in the park. There are serious dangers."

Geez, the apple doesn't fall far from the tree. Jake and his father would have to learn that she was a hands-on, do-it-herself kind of girl. She didn't need men telling her the ways of the world. She could handle this, and nothing would stop her from taking this solo trip.

"We're going to talk about that." Jake nudged her. "Right, Ad?"

Not that I was aware of. "Um, sure. Right. But really, Mr. Ryder—"

"Honey, how many times have I told you to call me Ned? Don't give me more gray before my time." He rubbed his goatee, which was more silver than brown.

"Ned," she said. "I'm not a pampered princess. I assure you, I can handle myself."

"I never considered you overly pampered, sweetheart. But the wilderness is a beast in and of itself. Even the most skilled hikers can run into trouble." The look he and Jake had shared earlier made a repeat appearance.

"Oh, Ned, stop. You're going to frighten her," Andrea said, alleviating some of Addy's tension. "You can take the man off the mountain, but you can't take the SAR out of the man. Where are you camping?"

"In the Silver Mountains, not too far from the city. My friend Logan has a cabin there, so if I run into problems, I can always go there. Not that I anticipate having trouble." She felt Jake tense up again, and when she looked up, the green-eyed monster was baring down on her.

JAKE LOVED HIS parents, but *come on.* First they watched the sunrise with him and Addy, then they walked back to the resort together, and now everyone else was awake and milling about, preparing for Trish and Boone's wedding. The girls were running in and out of the bedrooms talking about dresses and shoes, and they'd absconded with Addy the second they'd arrived back at the resort. Boone's mother, Raine, and her boyfriend, Patrick, had disappeared with *his* mother, and Boone and his brothers were looking around as confused by the commotion as Jake was. At this rate he'd never get a moment alone with Addy, and he was so tightly wound over this *Logan* dude, he was sure he'd grown horns. How could he have gone thirty years without knowing he had a jealous bone in his body? That realization sucked, but it was what it was, and if he didn't get her alone and find out just how well she knew this guy and why the hell she hadn't mentioned him before, he might just explode. *A cabin in the mountains.* He wasn't sure he wanted to know how she knew about that.

"Hey, while you're chewing on nails over here, can you please hold Seth?" Cash handed Jake his little boy. "I'll be back in a few minutes. I have to go help Duke and Blue get something from the kitchen." Cash gave Seth a quick kiss, then lightly smacked Jake on the cheek. "Whatever it is, get over it," Cash said. "Trish needs your head in the game, and so does my boy."

Jake ground his teeth together and glanced down at his nephew, who blinked soundlessly up at him. Seth was only two months old, and holding him was a little like holding a squishy football. A football who looked a heck of a lot like Cash, from his light brown hair to his serious eyes. It was hard to stay pissed off with that cute little muffin in his arms. He lowered his face and kissed Seth's cheek.

"Let me tell you something, buddy." Seth's eyes widened at the sound of Jake's voice. "One day you're going to meet a woman who blows your mind, and she'll make you want to hold her and run from her at once." Seth's lower lip pushed out in a pout. "Yeah, it kind of sucks, but it's also pretty freaking cool. Unless, of course, this guy with the cabin in the woods is someone she's hooked up with. Then it's not cool at all. Then it bites. Then—"

Seth's face scrunched up tight, and he let out a high-pitched wail.

"Oh shit." Jake lifted the baby to his shoulder and patted his back, pacing the hallway. "It's okay. It's not like that. I'm sure it's not. She wouldn't have offered it up so casually." Why was he explaining this to a baby?

"Dude, need a little help?" Boone asked.

"Yeah, but not with the kid." Seth quieted, but Jake continued pacing, hoping to work out some of his frustration.

"With your girl?" Lucky asked. "Because I can help you out. Take her off your hands, give her a little thrill."

"Lucky!" Boone glared at him. "Ignore him."

"What?" Lucky stretched, eyeing Cage, who smacked him on the back of the head and told him to behave. "Whatever. I'm heading up to the villa to start carrying shit down to the beach."

"Watch your language," Boone called after him. "Sorry, man. He's still got some growing up to do."

"No big deal." Jake hadn't been so different from that cocky kid when he was his age. Hell, he wasn't so different a week ago. He paced, patting Seth on the back and listening to Boone and Cage talk about Lucky, and he realized that a few months ago he'd been proud of being the player who hooked up with a different girl every week. Now he wasn't sure he even knew who that guy was.

A gentle, familiar touch on his back pulled him from his thoughts. He turned, and Addy's eyes dropped to the baby in his arms.

She covered her mouth with her hand, eyes wide. "I think my ovaries just exploded."

He felt a smile tugging at his lips despite the jealousy gnawing at his gut. "He's pretty cute."

She shook her head. "Not just him, although he's a cutie pie, all right." She gave Seth's foot a playful shake. Seth smiled and kicked his legs with delight. Then her hand was on Jake's arm and her gaze turned dreamy. "Seeing you with a baby in your arms, *that's* what got me. It's like seeing a lion carrying a baby kitten by the scruff of its neck."

He kissed Seth's forehead, his frustration easing with Addy's expression. Before Seth and Coco were born Jake hadn't given kids a moment's thought, but his niece and nephew had instantly wormed their way into his heart—although that didn't mean he was ready for his own kids. "Don't get any ideas. I gotta be able to pick up and leave at a moment's notice to go on rescue missions."

"Getting a little ahead of yourself, aren't you?" She tickled Seth's cheek, earning another sweet grin. "I'm barely girlfriend material."

"Yeah, about that. Were you going to tell me about *Logan*?" The name shot off his tongue like a curse.

"I knew you were upset about that, which you have no right to be, by the way. I told you I didn't want to have to deal with any weird jealousy stuff, no matter how flattering it might be."

"Flattering?" He scoffed. "What do you mean I have no right to be upset? You won't let me go with you, but you'll stay with some guy at his cabin?"

She crossed her arms, scowling as Boone and Cage headed out of the resort, and lowered her voice. "Maybe you're not boyfriend material after all."

"What the hell, Addy?"

"How about asking me *who* Logan is before giving me a death stare and jumping to conclusions?"

"Shit," he grumbled. "Yeah, I could have done that. But what do you expect me to think?"

"Oh, I don't know. Maybe that I'm a professional paralegal with a life that goes beyond hookups and casual sex?"

The hurt in her voice cut him to his core.

"We just talked about not hitting each other's triggers. Do you really think I would be so cruel as to throw out some guy's name who I've slept with? In front of your *parents*, no less?" She stepped closer, her stare lethal. She glanced at the baby, and the tension in her face eased a little.

Not enough.

Not nearly enough.

"I screwed up," he said earnestly. "I'm sorry."

She stared at him for a long moment, sucking all the air from his lungs.

"What are we doing, Jake?" She spoke calmly, though he had the feeling it was for the baby's benefit, because she was breathing hard, and a mix of pleading and anger hovered in her eyes.

He couldn't tell if she wanted to yell, cry, or walk away, but he hoped for the first, because he had no idea how to deal with tears, and he sure as hell didn't want to lose her.

"Maybe we're not made for this type of relationship. I sure as heck never thought I was." She crossed her arms again, and all he wanted to do was take her in his and apologize, but before he could move a muscle she said, "I see Gabby and Duke, Trish and Boone, and everyone else, and they all seem so happy, like they were meant to be together. And your parents? God, what they have is so *real.* I grew up with air kisses and don't-wrinkle-my-clothes hugs. Being with you, the way you held me, touched me…" She pressed her mouth into a thin line and shifted her eyes away. "For a brief moment I let myself forget who I've always been. It's no wonder you jumped to that conclusion."

When she met his gaze again, her eyes were filled with determination, and that slayed him anew. She tried so hard to be strong, and this time it was his fault her walls had gone back up.

He reached for her hand. "Addy…"

She looked down at his hand without taking it, and his eyes caught on the baby. He shot a look down the empty hallway. Where the hell was everyone? Panic sparked inside him at the prospect of not being able to talk this out here and now, which was really hard when he was holding a little baby who, remarkably, was falling asleep. He took Addy's hand, holding it tight as he walked toward the doors that led to the veranda.

"We're talking this out." It took all his effort to speak quietly when he really wanted to let it all out, regardless of how loud or angry they became. Some things took yelling and slamming doors to get them out of a person's system, and that was okay. She was worth it. He pushed open the doors and stepped outside, bringing her with him.

"We can do this later," she said, shading her eyes from the bright sun.

"No, we can't." He pulled out a chair from beneath one of the round glass tables and motioned for her to sit down, taking the seat beside her. He resituated the baby so he was cradled against his chest. "Look, I was a dick for not asking you about the guy—"

"Logan," she said flatly.

"Right. *Logan*. I'm sorry for being an ass and jumping to conclusions. It turns out I *am* a jealous asshole, but not over just any woman, Addy. Over *you*. It's not an excuse. You know I'm not big on excuses. I might be a jerk sometimes, but I'm an honest guy." Acutely aware of the baby in his arms, he spoke in a harsh whisper, fighting the urge to raise his voice. "So, yeah, I might have some more jerky, jealous moves left in me, and it'll suck for both of us until I learn to get control of it. But that's no reason not to try to make this work. We both have pasts."

"Big ones," she added, glancing at the sleeping baby.

She ran her finger over Seth's hair with a faraway look in her eyes that stopped Jake cold. He looked down at his adorable, innocent nephew and was overwhelmed by the emotions swamping him. How did people get from where he and Addy were to being where Duke and Gabby were? Or Cash and Siena, with two beautiful babies? Duke was no saint. Hell, none of them were. Well, except maybe Gage. But if each of his brothers could figure out how to rein in jealousy and live with their partner's past, then so could he.

He looked up, catching Addy watching him, and realized he still hadn't asked her how she knew the guy with the cabin even after she'd pointed it out. God, he really was an ass.

"I'm sorry I didn't ask about how you knew Logan."

"He's a private investigator. Gabby hired him to do some research for a case. He's a nice guy with a new *wife*."

"Like I said, I'm a jealous asshole."

She narrowed her eyes. "Jealous *yes*, but you're not really an asshole. If the shoe had been on the other foot, I probably would have assumed the same thing."

"Thank Christ. Look, Addy, I want to say I don't care about who you were with before me, but that implies that I don't care about a part of you, and that would be a lie. Because I do care about you, even if whoever you were with before me doesn't matter. But that doesn't mean I won't have a visceral reaction in times like this."

She looked up at him with a tight-lipped expression.

"We can't change the past, Addy, and honestly, as much as I hate thinking about you with any other guy, changing your history would mean you'd be a different person. And I totally dig who you are." Her expression softened. "I can't change my reaction to hearing about that g—*Logan*. But I can try to change how I react in the future."

"Good," she said, her expression fierce once again. "Because I don't like to be accused, and I sure as heck don't want to fight or have to defend who I am. As much as I enjoy our snappy banter, fighting sucks, and accusations hurt, and I need that in my life like I need a hole in my head."

"Agreed. And I'm sorry. I will do whatever it takes to make this work if you're willing to try." He reached for her hand. "No one said this would be easy."

"You don't really believe that I thought this would be easy, do you?" She smiled, and it righted a few pieces of his upended world. "We're passionate people, and passion has two sides. The side that burns so deep you can't escape it, and the side that claws away the skin and leaves you raw. Nothing about either one of us is easy, but for some godforsaken reason, I seem to like that about you."

He moved to the edge of his chair and put his arm around her neck, drawing her close. Even that felt too far away. "You like a passionate asshole. What does that say about *you*?"

She shook her head with a silent laugh, closing her eyes for a beat. When she opened them, her walls had come down again.

"You're really frustrating."

"Thank you. My girlfriend likes me that way." He kissed her then, slow and sweet, full of apology and gratitude and something much deeper. "I'm sorry, baby. I'll try to rein in my reactions. But on a positive note, I think we just survived our first fight."

They both looked down at the sleeping baby nestled between them.

"I think every couple should hold a baby when they argue," she whispered.

"I'll have to thank Cash." He was thinking about everything she'd said, and he felt like there was still so much left to say. "Addy, I don't ever want to make you feel bad, or hurt, or angry, although I'm sure I'll make you angry plenty of times without realizing it. What you said earlier about when you were younger? Baby, I wish I had known you back then so I could make up for each of those air kisses and don't-wrinkle-my-clothes hugs."

She leaned forward and caressed his cheek. He loved that so freaking much, he pressed his hand to the back of hers so it wouldn't slip away.

"We can't change our pasts," she reminded him. "The real question is, can we move forward without losing our minds?"

"That's not even a question." He kissed her again, careful to keep enough space between them so Seth didn't get squished. "Of course we'll lose our minds. But I like losing my mind with you."

"Me too." She arched her neck so he could kiss her there, which he gladly did. "I'll be more careful about how I say things," she said breathlessly. "I love your mouth."

"You love my cock," he growled in her ear.

"Shh." She giggled. "You'll subliminally damage the baby."

"The little rascal made us fight in whispers, and now he's hamstringing my groping action."

"Mm. Hamstrung, huh? Then I'm free to do whatever I want." She slid a wandering hand beneath his shirt and groped his abs. "I'm liking this. If only it wasn't wrong to have a hand down your pants while you held him. Or to be naked on the veranda. Hm. Maybe we should have done that after everyone was asleep last night."

"Sexy girl, I promise to make all of your dirty fantasies come true." He kissed her again as her hand traveled down his belly, hanging by a finger on his waistband. The anticipation of her touch alone got him hard. Having her this close and not being able to touch her the way he wanted to made him *throb*. "I'm always yours for the taking."

"Not with my baby on your lap you're not."

Addy gasped at the sound of Cash's voice and trapped her unstoppable grin between her teeth. She peered over Jake's shoulder at his brother.

"Sorry…?" she said, making them all laugh.

Cash shook his head, lifting Seth from Jake's arms. "Fair warning. The girls are on their—"

"There they are!" Trish burst through the doors with her entourage on her heels.

Hands free of the cuddly, cumbersome baby, Jake gathered Addy in his arms before the girls could whisk her away. "Until later, beautiful girl."

He lowered his mouth to hers and kissed her with all the passion they'd been holding back. Reveling in Addy's laughter against his lips, he kissed her through the girls' whoops and cheers and through his brother's teasing. He took the kiss deeper with each interruption, until she finally abandoned her laughter and gave in to their passion.

And then he kissed her some more.

CHAPTER FOURTEEN

ADDY GLANCED OUT the window of the beach cabana where she and the girls were dressing for the wedding, hoping to catch another glimpse of Jake while the other girls fussed over their hair and makeup. He'd shown up at her room with a bouquet of fresh-picked wild flowers when she was getting her clothes together to bring down to the cabana, and she'd instantly teared up. Amid the craziness of carrying tables and chairs from the villa to the beach and building the altar with his brothers, he'd taken the time to *pick* flowers and bring them to her.

When she'd said the wedding shouldn't count as their first date since the girls were all getting ready together and attending as a group, his response made her happier than she could have ever imagined. *I know you're there with me. Nothing else matters.* She was so into him her head was spinning. They'd been busy with wedding preparations, and she'd only caught glimpses of him ever since, but each glimpse brought a smile, a wave, a kiss, or—true to Jake's nature—a discreet pelvic thrust or enticingly seductive expression.

Siena joined her by the window, looking gorgeous with her hair twisted up in a French knot, making her appear even taller than usual. She was a good eight or nine inches taller than Addy, and her peach minidress made her legs look like they went on forever. As much as Addy loved the faux-diamond-and-pearl barefoot sandals Maggie had brought for the girls to wear, she'd give anything for a little heel height. Not only was she the tiniest of all of them at five foot one, but she could use a few extra inches when she was with Jake.

"Looking for my brother-in-law?" Siena asked.

"Maybe."

"Did seeing him with a baby give you any ideas?"

"After only a weekend together? You're kidding, right?" Addy smoothed her vintage-inspired teal shift to take her mind off of how seeing Jake holding the baby *had* affected her. All the girls had worn pretty summer dresses, and her chicly styled shift, with the sheer ruffle of trim, open-stitched insets, and skin-flashing keyhole back, fit right in. She concentrated on those details, trying not to allow her backpedaling mind to grab hold of the image of Jake holding Seth. But it was no use. The image was seared into her mind. Seth had softened every sharp, brooding edge of him. He'd taken such immense care to hold him gently and keep his voice down, even when it was obvious that he wanted to pace and hammer out their differences with vehemence.

"You don't have to pretend," Siena whispered. "It's been longer, right? You and Jake have been hooking up for months, haven't you?"

Was that what everyone thought? "No, we haven't. Not once before we came here."

"But…" Siena's brow wrinkled. "Cash told me that Jake hasn't been with another woman in months. We assumed it was because he was hooking up with you."

Addy's mind spiraled back to the night of Gabriella's wedding. Jake had never answered her question about whether he'd lied that night at the bar a few months ago when he'd told Blue he hadn't gotten laid in weeks.

"I'm sorry," Siena whispered. "I hope I didn't offend you, or—"

"You didn't," Addy assured her. *Just the opposite.* Happiness bubbled up inside her. Could it be true? Could Jake have been so consumed with thoughts of her that he'd stopped playing around months ago?

Didn't I?

She peeked through the curtains again, spotting Jake talking with his father and Boone beside the beautiful white and gold wedding canopy. *Maybe this thing between us isn't happening too fast after all.*

"I'm glad," Siena said. "Did you guys get to sneak away for crazy good makeup sex?"

When the girls had stolen her away from Jake earlier that morning, they'd noticed how sidetracked she was and peppered her with questions. She'd confided in them about Jake's jealousy, and after talking it over, she realized that she probably would have reacted the same way. Now she remembered that Cash had come into the room during their conversation, and not long after that she'd found Jake with Seth. She wondered if Cash and Siena had planted the baby in his arms to ease their tension. She wasn't sure if she should be thankful or annoyed at their intrusion into her and Jake's privacy. *Thankful. Definitely thankful.* After all, wasn't that what friends were for? Helping each other out in good times and bad?

"Should I take that silence as confirmation of the amazing makeup sex?" Siena asked.

"Are you kidding?" Addy laughed, although the panty-melting kiss he'd given her on the veranda had left her hungry for more. "With how busy we've been today? I've barely seen him."

"At least you have something to look forward to. *Lots* of makeup sex. Our Ryder men are *so* jealous."

Our Ryder men. She liked the sound of that.

"It's kind of cute the way they try to hide it," Siena added. "I knew the second I saw Jake's face all twisted up this morning when you guys came back from the beach with Ned and Andrea that he was jealous. You'll learn. If there's a male in your life, your man will be jealous over him. Period."

Addy didn't like the sound of that. "If that's true, he'll push me away quicker than he can say he's sorry."

"They're trainable," Siena assured her. "Just like we are. Guys are jealous and cocky; girls are jealous, needy, chatty…That's how it works."

Addy had never been needy a day in her life. Except she *was* sexually needy when she was with Jake. Did that count? No, she decided, it didn't, because that was different from needing his attention outside the bedroom. Maybe she and Jake really were wired differently than most other couples. Other couples could temper their sexual needs, but she and Jake were like raging infernos all the time. *Like Grandma*. Her hand moved over her tattoo. The similarities between her and Jake and her grandmother's first, happy marriage made her feel warm all over.

"Girls, come on." Andrea waved them over. She looked gorgeous and youthful in a navy short-sleeved dress that stopped just above her knees, with pretty pearls dangling from her ears. "We're ready to take pictures."

Gabriella's aunts had made sure they had enough flowers to create the feel of a magical beachside garden, transforming the beach cabana into a wedding haven. Trish looked gorgeous in her mother's wedding gown and a pair of her mother's diamond earrings, boasting an ear-to-ear smile. Cash and Siena had given her a blue lapis bracelet, and Lizzie had loaned her a diamond necklace that went perfectly with the earrings. The white garter Maggie had given her counted as something *new*. She had all the requisite items for a perfect bride.

"You're only two words away from your happily ever after," Addy said, easing in between Andrea and Sally as Gabriella's cousin Marnie, the island's best photographer, came bustling through the doors.

"You girls look like old pros." Marnie stood back, admiring the girls in their varying colorful outfits and barefoot sandals. "Gorgeous. You could be on the cover of my next issue of *Weddings Done Right*." Marnie traveled often for her wedding photography business, but she was in town for Gabriella's wedding and had happily agreed to take Trish and Boone's wedding photos.

"We've had a lot of practice lately," Lizzie said. "I can't wait for mine and Blue's wedding."

"Ohmygod!" Trish exclaimed. "I have the *best* idea!"

"Uh-oh," Andrea said. "When my daughter gets that look, she's scheming."

Marnie moved around the group, capturing Trish's excitement on film.

"Why don't you and Blue get married now? With us?" Trish grabbed Lizzie's hands. "Really. Our family's all here!"

"That's so sweet," Lizzie said. "But…my family isn't."

"Ohmygod. I'm an idiot." Trish pulled her into a hug. "I'm so sorry. Of course. I was just so swept up in becoming sisters-in-law with you, I wasn't thinking clearly."

Andrea patted Trish on the back. "We love your enthusiasm, baby girl. But Lizzie's family definitely needs to be at her wedding. And besides, didn't you hear Blue when he said they were getting married when her sister was on break from school over the holidays?"

"Uh-uh. I was too busy being *proposed* to." Trish squealed. "Okay, the holidays it is! That's not too far off, and we'll help you get ready for the wedding of your dreams!"

Addy had never gotten particularly excited over weddings. But seeing Trish and Boone and Gabriella and Duke this weekend and knowing how happy they were brought a lump to her throat. She was excited for them to find their happy endings. She smiled to herself, thinking about the *happy ending* she wanted to give Jake tonight. Something a little extra special for the big brooding man who'd finally made her feel something. She'd make him *feel* something all right. *Oh yeah, we're definitely different. You girls are thinking of flowers and wedding dresses, and I can't wait to get my man naked.*

The room grew quiet, and Trish pinned Addy with a mischievous look. "Double wedding, Addy?"

"What?" Addy waved her hands, walking backward. "No, no, no. No wedding here. We've barely been together two days."

The girls laughed.

Addy held her breath.

Marnie continued taking pictures.

Great. Did you capture that ohmygod *look?*

"Oh, honey," Andrea said. "Time means nothing in matters of the heart. Why, I knew the moment I set eyes on Ned that he was the one for me."

"Aw," Maggie said. "I hope I find that one day."

"The way Niko was checking you out earlier, I think you

might be on your way," Gabriella said, causing Maggie to blush.

Addy had noticed Niko checking out Maggie, and she'd seen the spark between them, too. It was hard to miss. *Like the spark between me and Jake.*

Andrea touched Addy's hand. "Jake is just like Ned. More so than any of my other boys. Ned's relaxed a bit with age, but when he was younger, he was obsessive, just like Jake. When Ned set his mind on something—or in my case, *someone*—nothing stood in his way. Until you, Jake's only obsession was search and rescue. I wondered if anyone could pierce through his walls and get to his big, generous heart."

"I think *obsessed* is a little strong," Addy said. Jake's voice rolled through her mind. *You're mine, Addy.* Maybe his mother wasn't so far off after all.

"You're right. I don't mean obsessed like a serial killer. I meant he's single-minded. He knows what he wants and nothing will stop him from getting it." Andrea glanced at Trish and winked. "All of our kids are determined—"

"And loyal," Lizzie said, her eyes locked on Sally, who nodded in agreement.

"Yes. They are loyal," Andrea said. "I'm proud of them all for growing up to be responsible, caring adults. It's good to know we've done something right."

"There's no doubt that Jake's a great guy, and I don't mean to burst anyone's bubble, but really," Addy said. "We've hardly been together long enough to know if we like the same foods, much less want the same things out of life." The words came out rough and uncomfortable. She felt like she already knew him better than she knew most people.

"You keep telling yourself that, honey," Andrea said sweetly.

Addy wondered if she could see the panic blooming inside

her with the realization that everyone else knew how close she and Jake had become when they were still figuring it out themselves.

"Girls?" Marnie said. "I'm sorry to interrupt, but if we don't get the pictures soon, I'll miss my boat back to the mainland, and I have to be in Chicago tonight."

Boat? Addy's mind reeled. She was leaving in a few hours. They'd been running around so much it had totally slipped her mind. There would be no awesome makeup sex, no waking up in Jake's arms tomorrow morning. There would be no *Jake* for ten long days.

Andrea stepped closer. "Your heart has woken up, sweetheart, and love always wins. It's stronger than anything. Even our sense of self-preservation."

She hadn't set out to sleep with Jake, much less be in a monogamous relationship. And now she couldn't imagine going ten days without him.

TRISH AND BOONE exchanged their vows beneath the white and gold wedding canopy Blue had masterminded and Jake and his brothers had helped build. Addy's eyes teared up when they'd said their vows, and she was adorable trying to hide it by fluttering her long lashes into the breeze. Jake hadn't been able to take his eyes off of her during the entire wedding ceremony, which had been almost as beautiful as she was. That was two hours ago, and now his brothers were deep in conversation about their fishing trip later that evening, and the girls were excited about having another girls' night up on the bluff. But there would be no swooping in and kidnapping Addy tonight.

She was leaving in a few hours, and Jake was doing all he could to not think about it.

Addy stood by the water's edge with Gabriella and his mother, swinging her hips to the beat of the music. They'd just danced to five songs together, and he already missed the feel of her in his arms. The late-afternoon wind whipped her long dark hair across her back like a wild mane, pressing her short, sexy dress against her body, leaving nothing to the imagination. She'd been talking to his mother for a while now, and he wondered what his mother was telling her. Embarrassing stories of his childhood? Not likely. His mother tended to pull those out when she could get the most bang for her buck and see the blush rise on her children's faces. Jake guessed they were talking about girl stuff. Clothes, shoes…That didn't sit right either. Addy didn't seem to get into those things the way he'd seen other women get giddy over them. What did she get giddy about? He laughed to himself. Addy didn't do *giddy*. She did serious, sexy, seductive, and lately he'd been gifted peeks into her softer, vulnerable side. But if he knew his girl, and after months of watching her reactions and thinking about her, he was pretty sure he did, he knew how rare and special those glimpses were.

He felt his father's presence before he appeared beside him. It had always been that way with them. His father had been the one to teach him how to hone his senses for search and rescue, and as he got older, those skills overflowed to the other parts of his life.

"Hey, Dad. How's it going?"

"I think I should be asking you that." His father nodded in Addy's direction. "She's really gotten under your skin."

"You could say that." Jake and his father had a special bond.

He'd spent his formative years trekking along in his father's shadow, soaking up every ounce of knowledge his father was willing to share. They shared more than just a love of helping others and pushing themselves past their limits. Jake shared his father's nearly fearless disposition. Facing nature's elements, wild animals, harsh weather, or the unknown didn't scare them. But *failing* a rescue mission did. That was one reason Jake lived an unencumbered life. He'd long ago separated his emotions from everything but family and search and rescue. He couldn't afford to be distracted when there were lives depending on him. Watching Addy gather her hair over her shoulder, he knew he was facing the biggest distraction of all, and he was glad he'd taken two weeks off while she was traveling. That gave him time to get a handle on things.

"What's your plan?" his father asked.

"Plan?" he asked. "About…?"

"Her trip. Come on, son. I know you pretty well." His father's lips tipped up. "Right about now you're looking at her and either concocting a plan to ask her not to go, or you're figuring out how to get her to let you go with her."

"Already tried both."

His father laughed and patted him on the back. "You've got no jurisdiction over her."

"No shit." Leave it to his father to liken this to search and rescue. In every rescue there was an AHJ, or Agency Having Jurisdiction, who oversaw the mission. Addy had made it crystal clear that he had no such authority over her.

"Give her space, Jake."

Yeah, right.

"You were never good at backing off. You see a crisis and you tackle it. You've always faced things head-on, hated the unknown."

"I face the unknown every time I set foot on a recovery mission. You know that. You do the same thing." His father had worked in search and rescue his whole life and had eventually founded East Coast Search and Rescue. Now he claimed he was retired, but Jake didn't think his father would ever truly retire. He still spent a good deal of time directing volunteers and overseeing training courses.

"Yes, we face it with this." His father tapped his head. "But you've never faced it with this." He tapped Jake's chest, over his heart. "You protect that with everything you've got."

Jake scoffed. "I never even thought about that particular organ before Addy. And now, I'm all fu—messed up."

"Fucked up? Yeah, that sounds about right."

Crossing his arms, Jake faced his father. "Why's that?"

"It's the nature of the beast. When the right woman comes around, she turns your world upside down."

"Yeah? Well, I think it's more than that. I suck at relationships, and I'm pretty sure I'll screw this up."

"How can you know? You've never *tried* a relationship."

"Never wanted the distraction. And now that I found someone worth being distracted for, I feel totally unprepared. *Me. Unprepared.* Dad, I've been prepared for every single thing in my life since I was five years old. *Over*prepared." He paused at the amusement in his father's eyes. "What could possibly be funny about this?"

"You can't prepare for love. It hits like a storm and blows everything to smithereens." He touched Jake's shoulder, turning him toward Addy. "She's a smart girl, Jake. She's tough, and from what Gabriella has told us, she took quite a risk going against her father's wishes. She turned her back on everything her parents offered, determined to make it on her own. That's not a woman who will bend to your will, son. And trust me, you wouldn't be satisfied with a woman who would."

Jake blew out a breath of frustration. "You know the dangers of camping alone."

"Yes, and the idea of that little pixie out in the wilderness alone scares the daylights out of me. But you caging her in? That's even more dangerous territory, Jake. Educate her. Be there for her if she calls for help. But this time, I think you need to take a page from Gage's playbook. Step back and let her lead."

Jake scoffed. "Gage? He's been hanging on for *years*."

His father shook his head. "He's been *in love* for years. There's a difference. Gage is a smart man. He might not blow through life like you do, but he knows when to step up and when to back down. Trust me on this. It's time to step back. You cage that girl in and you're liable to get bitten."

Addy turned, and their eyes connected, igniting the very air between them.

"Tread carefully," his father said before walking away.

Jake headed for Addy. She tilted her head in a thoughtful pose, watching him watch her. *What are you thinking, sexy girl?*

Every step brought more heat, a deeper need to have her in his arms. In his bed. In his *life*.

Step back. Let her lead.

He tried to wrap his mind around his father's suggestion, but Jake wasn't good at stepping back. He was a born leader. A fixer. The rescue guy who scaled the side of mountains to check every dangerous cave, even in the most treacherous conditions, because someone's life was on the line.

No one's life was on the line now, but he sure felt like it

was.

Addy said something to Gabriella, her sexy smile doing funky things to his stomach again. *Jesus.* Would that shit ever settle down? She walked toward him, her hips swaying seductively, her dress swishing around her thighs, and her gorgeous eyes locked on him. Then she was in his arms, reaching up and circling his neck, causing his heart to swell.

"Hey there, big boy," she said with heat in her eyes. "Looking for a date?"

How could he step back when the woman who had blown his mind before she'd ever agreed to go out with him was right there in his arms?

They moved seamlessly to the music, as if they'd been dancing together forever. "Only if it's with you." He leaned down for a kiss and she pressed her finger over his lips. "You're *kiss blocking* me?"

"I'm slowing us down for one second, because the minute our lips touch, my brain goes in one of two directions—the gutter or out the door. And right now I have to focus or I'll miss my boat."

"There's an easy way to fix that. *Stay.*"

CHAPTER FIFTEEN

OKAY, WAS ON the tip of Addy's tongue. There was no place on earth she'd rather be than in Jake's arms. She'd just admitted as much to Gabriella and his mother, but staying would mean putting off her plans for a day. Though it didn't sound like much, it *was* to Addy. It was giving Jake power over her decisions.

"Jake," she said softly, trying to figure out how to explain what she'd just explained to Gabriella—who had called her *crazy*—and his mother—who had called her *strong*—without sounding like she didn't want to be with him. "You have to know I want to stay. I want to wake up in your arms tomorrow and watch the sunrise and smell the flowers you picked for me."

Her eyes dampened, and she drew deep, willing herself to be strong. "I debated staying, but I can't."

He pulled back only a fraction of an inch, but she noticed. *Boy* did she notice.

"*Won't,* Addy. There's a difference."

She sank back down on her heels. "Yes, you're right. There is, and I'm sorry, but changing my plans is..." This was where she'd stumbled with Gabriella, and it was even harder trying to find the right words for Jake when he was looking at her like she was all he ever wanted. "I told you I wouldn't change my plans when we first got together."

"Things change," he said a little softer. "Addy, it's a day, not a week. I'm not asking to go with you or trying to keep you from going. I want one more night with you, and I really want to go over some general safety guidelines and make sure you know what to do in case of an emergency. I can show you the things you may not have thought of, like what plants and snakes are poisonous and what knots to use for certain things, and—"

"Stop." It was another knee-jerk reaction, but knowing that didn't make it any easier to try to slip out from under its grip. "I appreciate your offer, but I told you I've done my research. I'm fully capable of preparing for a camping trip, and if I'm not, then I'll deal with it when something goes wrong." She had bought books on knots and basic camping skills, and although she hadn't read them yet, she would have plenty of time to do so once she got situated on the mountain. She'd looked up the important things, like what to pack, what to expect, and what wild animals she might run in to. Besides that, she definitely knew how to sit by a campfire, heat up a bowl of soup, and sleep in a frigging tent.

"It's not like there are lions, tigers, and bears up there," she said to lighten the air. "I mean, there are black bears, but I'm not a berry, so I think I'm pretty safe. And yes, I know I could see a mountain lion, but it would be rare, so can we please not argue about this? You know I'm not going to give in."

He pulled her against him, hugging her as he kissed the top of her head. Tension radiated from every inch of his body, but his touch was caring and tender, and the dichotomy shook her to her core. Her heart said *stay, stay, stay*, but her head fought tooth and nail against changing her plans. She'd already changed so much, and giving in would tell Jake he could get her to change her plans anytime, wouldn't it? That was a little too close to home.

Tipping up her chin, she met his gaze, and her heart whispered *stay* again. How on earth could she stick to her guns when all she wanted was to stay right there in his arms? Was this how women lost themselves? Their independence? Was this how she'd turn into her mother? By first giving in to one small thing, then the next and the next, until the need for her problem-solving and decision-making skills were erased completely and she flitted through life letting him take care of everything? She shuddered at the thought.

"I can't stay, Jake. Besides, you have the fishing trip tonight with the guys, and I refuse to be the cause of you missing that." She reached for his hand, feeling the tension in his grip. "We still have a little while before I leave. I have to pack and say goodbye to everyone, but I'd like to do those things together if you're willing."

He ground his teeth together, disappointment swimming in his eyes.

TIME MOVED TOO fast as Jake and Addy packed her things, making small talk about the weather, the wedding, and the island. Everything except the elephant in the room. She'd begun this weekend by setting up rules and expectations, as much for herself as for him, and she'd already blown those out of the water. She didn't like the feeling of not being able to imagine a day without him—or anyone. It went against everything she knew about herself, but her trip loomed over her like a long, dark stretch of loneliness.

Jake carried her suitcase out of the resort. "How are you

getting to the mountains tomorrow?"

"I rented a car, which I'll return in Sweetwater, a small town not far from the trailhead where I'm starting my hike. The girl at the rental agency said they could drop me off."

He nodded, and she could see the gears in his mind churning. She knew this was killing him as much as it was killing her.

"I really don't want to talk about the trip," she said honestly. Even the little they'd already said made her waffle about leaving.

He set down her suitcase and hauled her against him. They were on the curved part of the dusty road between the resort and town, buffered by a fringe of trees, giving them a modicum of privacy.

"You're too stubborn for such a petite little thing." With his hands around her rib cage, he lifted her into the air, her legs dangling beneath her, and he gazed heatedly into her eyes. "You'll miss me when you're all alone at night on that trip we're not talking about." He pressed his lips to hers, still holding her in the air like a rag doll. "But not half as much as I'll miss you." Circling her waist with one strong arm, he held her against him. "How do you pack so much power into silence?"

Swallowing past the lump clogging her throat, she managed, "Thinking..."

He lowered her feet to the ground, the hope in his eyes too blatant to ignore. She touched her forehead to his chest and closed her eyes, willing herself not to admit what was going on inside her, but it was too consuming, too distracting, too determined to escape.

"I didn't want to fall for you," she said, pressing her palms to his chest. "I just wanted to sleep with you."

Taking her chin between his fingers and thumb, he lifted

her face and lowered his lips to hers in another tender kiss. "I was falling for you before we ever came to the island. It's only fair that you endure at least a little bit of torture."

How did he make her smile when she felt on the verge of tears? "You're taking too much pleasure in the fact that I don't know who I'm becoming and I don't want to lose who I am."

"Don't kid yourself, sexy girl. I'm taking great pleasure in the fact that you're letting me into your world. You're not changing who you are." He lifted the suitcase as evidence and set it back down on the ground. "We're just too strong of a force to deny."

His arrogant grin told her what was coming next. She put her hand over his mouth and narrowed her eyes, trying to ignore the sensual, teasing slick of his tongue against her palm.

"Don't you dare follow that up with you told me so." Her voice was shaking despite her efforts to hide it. "It'll just make me want to fight these feelings to prove you wrong."

He grabbed her wrist, the cockiness turned to pure seduction. "You think a little rebellion will deter me?" Eyes locked on hers, he sealed his mouth over her neck.

Every slick of his talented tongue sent heat to the juncture of her thighs. She grabbed hold of his waist, battling her weakening knees as he continued the sensual torture. His free hand traveled over her hip. The thin material of her dress did nothing to block the blaze of his seduction as he caressed her bottom, obliterating her ability to think past the need mounting inside her. When he nibbled on her shoulder, then returned to her neck—*Oh God, yes, there*—her toes curled against her sandals and she leaned in to him. A single rock of his hips brought his hard length against her belly. She closed her eyes, willing herself to pull back, to fight the lust coiling deep inside her. He captured her mouth, his long, thick fingers slipping beneath her dress, beneath her panties, and plunging into her slick heat. Her breath rushed from her lungs, and she felt him smile against her lips. She went up on her toes, sinking back down along his fingers, urging him to take what he wanted—to give her what she needed.

"Fuck, Addy," he growled against her lips.

"Don't stop." She clutched his wrist, holding his hand prisoner between her legs.

"Not a chance. I want to haul your ass over my shoulder and drag you into the woods."

She met his piercing gaze. A silent and very clear message of assent exploded between them, and in the next breath she was over his shoulder and he was charging into the woods, both of them laughing. He laid her on the ground among leaves and grass, buffered on all sides by thick bushes, and made quick work of dropping his pants.

"Hurry," she pleaded as he came down over her.

In one hard thrust he drove into her, and she cried out. He silenced her with a mind-numbing kiss, sending more waves of erotic pleasure crashing over her, each one drowning out the one before, taking her higher, bringing them closer together. Beneath her closed lids, flashes of the time they shared burst in quick succession—the laughter, the teasing, the lovemaking. The *fucking*. He was the fierce and passionate man she never allowed herself to hope for, careful enough to know when to pull back but manly enough to know when she needed to be pushed. Craving the sight of the man who had awoken her heart and taken her body to heights she'd only dreamed of, she met his gaze. His eyes brimmed with desire so intense she was sure it must be sizzling in his veins. The risk of being seen, the fierce look of hunger in his eyes, and the way he gave her exactly what she needed, wound together, bringing all of her emotions to the surface. Their connection was so raw, so powerful. It was brutally beautiful. He claimed her in another possessive kiss, taking her deeper, harder, as if he were trying to claim every ounce of her, pounding into her again and again, until all she felt was the soul-sucking, earth-shattering greed of their mutual release.

Chapter Sixteen

JAKE TOSSED OUT his fishing line, hiked his foot up on the bench, and wondered how he was going to get through ten Addyless days.

"She actually left." Duke leaned against the side of the boat with a beer in his hand. "Bet you never thought that would happen."

Jake kept his eyes on the dark water, thinking about how he and Addy had run back to the resort because she had insisted on taking a quick shower—alone—and she'd nearly missed the boat. He should have gotten in that shower and made her miss it. "Do you even know Addy? Of course I knew she'd leave. She's not exactly someone who listens to others."

Duke chuckled. "I guess I'm the one who didn't see it coming." He sipped his beer. "Sounds like you're pretty upset."

Jake scoffed. "What tipped you off?"

They'd been fishing for more than an hour and hadn't caught a damn thing. Normally Jake wouldn't care, as spending time with his brothers was fun no matter what, but not only was it taking all his willpower not to gun the boat toward the mainland and catch a plane to New York, but all the guys had talked about was getting back to their significant others.

"There's no beer in your hand, for starters," Duke pointed out.

Because I haven't written off the idea of leaving yet, and I need to be sober to drive a boat, navigate through an airport, and drive a fricking rental car.

ADDY HAD BEEN trying not to think about Jake since Elpitha Island had faded into the distance as the boat carried her to South Carolina. She'd stood gripping the railing, blinking into the wind for the second time that day. Her emotions had sure picked a grand time to kick into gear. She'd tried to push the image of Jake and Gabriella waving from the dock from her mind as she boarded the crowded plane. She'd even tried to close her eyes for a nap on the flight to New York. Their decadent weekend should have taken its toll, considering they hadn't slept more than a few hours, but Jake's voice kept whispering through her mind, keeping sleep at bay. *You own so much of me*, he'd said as he hugged her so tight she could barely breathe. *It'll kill me if anything happens to you*. But he'd stopped asking her to stay. He'd respected her wishes despite how much he hated her leaving.

Now, as she tossed an armful of camping supplies on the couch, a harsher reality was staring her in the face. Where among the mounds of clothes, blankets, lighters, compass, maps, and a zillion other wilderness necessities did her lonely heart fit in? She'd gotten exactly what she wanted. She just never expected it to hurt so much. She couldn't even call Gabriella to meet her for a drink and drown her sorrows. A seaplane was picking up her and Duke after the fishing trip and whisking them away for their honeymoon.

She set her hands on her hips and turned to the mirror she'd had inset in the fireplace. She may not have wanted her parents' posh lifestyle, but in some respects the apple didn't fall far from the tree. Addy had her father's flair for design. The mirror made her cozy space look bigger and classed up her eclectic style of mismatched greens, salmon, and distressed grays. When she'd rented the apartment, she hadn't imagined ever using a fireplace when she could simply kick up the thermostat a notch. The irony was not lost on her that she was embarking on a trip where fire would be the only element to keep her warm on cold mountain nights.

She sank down to the couch, sighing heavily and sending her neatly packaged lightweight tent, one of her pink hiking boots, and her first-aid kit tumbling off the cushions. They landed with *thunks* on the plush area rug.

What the hell am I doing?

Addy wasn't a second guesser or a wallower, and the fact that she was doing both simmered uncomfortably in her stomach. She pushed from the couch, sending another pile of supplies to the floor, and stalked into the kitchen for a bottle of wine. She took one from the rack without even looking at the label, uncorked it, and guzzled it.

"Okay, Addison. Time to get your ass in gear." Carrying the open bottle, she went into her bedroom and grabbed the backpack she'd purchased for the trip, hooked it over her shoulder, and swigged another mouthful of wine. She could do this. Like everything else in life, she'd put one foot in front of the other and refuse to think about the big, brooding boyfriend she'd left behind. Feeling better already, she picked up the camping books she'd nearly forgotten to pack, and her mind traveled back to Jake asking her to let him go over safety precautions. He was so earnest and sincere in his desire to help.

Her mind instantly found the image of him crouched in the shower as he spotted her tattoo while he lovingly washed her. He'd looked as worried as he'd been curious. A lump lodged in her throat. *Do not go there.* She swallowed the guilt of not spilling her secret and shifted the books to the crook of her arm, taking another swig of the liquid courage.

An hour later she sat in the middle of her living room floor in her pajamas, among her supplies, eyeing her laptop. She needed to get Jake off her mind. What better way than to get her mind *on* someone else? Grabbing her technological friend, she remembered her promise to Jake. *No looking at my Tumblr page.*

For the weekend.

She eyed the clock on the screen. It *was* after midnight.

Tapping her finger on the edge of the laptop, she debated taking just a peek. *Right, like I ever just peek? Would I mind if Jake just peeked at a hot girls Tumblr page?* Jealousy gnawed at her. *Unless we were looking at hot couple Tumblr pages together.*

Hmm...

She grabbed her cell phone from the coffee table and called Jake. The call went directly to voice mail. *Of course.* Elpitha's cell reception sucked. She closed her laptop and took another drink. She didn't want to look at anyone else. She wanted Jake, and it was her own damn fault he wasn't there.

Chapter Seventeen

ADDY DIDN'T KNOW how long she'd incorporated the incessant pounding on her apartment door into her dreams, but as she tried to get her foggy brain to focus, reaching blindly for her phone on the floor beside the couch, the pounding began anew. *Someone has a death wish.* Her phone was dead. Another knock on the door brought her to her feet. She stumbled through her living room, guided only by a sliver of moonlight streaking through the curtains, and tripped over the pile of camping supplies she'd failed to pack before she fell asleep.

Another knock sounded.

"Hold on!" *What the hell?* "You better hope the complex is on fire."

She put her tired eye up to the peephole, but whoever was on the other side of it was leaning at an odd angle, and she couldn't see anything but a shoulder. *Great. Some drunk guy probably has the wrong apartment.* The guy reached up and rubbed the back of his neck, and her breath left her lungs.

Her stomach flipped as she tugged the door open and Jake lifted his head, one forearm still resting on the doorframe.

"Hey there, sexy girl," Jake said with an easy smile. He wore the low-slung jeans he'd had on earlier and a dark T-shirt that clung to his broad chest. But it was the look of longing in his eyes that made her heart nearly stop.

"What are you doing here?"

His arm slid around her waist, gathering her against him. "I missed you, too." His lips met hers in a toe-curling kiss that left no room for anything but the inferno between them.

She came away breathless, her hands pressed firmly on his chest. She curled her fingers under, wanting to stay close. "Why are you here?"

He nuzzled against her neck. "Is that any way to greet your boyfriend at two in the morning?"

She dragged him inside by his collar and closed the door behind them. He was grinning like a fool as he hauled her toward him again, his back against the door. He spread his legs and sank down so they were eye to eye. She'd missed his greedy stare and arrogant grin. She pressed her hand to his scruffy cheek, feeling like she should be annoyed with the intrusion, but all she felt was relief and overwhelming happiness.

"Are you checking up on me?" she teased.

"Do I *need* to check up on you?" He dragged his eyes down her tank top, lingering on the words emblazoned across her chest: EAT CLEAN PLAY DIRTY. His eyes darkened and flicked to hers for half a second before dropping to her boy shorts, where they lingered on the words printed from hip to hip, ALL-NIGHT BUFFET.

She cringed.

He grabbed her butt, pulling her firmly against him. "It just so happens I'm starved."

Her body was vibrating with desire, but a hint of worry tiptoed in. Had he come to change her mind about the trip? "Is that right?" She kissed him just below his ear, then bit down hard.

"Ouch! Damn, woman." He spanked her ass.

She drew back, holding his biceps, and glared at him. "Are you here to get me to change my mind about the trip?"

"No. I'm here because—" His eyes drifted over her shoulder, and he huffed out a disbelieving laugh before meeting her gaze again. "Because I missed you, and someone has to make sure you're taken care of before you go. Safety-wise, of course." He reached behind him and handed her a leather journal that he must have had stuffed in the back of his pants, because there was no way it would fit in his pocket. "And I brought you this. In case you want to keep a journal about your adventure."

She narrowed her eyes. "Really? That's so sweet, but…this isn't to soften me up, is it? To get me into an incredible sexathon meant to convince me that I need a six-foot-three tour guide?"

He set the beautiful journal on the floor and brushed one hand over her hair, which she was sure looked like Medusa's. "I'll never forgive myself if something happens to you and I wasn't there to protect you, but I know you want to do this alone. So no, this visit isn't meant to convince you to let me go. I want to run through the basic safety rules with you, and…" He gathered her closer, holding her like he never wanted to let her go. "I needed you in my arms one last time. Ten days is a long fucking time."

She'd never thought so before, but ten *hours* without him had seemed like forever.

"Baby?" he whispered in her ear.

"Mm-hm." She wanted to stake a tent right there in his arms.

"Is that a *pink* hiking boot?"

"You have a problem with pink?" She tried to sound offended, but she couldn't stop smiling. He was there, like he'd somehow known she was missing him, and he wasn't pushing her to change her mind about the trip.

He rose to his full height, lifting her in his arms as he did. Her legs wound around his waist. She never imagined herself being carried by anyone, and Jake took her from fighting it to wanting it in the blink of an eye.

"Let me show you just how much I love *pink.*" He carried her through the living room. "Nice packing job."

"No comments from the peanut gallery. You're not here to critique me. You're here to…" She studied his face. Was he really there with no ulterior motive? He missed her? Wanted to teach her a few safety rules?

He stopped at the threshold to the bedroom, pressing his lips to hers. His hand slid beneath her boy shorts and she drew back from the kiss.

"You're here for a booty call," she teased.

He carried her into the bedroom and sat on the edge of the bed with her straddling his lap. "That's a long way to go for a booty call."

She flipped her hair dramatically and batted her lashes. "I'm worth it. I've ruined you for all other women."

He lifted her top over her head and tossed it aside. Her nipples puckered at the cool air whisking over them.

"Cocky, aren't we?" he teased, before bringing his glorious mouth to her breast. His tongue slid over the taut peak, making her shiver all over.

She ran her fingers through his hair. Oh, how she'd missed that. "Just like you've ruined me for all other men."

Turning with her in his arms, he laid her on the bed beneath him and inched down her body one kiss at a time until he reached her shorts. "Baby, I haven't even begun to ruin you.

Now, let's see what's on the menu tonight."

He took her shorts down slowly, licking his lips as he tossed them aside. The predatory look in his eyes made her ache.

She covered her privates with her hands, a big grin tugging at her lips. "Fair's fair. Naked, big guy. *Now.*"

A low laugh sailed from his lungs. "My, my. I do love your demanding side." He tugged off his shirt, swung it over his head, and tossed it across the room.

"Woo-hoo," she cheered, pushing up on her elbows to take in the show.

He unbuttoned his jeans and swayed his hips as he unzipped them, revealing a tuft of dark hair. Sweet baby Jesus, the man had moves *and* he'd gone commando.

"You'd better hurry. Knowing you weren't wearing undercrackers is an instant aphrodisiac."

"Undercrackers," he mumbled with a sexy smile. "I'll remember my girl likes me ready and willing."

While she reveled in the endearment, he raised his brows, taking his sweet old time as he pushed his jeans down to his knees. His cock sprang free, and she scrambled to the edge of the bed and crooked her finger. He began pushing his jeans down further and she shook her head, taking his hard length in her hand.

"Leave them on." She slicked her tongue from base to tip, and he groaned.

"Damn, you are my naughty girl."

She reached around, grabbing his ass as she took him in her mouth, earning another heady noise.

"Fuck, Addy. How will I survive ten days without you?" He tangled his hands in her hair and she met his gaze, circling the broad head of his arousal with her tongue.

"How do you think I feel?" She slicked her tongue along his length again and stroked him with her hand. "I'll be hiking without any of my toys." Her eyes widened. Why hadn't she thought of bringing them?

"Shit," he ground out. "You're bringing them, aren't you?"

She shrugged, sure she looked like the cat who ate the canary, but even as she teased him, she knew she could no longer be satisfied by a battery-operated boyfriend. He stepped from his jeans, flipped her onto her stomach, and smacked her ass. She *yelp*ed and laughed, trying to crawl away, but he tugged her back by the ankles and laid his full, delicious weight on top of her. She was so full of him she could barely think straight.

"You'd rather have a toy than me?" he said heatedly into her ear.

She lifted her ass, grinding against his cock, and couldn't help teasing him a little more. "My Neanderthal won't be there to satisfy me."

He scratched his scruff along her cheek, and she couldn't suppress the wanton moan from escaping.

"And who's fault is *that*?" he growled.

She laughed, trying to turn over beneath him, but he was too heavy, too strong.

"Don't try to avoid the question." He kissed the back of her neck.

"Are you kidding? I'm trying to turn over so I can take *full* responsibility for my actions." He seemed to like that, and lifted up, allowing her to turn onto her back. While he was still perched on his palms, she lifted her hips, dragging her sex along his arousal.

"You think you're going to sidetrack me and make me forget about those *toys*?"

Grinning like a fool, she shook her head. "I'd rather have you than a toy any day, but just in case, and since you're *hungry*, maybe you should take your fill and make me forget those toys. Otherwise…"

"Sexy girl, it'll be a miracle if you can still walk when I'm done with you."

JAKE DIDN'T SLEEP a wink. He'd fulfilled his promise and worn Addy out to the point of exhaustion, and she'd fallen asleep lying on top of him. He didn't want to move her. As he lay beneath her, her hair cascading over his side, her hand over his chest, he memorized the feel of her, the sure and steady cadence of her heart beating against his. He wanted to tell her he was going with her today and make her deal with it, but his father's words held him back. *You cage that girl in and you're liable to get bitten.*

He wrestled with that thought over the course of the morning, tempted to tell her anyway when they were making love in the shower and again now, as he watched her dress in a cute pair of cutoffs and a white T-shirt with a red flannel shirt tied around her waist. Her hair curtained her face as she tightened the knot on the shirtsleeves, and she tipped a sweet smile in his direction. He was so high on her he couldn't think straight.

She crossed the floor slowly, reaching for him, and hooked her finger in the waistband of his jeans.

"Did you drop your luggage at your place?"

He shook his head, too messed up to speak.

"Is it in the hall?" She gazed out of the bedroom.

He shook his head again, cleared his throat, and forced his

pussy-whipped self to man up. "During the fishing trip my brothers were going on and on about how sexy their wives were at the wedding."

She trapped her lower lip between her teeth, that raging smile she'd been flashing since he'd arrived refusing to be erased. "I might have given them a few pointers in seduction."

"Of course you did." He tugged her against him, kissing the top of her sexy, stubborn head. "Jesus, those men don't know what they're in for."

She kissed his chest and peered up at him. "How does that explain your lack of luggage?"

"I couldn't stand listening to them and thinking about you. We cut the fishing trip short, I asked my father to get my stuff in the morning, and I hijacked Lucky and Cage. And the boat."

She laughed. "Do they even know how to drive a boat?"

"That's why I took Cage with me. My brothers were too horny to sit still another minute, and I couldn't drag my father out because he'd give me shit for not giving you space. When we got back to the island I saw Lucky and Cage at the tavern. Lucky jumped at the chance to help me out. Apparently Cage owns a boat, and taught Lucky how to drive, but I guess he's a bit of a wild child, so Cage came along."

She wound her arms around his middle. "So you dropped everything, stole a boat, and probably bought an outrageously expensive last-minute plane ticket just to see me."

He leaned down for a kiss. "And to make sure you're safe, baby."

She pressed her lips together, narrowing her eyes. He expected a fight, and when she said, "That might be the sweetest, most romantic thing a person has ever done," he let out a relieved breath.

"That's an overstatement, and I didn't do it to be romantic."

She touched his chest, and he flattened his hand over hers.

"And I didn't think I liked romance," she said tenderly. "But we're both testing new boundaries."

Yeah, baby, I'd love to test your boundaries. He dragged her out of the bedroom.

"What's wrong?"

"The minute 'boundaries' comes out of your sexy mouth, my mind goes to dark places." He tugged her against him again, needing to soak in as much of her as possible. "I'm going to cook you breakfast and pretend that word doesn't exist, or you're never going to make it to the mountains."

Chapter Eighteen

ADDY SAT ON a stool at the counter watching Jake move around the kitchen like he belonged there, easily finding her pans and dishes and cutting up vegetables like a chef. "You didn't strike me as a guy who knew how to cook. It makes you even hotter. Not that you need an ego stroke."

"I told you my parents taught us to be prepared." Leaning over the counter, he gave her a chaste kiss. "And I need to hear that every single day if it's coming from you."

"Flirt." She sipped her coffee. "I thought you meant in the wilderness, and pushing you career-wise."

He waved the spatula in her direction. "Preparedness in all aspects of life. Cooking, cleaning, laundry. You name it, we did it. And it's probably a good thing, or we all would have starved after we left home. You can only put up with pizza for so long." He turned back to the stove and loaded up two plates with mounds of vegetable and cheese omelets and toast, then plunked one plate down in front of Addy.

"That's good parenting. My parents taught me how to speak to the chef." She stared down at the heap of omelets and toast. "This looks amazing, but I'm not really a breakfast person."

"Sexy girl, that is not a proper response to the chef. I might need to have a talk with your parents. You are about to go hiking for ten days. Ten. Days. You need all the nourishment you can get." He handed her a fork and took a bite from his own plate.

She gazed into Jake's warm hazel eyes, thrills chasing through her veins. She still couldn't believe he was there. "Thank you, but seriously, I never eat breakfast. I'm good with coffee."

He leaned his forearms on the counter, bringing his serious face within inches of hers. "You don't have enough meat on your bones to argue this point. You need to eat."

She crossed her arms, feeling bad for refusing him, but she really wasn't a breakfast person.

"You've never done this, Addy. Backpacking is hard work, probably the hardest thing you'll ever do. You'll burn through thousands of calories just making it up to Riser's Ridge."

"You have no idea what else I'll do in my lifetime. Maybe this won't be the hardest thing." She hated the automatic response, but she'd obviously spent too many years tying up the obedient girl and releasing her counterpart, Little Miss Independent.

He rose, his eyes boring into her. "Addy, this isn't a battle of wills. It's simple math. The average person needs a certain amount of calories every day. You add to that the three to five thousand calories they'll burn by carrying a pack and hiking for four or five hours a day, and you've got a bigger calorie requirement than you can imagine. If you don't replenish your calories, you'll waste away." His gaze softened, and he leaned in close again. "This isn't me trying to bully you, sweetheart. It's me trying to make sure you don't end up too sick to make it down the fucking mountain."

She clenched her teeth, wishing he didn't make sense.

"You're not giving in by taking care of yourself. Learning

from others doesn't make you weak, Addy. It makes you smart."

She stared at him for a long moment, battling herself more than him. "I'm not trying to be stubborn, and I appreciate your advice." She picked up the fork, and as she scooped eggs onto it, she smiled up at him. "I'll try, but don't let this be like opening a door to you bossing me around or picking apart my abilities. Just because you make sense once doesn't mean you're Superman. Despite that tattoo."

"Are you going to be this belligerent the whole time we're packing?"

She shrugged. "I would say no, but we both know it would be a lie." She ate the eggs, and the mix of spices and vegetables caused an explosion of flavor in her mouth. "Mm. Okay, this is seriously amazing."

He grinned.

She pointed her fork at him. "I deserved that one, but watch it, buster. Tell me about your Superman status." As she scooped up more eggs, she added, "But not if it has to do with a girl. No triggers today."

As he ate, his eyes drifted to her plate, nudging her along to put another mouthful down the hatch, which she did.

"'No triggers.' I think I'm going to have that tattooed on your wrist." He finished his plateful of eggs in a few fast bites and rubbed his hand over his tattoo.

She felt her cheeks heat up, thinking about her earlier mention of *toys*. Maybe she did need a little reminder to behave after all. "I think I like 'taken' better."

He climbed onto the stool beside her and kissed her. "I'm glad you can finally admit it." He lifted his shirtsleeve, his muscle flexing beneath the ink. "Do you really think I'd get a Superman tat because I think I deserve Superman status?"

Her eyes slid down his chest. "If I were you I might."

He leaned forward with a sexy smile and said, "I'm not quite that arrogant."

She arched a brow, and he laughed.

"Okay, maybe I am, but not in this case." He pulled his sleeve down over the tattoo, but his hand remained on the cotton as he spoke. "I told you about my college buddy Chris. Well, Superman—Samson—was his older brother."

Addy placed her hand on his leg, drawn by the emotion in his voice.

"Sammy was like a brother to me. He was funny as hell, and he gave me and Chris shit for being idiots, you know, like most college guys are. But he also took every chance he could to pound responsibility into our heads."

"What happened to him?"

"We used to take an annual fishing trip up the Aucilla River. We'd camp, go fishing, hiking, and talk about how we'd still be taking the same trip when we were seventy. Sammy was a big guy. He had two inches and a good twenty pounds on me. There was nothing he couldn't do. Sports, academics, you name it, he nailed it. The girls dug him. He had a clean-cut look. Dark eyes, pitch-black hair, muscles on top of muscles, but a warm, friendly demeanor despite his size. Clark Kent. *Superman.*" His voice got lower, and he looked away, blinking repeatedly, revealing the sensitive man behind the bravado.

She'd seen glimpses of that side of him, but witnessing him struggling tore at her heart.

Jake cleared his throat and placed his hand over hers. His thick fingers curled around her hand. "It was the summer before our senior year of college. We were fishing from the boat, having a good time, and Samson leaned over the boat to pull up a line of fish." He swallowed hard, his eyes downcast, and nodded to her food. "Please eat, baby."

She picked up her toast and absently took a bite, wondering how he could think of her when he was in the middle of talking about something that brought heaviness to the air around them. "Keep going."

"I can still see him laughing at something Chris said as he leaned over the boat to grab the line. He was smiling so *hard.* We knew the river. Knew the dangers. We were always careful. But he didn't look before he reached. A water moccasin got hold of his radial artery. What are the chances? Sammy's eyes opened so wide, and there were two, maybe three seconds when we didn't realize anything had happened, and then he let out a wail so loud it echoed against the trees. The goddamn snake had latched on and he was shaking it off."

His voice cracked, his eyes glazed over, and he shook his arm as if it were Sammy's, shaking off the snake. "He grabbed it by the back of the neck and tore it off. And we knew. We *knew*..." His voice trailed off, and he released her hand to rub the tattoo again. "We were too busy talking shit. We never saw it coming." Unabashedly turning damp eyes to Addy, he said, "It was over fast. When poisonous venom gets in a main blood vessel, there's no slowing it down. He knew. We knew. The two minutes that followed were the worst of my entire life."

Addy couldn't stop her tears from falling, even though she knew she should be strong for Jake. She climbed onto his lap, thinking of the look that had passed between him and his father at breakfast yesterday morning. Goose bumps rose on her arms. He held her in silence, the weight of his confession binding them together.

A minute, or maybe ten, later, he said, "Come on, baby.

You need to eat."

Addy finished most of her breakfast, even though she didn't have the stomach for it, while Jake busied himself cleaning up the kitchen.

"I'm sorry about your friend," she finally said, feeling like there were no words that could possibly convey how deeply sorry she truly was.

He nodded, forced a half smile. "Yeah, me too."

Jake was quiet as he dried the frying pan and put it back where he'd found it. Addy washed her dishes, and they went into the living room. As he looked through her supplies, showing her how to use the compass and leafing through her unread wilderness books, dog-earring pages he insisted she read, she realized everything had changed again. While she was busy demanding to keep her independence the last few days, he was reliving a nightmare in his head. How often did he think of Samson? *Superman.* Sinking down to the floor beside him, she looked at the pointy design of his tattoo peeking out from beneath his sleeve, and she knew he thought of his friend every single day, whether he wanted to or not.

THREE HOURS LATER Addy stood at the trailhead in her pink hiking boots and cutoff shorts, hands on hips, shaking her beautiful head at Jake and looking cuter than any woman should be allowed to.

"Jake…"

"Don't look at me like I'm ridiculous, Addy." After he told her about losing Samson, she'd eased up on her insistence about doing this whole camping thing on her own. She'd allowed him to teach her the basics about camping, hiking, and first aid, but she'd shut him down when he wanted to go over her meal plans and go through the food she'd packed. There was nowhere near enough time to cover everything he wanted to, and he'd given in, because fighting with Addy wouldn't make saying goodbye any easier. But on the drive to the mountains, with the loss of his friend fresh on his mind, the realization of what she was taking on hit him head-on. He hadn't expected to feel the need to *push* his way into her trip, but the idea of her walking up that trail without him went against everything he felt.

"Anything can happen to you out here," he insisted.

She stepped forward, her smile reaching her eyes as she took his hand. "I know you have all sorts of scary thoughts going through your head about what's going to happen to me. And after what you told me about Samson, I have to admit, I'm a little more nervous about doing this, too."

"Then let me go with you. At least for the first day."

She shook her head, and Jake's stomach plummeted.

"I don't blame you for being mad, especially since things have changed so much between us. I honestly have no idea how I'll make it through the next ten days without arguing with you." She smiled and touched his cheek. She was his kryptonite. "Or kissing you, or being in your arms. But even with all those wonderful new feelings, nothing has changed with regard to my trip. I'm sure it sounds selfish, and I don't mean to make you worry, but I *need* to do this alone. I have a plan. A goal. And I have been up front and honest about it the whole time. I need to follow through with my plans or I'll never forgive myself, and I'll probably blame you for it."

Clenching his jaw, he pulled her against him. "You are a roaring pain in the ass."

She laughed. "We've already established that. What else ya got? And don't even think about going all Neanderthal on my ass and traipsing after me, because that's one sure way to piss me off."

He glared at her.

She pressed her lips to the center of his chest, palms flat against his pecs. Those delicate hands *belonged* there. He was going to miss her touch, her voice, her sassy backtalk. When she lifted her eyes again they were suspiciously glassy, and hell if his gut didn't wrench again.

"I'll tell you what," she said. "I'll text you tonight and let you know I found a safe spot to camp."

He nodded, knowing he had to take whatever she'd give, even if it was nowhere near enough.

"Every night," he said more sternly than he meant to. She went silent, and he knew he'd pushed her too far. "Fine. Jesus, Addy. Do you even realize what you're going to put me through?"

"Yes, because I'm going through it, too."

"Are you?" His voice rose despite his trying to remain calm. Fisting his hands to channel his frustration elsewhere, he paced.

"That's a jerky thing to say." She turned away, looking impossibly small and delicate against the backdrop of towering trees and mountainous terrain.

All he wanted to do was keep her safe, but he heard in her voice the hurt he'd caused. She reached for her pack, which they'd also argued about because it was too heavy for her. He grabbed it before she could. The damn thing weighed nearly a third of what she did, but true to her stubborn nature, she insisted she was *fine*.

He held it up for her to slip her arms through. "I'm sorry

for being a prick, but I care about you, Addy."

Instead of putting her arms through the straps, she wound them around his waist and hugged him so tight he could feel her body trembling, and he choked up.

"I'm sorry, sexy girl." This was hard for her, too. He'd been so frustrated he'd missed that she was also scared. As hard as it was not to use that to his advantage, he knew he had to build her up, because if she worried, she'd be less ready if she ran into trouble. "I know you're capable of anything you set your beautiful mind to."

She nodded and held him tighter, chipping away at his frustration and redirecting it at himself. He framed her face in his hands and gazed into her eyes. "You can do this. Just promise me you'll be extra careful. Think, plan ahead, and you know"—he knew better than to say he'd come running if she had any trouble—"there's no shame in cutting the trip short if you get bored."

She wound her arms around his neck. "Kiss me, Jake. Please just kiss me, toss that pack on my back, and drive away. Meet me back here in ten days with a smile on your face, a steel rod in your pants, and a foot rub at the ready."

How could he argue with that? He kissed her deeply, and then he kissed her again and again, until they were both so stirred up she pushed him away. He helped her with the mammoth-sized pack, and he hoped to hell she'd brought the right foods to eat, enough to drink, and the good sense to come down the fucking mountain early and back into his arms where she belonged.

Chapter Nineteen

ADDY FELT LIKE she had a five-hundred-pound gorilla on her back as she trudged up the mountain. The pack was digging into the back of her hips, and the shoulder straps made her shirt grind like sandpaper against her skin. Jake had warned her that the pack was too heavy, but what was she supposed to do? Jake had said she didn't need the small hand shovel she'd packed. *You're in the woods. You can use a rock.* But she'd scoured a girls' camping forum and she'd learned all about water-purifying tablets, biodegradable toilet paper, and burying her poop, which she wasn't looking forward to. But hey, if she was going to rough it, she was going to do it all the way. *Almost.* She needed the damn shovel.

The first leg of her adventure was a straight eight-mile shot up the mountain to Riser's Ridge. There was a stream nearby for water, and it was off the trails, so she shouldn't be bothered by other hikers. It looked like such a short distance on the map, and nowhere near as steep of a climb as it actually was. She grabbed hold of a tree, using it for leverage to propel her up the mountain. The rough bark scratched her hand, but she'd get used to that, too. She stopped, huffing for air, and slid the pack from her shoulders, rolling them back to ease the pain. She'd envisioned being embraced by a euphoric feeling as she hiked up the mountain taking in the beauty around her. But all she could think about was the ache inside her chest that had nothing to do with the grueling climb.

She dragged the pack along the ground and continued climbing. She had to be nearly there. She'd been walking forever. As she reached for another tree, snagging her finger on a sharp piece of bark, she wondered what the hell she was doing climbing this big-ass mountain when she could be sprawled across Jake's naked body.

She couldn't allow herself to go down that path. Not on day one of the hike she'd been looking forward to for months. Her pack got caught on a rock, and she heaved it back onto her shoulders, pushing thoughts of Jake aside. *Again.* When they lingered like sunburn, she buried them deeper and pushed on.

After several hours her legs felt like rubber, her feet were sore, and her heart hammered out its complaints. She was tempted to stop and rest, but she wasn't sure she'd have the energy to get back up once she sat down. Maybe she should have started an exercise program before setting out for this trip, as Gabriella had suggested a number of times over the preceding months. But Addy hadn't expected it to be *this* hard. Just as the grayish hue of evening began to close in on her, she saw a break in the trees and her pulse sped up. Clinging to the shoulder straps of her pack, she upped her pace, forcing her noodle legs to carry her up the last fifty feet to the clearing. She stepped through the line of trees and into a rocky area. Exhaling loudly, she was struck by the magnificent view of rolling hills in every direction.

She peeled her pack from her shoulders, dropping it to the dirt with a *thud.* A cloud of dust billowed up at her feet as she gazed out at the sweeping views of trees and mountains. Inhaling a lungful of crisp air, she laughed, unable to believe she'd done it. Just over twenty-four hours ago she thought the view of the ocean was one of the most spectacular she'd ever seen. But this was even more incredible. Glorious mountains kissed the sky as far as she could see, fading to blue in the distance, then to a ghostly shade of gray. She'd been all over the world with her parents, and she'd never seen anything so amazing in all her life. *And I got here all by myself.* She felt silly taking pride in having hiked for only a day. But she *was* proud. She didn't quit when it got hard. She didn't give in to the ache of missing Jake and head back to his open arms. No, the girl who was born into a world of celebrity, diamonds, furs, mansions, and private jets had put on her fifty-dollar hiking boots and trekked up a mountain all by herself, hauling a boatload of supplies.

She'd done it.

And this was just the beginning. Ten days of exploring lay ahead of her.

She crouched to dig her phone from her pack, feeling the strain on every muscle as she waited for it to power on and guzzled some water. She'd been so determined to prove she could spend ten days in the mountains, with a secondary goal of getting Jake out of her head. Now the time alone was within her reach, and *forgetting* the man who made her feel more than she ever imagined was no longer even on her radar. Her phone vibrated with incoming texts she'd missed when it was off. Two from Jake and one from Gabriella, which was surprising since she was on her honeymoon. She read Gabriella's first, wanting to savor Jake's.

"Whoa," she whispered to herself, wondering when she had turned into one of *those* girls.

Shaking off that thought, she read Gabriella's text. *Did you go? Are you okay? Is Jake with you?*

Addy stood with her back to the gorgeous view and held up her phone, smiling as she took a selfie. Then she took another, blowing a kiss to the camera.

She sent a quick text to Gabriella with the first picture. *I'm here! Riser's Ridge is beautiful and Jake isn't here. But…are you ready? I miss him like crazy! Who would've thought?? Enjoy your honeymoon, MRS. RYDER! Love and hugs, your mountaineering assistant (Can you believe it!?!?!?).*

Addy opened Jake's text and was surprised to find a selfie. He was sitting in the driver's seat of his SUV beside a piece of cardboard, on which he'd written *You should be here.* He was holding the phone out with one hand and pointing to the seat beside him, his expression dead serious. She read the text bubble. *I'm saving a seat for my sweet pain-in-the-ass girlfriend. I'm proud of you. Be safe, sexy girl. I miss you already. Yeah, I admitted it. What have you done to me?*

Emotions bloomed in her chest again. She read it three times before responding, imagining his tight jaw after he typed that he missed her, and the struggle he must have felt when he'd written the last line. She had no idea how it happened, but all those months of wanting coalesced, and she felt herself tumbling down a slippery slope with three terrifying words at the bottom.

She scrolled to the picture of her blowing a kiss. Her hair was tousled, a few strands blowing against her cheek. She had a streak of dirt on her chin, and her shirt had fingerprints at her waist. She glanced at her hand, finding the source, and wiped the dirt on her pants before typing a response to send with the picture.

Look at your kick-ass girlfriend. No major catastrophes yet! I'm at Riser's Ridge, and I'm going to set up camp and write in my beautiful new journal. I miss you, too, so whatever I've done to you you've done right back. Wish I could kiss you right now.

Adding a few heart emoticons to the text, she sent it off and clutched the phone to her chest. She'd known this trip would be one of the most difficult things she'd ever set out to accomplish, but that was before she'd begun falling for Jake. Getting out from under her parents' thumbs had been stressful, mostly because she knew she was hurting them by doing so, but even at eighteen she'd known she wasn't made to live a life where someone else handled her affairs, or where she was expected to fit into a mold of any type. College and her professional life had taken hard work and the drive to succeed, both of which she controlled. But ten days without Jake would tax parts of her she had no control over. She barely knew what her heart needed, much less how to handle it when it longed to be with him. This would be *the* most difficult thing she'd ever set out to do. And if today's aches were any indication, she was in for a painful few weeks.

But she *would* get through this, and she knew she'd be stronger for it.

Her phone vibrated and her pulse kicked up again. *Gabriella.* She opened the text, fighting a wave of disappointment, and couldn't help but smile at the picture of her bestie and her new husband, their cheeks pressed together with wide smiles that reached all the way up to their eyes. She couldn't even be envious, because she could have had that with Jake. He could be with her right now, getting ready to share another hot and sexy night under the stars.

Oh shit. The sun was setting and she still had to set up camp.

She typed another quick text to Jake. *Shutting off my phone to conserve the battery.* She held her breath as she added what had seemed impossible two days ago but now was inescapable. *You were right. There's no shutting off thoughts of you.*

As she sent the text and powered off her phone, she wondered if she was in over her head—on the trip or with Jake.

One day at a time, she reminded herself, and set to work putting up her tent.

After unrolling the nylon protective sheathing that was supposed to protect the floor of the tent, she slid a thin metal spike through the nylon rings at each corner and used a rock to hammer them in. *Easy-peasy.* Soon she'd have a place to call home for the duration of her trip. Against the advice of the salesman, she'd splurged on a four-person tent so she'd have plenty of room to unpack her things and move around.

True to the salesman's promise, the pop-up tent was easy to erect, and within half an hour she had it secured over the protective flooring. She tugged her backpack to the edge of the nylon sheathing, which extended beyond the frame of the tent, creating a small, clean place for her to sit, and began unpacking. She unrolled her sleeping bag and set it up inside the tent, set her clothes out in neat piles, blew up the inflatable pillow, and having forgotten a pillowcase, wrapped it in one of her T-shirts. She didn't know what everyone had been so worried about. Besides the hike up the mountain, this camping stuff was a breeze. It wasn't the Hilton, but the tent was spacious enough for her to keep her cooking supplies and food in one corner and still have room to move around.

After Jake had insisted she eat that enormous breakfast, she hadn't wanted to discuss her meal plans with him. She was pretty sure he'd balk at her choices. Energy bars, soups, and prepackaged camping meals she'd found online were light and easy to prepare. She opened one of the collapsible bowls she'd bought and tossed in the energy bars. She lined up the prepackaged meals and cans of soup, bottles of water, and water-purification tablets and sat back to take it all in. She was *really* doing this. Ten days in the wilderness. Alone. So far so good, except for the dull ache of missing her boyfriend.

Boyfriend.

Even with how happy she'd been for Gabriella when she'd met Duke, she'd been a little envious, too. She never thought she'd find a man who could make her feel all swoony like Duke made Gabriella feel. She was so very wrong.

Her stomach growled, and she looked at her food. It seemed silly to start a fire when it was almost dark, and she was too exhausted to go in search of the stream to clean dishes. She grabbed an energy bar and went back outside to finish setting up her campsite.

She hung her lantern on the limb of a tree and used her hand shovel to dig a small fire pit. By the time she was done collecting rocks and lining the pit, she was so tired it was all she could do to lower herself to the little vinyl front porch. She grabbed the leather journal Jake had given her, wishing she could crawl into his lap and let his big, strong hands ease all her aches. She smiled as she ran her hand over the distressed leather. When he'd given her the gift, she hadn't taken the time to appreciate just how thoughtful it was. She gazed out at the inky sky, wondering what he was doing. Was he at his place? Out with friends? Was he thinking of her? She could call him, but that would make her seem needy.

She flipped open the journal and lifted it from her lap to read Jake's handwritten note. *Sexy girl, you can hike for miles, but everything you're looking for is waiting for you right back here. Your Neanderthal, J.R.*

Butterflies took flight in her stomach, and she reached for her phone.

Maybe I am a little needy after all.

AFTER HAVING DINNER with his parents and picking up his luggage they'd brought home from the island, he hugged them goodbye, tossed his suitcase into the back of his SUV, and headed home. His parents still lived in his childhood home, just outside of New York City. He debated staying at his cabin, which was only twenty minutes farther out than his parents' house, but his place in the city put him that much closer to Addy. He wanted to be as close as possible in case she ran into trouble. He never minded the drive, but tonight, as the lights of the city came into focus, it took all of his resolve not to hit the highway and head for the mountains. When he'd received Addy's text earlier in the evening he and his parents had been eating dinner out on their deck, and it had sparked a lengthy conversation about how he was doing the right thing by giving her the space she'd asked for. But that didn't mean it didn't suck.

He navigated through the busy city streets, trying to distract himself. He'd been doing that a lot lately. Trying to distract himself from the woman who was staking claim to such a large piece of him he didn't think he'd ever recover if she walked away.

As he pulled into the parking garage his phone vibrated, and Addy's picture filled the screen. He snatched it from the console, swiping the screen as he parked between two cars.

"Hey, baby. You okay?" Static filled the line. He jumped from the truck and sprinted out of the parking garage. *God-damn concrete jungle.* "Addy? Are you there? Are you okay?"

"Yeah, that's better."

Her sweet, calm voice brought a smile to his face. "You're okay?"

"Of course. But you sound stressed. You okay?"

He paced the sidewalk. "I didn't expect you to call. I was worried something happened."

"Aw, you were worried about me."

"Of course I'm worried about you." *Jesus, woman.* "How are you? Are you staying hydrated? Did you get the tent set up okay?"

"I'm...pretty great, actually. Yes, I'm staying hydrated, and I got the tent up. I told you I could do it."

"I knew you could do it, but that doesn't mean I don't wish I was there with you. You sure you're okay?"

"Mm-hm."

The stretch of silence that followed made his stomach knot up. "Addy, what's wrong?" She sighed, cinching the knot even tighter. "Baby, what is it? Are you scared?"

"No," she snapped. "Why do you jump directly to that? I told you I could handle this."

He rubbed the back of his neck. "You were so adamant about not calling me, and then you did, and I'm glad you did, but you sound like something is wrong."

"Maybe it is," she said softer. "But not because I'm scared of the dark."

Could she be more frustrating? "Addy, you're freaking me out here. Please tell me what's wrong, or I swear I'll be up that mountain faster than you can get pissed off at me for doing it."

She laughed. "Right now that's not exactly a threat, because I miss you a lot. More than I probably should."

He breathed a sigh of relief and leaned against his building. "I miss you, too, baby, but you *should* miss me. That's what girlfriends do."

"Yeah, I'm getting a real good dose of the whole girlfriend thing right now. I just opened the journal."

He was wondering when she'd open it up, and he wasn't sure how she'd react to his note. "And?"

"And…it's a good thing you're there, because I kind of want to throw myself at you right now."

"That is *not* a good thing. Want me to come up?"

"That's a loaded question."

Hope sparked inside him.

"But I need to do this alone, Jake."

He bit back the terse response vying for release. "Right. Listen, I'm out on the sidewalk. Let me get up to my place and call you right back."

"You don't have to—"

"Addy, I *want* to. You've been on my mind all day. I just don't want to stand on the sidewalk while we talk." After they ended the call, he took the elevator up to his apartment, grabbed a beer from the fridge, and headed out to the terrace as he called her back.

"So this is what it feels like to miss a boyfriend?" she said without saying hello.

"It's pretty new for me, too, this whole missing you thing."

"I don't hate it, but it's hard on the heart. So tell me, *boyfriend*, where do you live, anyway?"

Jake stretched out on the lounge chair of his penthouse

terrace. "I've got a little place not far from yours."

"I'm trying to picture what your place might look like, but all that comes to mind is us lying on a blanket on the bluff. What's your place like?"

He smiled with the memory of her freaking out when Gabriella's relatives showed up at the villa the morning after the wedding. "I'll show it to you when you get back from your trip. What are you doing right now?"

"Lying down outside my tent, looking up at the stars. *Please* tell me about your place. I want to picture you there."

"Why is it impossible for me to deny you a damn thing?"

She laughed. "I don't know, but I'll use that to my advantage someday."

He missed her so much, he ached with it. "I hope you do," he said honestly. "I bought this place from my college buddy Jett Masters. He's a real estate investor, and when I told him I needed a place in the city where I could live outdoors, he hooked me up."

"Live outdoors? What did he do, walk you down to a bridge and point to the space under it?"

"No. He showed me to a rooftop apartment. His brother Dean owns a landscape design business, and he created an outdoor living space complete with a lawn, plants, rock gardens, and a covered sleeping deck, which is where I am now."

"So, you have a *penthouse*? I can't even picture you in a penthouse."

He took a swig of his beer. "Neither can I, which is why I also have a cabin out by my parents, but I can't exactly hang out with my brothers at a bar and then drive, now, can I? Besides, this isn't a penthouse. It's a *rooftop apartment*, and it was the only way to get this outdoor space. I wish you were here right now, lying next to me."

"Yeah," she whispered. "Me too."

He listened to her breathing in comfortable silence, maybe even necessary silence, while they each dealt with the strength of their connection.

"Tell me a secret," she said. "Something no one else knows."

The answer came without thought. "I can't stand being away from you."

"Jake." His name came out breathy.

"I'm serious, Addy. For months I tried not to think about what it would be like if you were mine, and now that we're together it's like everything I tried not to think about exploded into epic proportions."

She went silent again.

"Too much honesty?" he asked, taking another drink of his beer to settle his nerves.

"No. Maybe. I don't know."

He heard her smile again and pictured that sweet vulnerability in her eyes, wishing he was there to see it firsthand.

"Don't you think it's weird that a girl who doesn't want to be told what to do is with a guy who uses terms like 'mine'?"

"No." He finished his beer and set the empty bottle on the deck. "You want your independence, but you need someone strong enough to know you really want more."

"You think you have me all figured out."

"Hardly. We click, Addy. We feed off each other in a way I never knew was possible, and you feel it. I know you do. Otherwise you wouldn't be on the phone with me right now."

She was quiet again, and he waited her out. When the silence stretched too long, he worried he'd pushed her too far. "Tell me I'm wrong, and I'll back off."

"No, you won't," she said just above a whisper. "Because you can't. The same way I can't."

He closed his eyes, reveling in her confession. "Let me come to you, Addy. Let me spend the next ten days experiencing your first hiking trip *with* you."

He was answered in silence again.

"Addy, don't get scared off." Damn it. He shouldn't have pushed.

"It'll take more than that to scare me off," she said softly. "But I should go. I need to conserve my phone battery or my boyfriend will worry. I'll text you tomorrow night."

He sat upright, his emotions lodged in his throat. "Wait, Addy. Don't go—"

She'd already gone.

Chapter Twenty

GOD DID NOT make muscles for climbing mountains. That much was obvious. Addy rolled onto her side early Tuesday morning, wincing in pain. Her shoulders ached, her legs were on fire, and her stomach felt like small children had been using it as a trampoline. She inhaled the crisp mountain air and pulled her sleeping bag around her shoulders. Big mistake. She sucked in a sharp breath at the ache in her upper arm. She wasn't used to hiking, digging, or carrying the equivalent of a large man on her shoulders.

She rolled onto her back, blinking up at the ceiling of her tent and thinking about how cowardly she'd been to end the call with Jake so suddenly. She hated that her need for independence was so deeply rooted her first reaction to his thoughtful suggestion was to clam up. But what had scared her even more was her second reaction, the one that had made her end the call. She'd wanted to agree to having him join her so badly, she knew if she didn't hang up it might slip out.

Pushing up to a sitting position, and groaning in pain, she refused to allow herself to pick up the phone and call Jake. It wasn't fair for him to have to deal with her mixed-up emotions. She needed to get her butt out of that sleeping bag, find the stream, stop wallowing in that crazy middle ground, and clear her head. *I've got miles to cover, wilderness to conquer!*

And a man to miss! He was definitely right. Every single thought led right back to him.

And…she had to pee.

Badly.

As she rose to her feet, her muscles retaliated, making her walk like Frankenstein, and she emitted pathetic whimpering noises with every step. She dug the Motrin from her first-aid kit, downed it, and unzipped her tent, bristling against the morning chill. Her bladder hurt she needed to pee so badly. She could brave a little chilly weather. After talking to Jake last night and then writing in her journal, she'd had just enough energy to strip off her shorts and pass out. She slipped her feet into her boots, which she'd left just outside the tent, and headed into the woods. Something wiggled beneath the sole of her foot and she screamed, kicking and shrieking as she hopped on one foot, sending her boot flying across the campsite. She grabbed hold of a tree to steady herself and lifted her foot to inspect the bottom. No bites or evidence of whatever evil creature had stowed away in her boot for the night. But now she had to pee even worse. Half tiptoeing, half hopping, she went deeper into the woods, paranoid about something—*anything*—crawling on her, but there was no way she'd go in search of her boot until she peed. She found a spot behind a group of bushes, dropped her panties, and crouched. As sweet relief took hold, she realized she'd forgotten toilet paper.

Great.

Nothing like a drip-dry morning.

She slipped off her skivvies and peered around the bushes. *What the hell am I looking for?* Visions of animated deer popped into her mind. Laughing at herself, she half tiptoed her way back to the tent and cleaned up *down there*, put on clean underwear and shorts, grabbed a hoodie and slipped it over her head. She tugged on thick socks, and wearing only one boot, she tiptoed and hopped in the direction of the boot she'd flung.

At least she'd forgotten about the pain in her muscles.

Her pink boot lay on the ground looking eerily out of place among the dark leaves and twigs. Her mind spiraled back to Jake. Was this the type of scene Jake came across when he was searching for a missing person? A single piece of footwear lying in the forest? The desperation of such a sight caught hold, and pieces of Jake continued falling into place. He wasn't just being overprotective. He lived out his worst fears every time he went searching for a missing person. *Only now it's me he's worried about.* Guilt settled into her achy muscles.

She retrieved her boot and shook it out. Nothing but a few pieces of a twig fell out. She bent back the tongue and peered into it, fishing around inside for any lingering stowaways of the four-or-more-footed variety. Thankfully, whatever was in there had vacated. She wiped off her sock and shoved her foot in the boot, making a mental note to keep her boots *inside* the tent from now on.

Back at the tent, she brushed her teeth using bottled water, gathered her toiletries and soap in a backpack, tossed in a water bottle and a hand towel, and headed in search of the stream. Addy wasn't big on north, south, east, west, but she knew she'd walked straight up the mountain and the stream should be off to her right.

Birds took flight overhead, their noises amplified in the peaceful forest. Shielding her eyes from the morning sun, she watched them fly away. She couldn't remember the last time she'd taken the time to watch birds do anything, and took a moment to enjoy her surroundings. The scent of pine and damp earth hung in the air, so different from the smells of the city. She inhaled deeply, closing her eyes and focusing on the serenity around her, and the ache in her lower back and legs. It was good pain. It meant she was pushing herself outside her comfort zone. The sounds of the stream trickled in and she opened her eyes. How had she missed that sound before? She followed the tranquil sounds to the wide, rolling stream and set her supplies at the edge of the water. As her mind revisited Jake, she told herself this was just what she needed, a few days of pushing herself out of her comfort zone without the constant barrage and hustle and bustle of the city.

But she wasn't buying it as earnestly as she had a few days ago.

With a quick scan of the area to make sure there were no animated deer watching, she stripped off her clothes, grabbed her soap, and stepped into the stream.

"Holy cow!" Lifting her feet in quick succession, as goose bumps raced up her body like scales, she hurried into the middle of the frigid stream and washed up in the icy water. She crouched, hoping no fish decided to explore her private cavern, and rinsed the soap off as fast as she could. Her teeth chattered, but this was good, too. She was roughing it. Now she could say she'd done it.

Running out of the water was worse than being in it. Shivering, she dried off with the washcloth, wishing she'd packed a bigger towel, and tugged on her shirt and sweatshirt. She realized she'd forgotten her bra and made a command decision to forgo bras for the rest of the trip. That seemed like prize enough for making it through an achy body and frigid bath. Her feet were muddy, which presented another problem. She couldn't put on her underwear without getting it muddy. Bare-assed, she carried her boots and towel to the water's edge. She spied a log and headed for it, telling herself she could figure this out like she did everything else.

She set the towel and her boots on the log, which was only about six inches from the water's edge, and stepped into the water to wash off her feet. See? Easy. After rinsing them off she stepped over the muddy shore and onto the log. She wobbled, but managed to sit on it while she wiped off her feet. She swatted at something crawling up her leg, then her hip, then—*holy shit*—there were ants *everywhere*—crawling along her butt, her thighs, her lower back. She ran into the water, holding her shirt up to her neck and swatting at the offending bugs, shrieking at the top of her lungs as she tried to scrub them off.

By the time she got back to her campsite, hair drenched, sweatshirt not much drier, she was frustrated and achy and angry at herself for not thinking ahead enough to have her morning routine figured out before plunging into it. *That* would never happen again.

She changed into dry clothes, brushed her hair and tied it back in a ponytail to avoid any other creatures latching on to her, tied a rope from one tree to another and hung her wet clothes on it, and started a small fire to boil water for coffee.

Lots of coffee.

She nibbled on an energy bar and skimmed through the journal pages she'd written in last night. Though she'd started out writing about her hike up the mountain, she'd ended up writing pages and pages about her feelings for Jake. Once she began, her emotions had flowed like a river. Her feelings were *real* and frightening. *And unfair to Jake.* She had to learn to handle them like she handled everything else in her life. Head-on.

Setting the journal aside, she took a selfie for Jake, adding the caption *Wilderness beauty at its best. Day two has arrived, and I'm ready!*

She stared at the words she'd typed. They were not at all what she felt. It took all of her courage to delete what she'd written and give voice to the truth, but once she started, it got easier with each word. *I'm sorry I chickened out of our conversation and hung up. I'm sure you want to come up here and drag me by my hair into a cave and make me listen, but I have to learn to listen to myself before I can listen to anyone else. I miss you. Truly I do. Thanks for being patient with me.* She sent it off and opened the journal again. Her phone vibrated seconds later with a text from Jake, and she couldn't open it fast enough.

If you find the secret to making my sexy girl listen, please share it with me.

She smiled, relief consuming her. Feeling luckier than she ever had, she typed a response that she knew would make him smile, too. *Where's the fun in that?* She added hearts and a smiley emoticon, and then typed, *Turning phone off again to conserve battery. NOT hanging up on you. xox.*

Feeling more at ease, despite her rough start to the morning, she made coffee, reveling in the way Jake seemed to understand her. As the hot liquid warmed her from the inside out, she realized he sounded as though he knew her better than she knew herself. It was time for her to get to know Addison Dahl.

She pressed pen to paper, more of her heart pouring out.

I never imagined that wanting my independence so badly would make me afraid to let any piece of it go. Thinking of her grandmother, she wrote, *You taught me to own my pride, my lust, my anger, and I wear those things like badges of honor. And now I'm here alone, and I can't stop wishing Jake was here with me. I'm greedy for him. For his time, the sound of his voice, the feel of his hands on my skin. Even for our banter, because that's what makes us who we are. I can't pretend those feelings that I've never had before haven't consumed me since our very first kiss. But giving in terrifies me, because I look back at you and Mom and I know I can't survive the kind of relationships you had, and I'm afraid of backsliding. Of letting him in and then becoming the very person I fear.*

She closed the journal and drew in a deep breath, wondering if she was destined to spend her life fighting to retain the independence she'd worked so hard to claim—or fighting against it.

JAKE STEPPED FROM the shower to answer his vibrating phone after a late run Tuesday evening. He wrapped a towel around his hips as he read Addy's text, and headed in to the bedroom. *How's my Neanderthal?*

He stood at the end of his bed and texted, *Just got out of the shower after a long run. Miss you. You okay?*

She responded immediately. *I was until you put THAT image into my head.*

Wish you'd been in it with me. He ran a hand through his hair and took a selfie, capturing the cocky grin she teased him about straight down to the towel around his hips and sent it off with the text *Does my girl want to play?*

He sank down to the bed and her answer arrived the second he hit the mattress. He drank in the selfie she'd sent, of her body from the neck down. She was lying on a blanket wearing a blue sweatshirt, unzipped to expose the smooth skin between her breasts. *No bra. Nice.* Her hand rested on her thigh, her finger tucked just beneath the fringe of her cutoffs.

"Oh yeah, baby, you want to play." He leaned back against the pillow, relieved that she was safe, and typed another text. *Slide those fingers into your panties and send me another pic.*

He was hard just thinking about her touching herself. He took off his tented towel and fisted his shaft, giving it a long, tight stroke. His phone vibrated and he opened the text one-handed, admiring the image of her, shorts unzipped, her hand pushed down between her legs. His pulse spiked, and he stroked himself again as the next image rolled in of Addy with her shorts off and her fingers resting on her sex.

"Fuck, sexy girl. You're killing me," he said as he texted the same words. Then he took a picture of his hand wrapped around his cock and sent it. *You wanna play? I'm all in, baby.* He grabbed a bottle of lotion from the bedside table, poured some in his left hand, needing his right to text, set the phone on his abs where he could see the picture of his dirty girl, and wrapped his hand around his shaft again. His phone vibrated with a picture of Addy's sweatshirt unzipped, her beautiful breasts on display and one nipple between her finger and thumb.

"Fuck," he ground out, stroking himself harder. He put his phone on speech-to-text and said, "Fuck, Addy. Call me." He took another picture of his slick, swollen cock, with a glistening bead at the tip, and sent it off.

His phone vibrated with another picture of Addy's naked body from neck to knees, her back arched, knees bent, one hand flat above her mound, her slick fingers on her clit. Another picture popped up of her from the waist down, two fingers buried inside her. He imagined his hand as hers as he stroked himself to the image of her getting off to thoughts of him. It'd been too many days since he'd kissed her, touched her—made love to her. Another picture of her popped up, the same as before, from the waist down, but her back was bowed off the blanket, all her muscles straining. Fuck, he could taste her come on his tongue, feel her body quivering against him. One more look was all it took. Warm, white jets streaked over his stomach as he grunted out her name, images of her flying through his mind—her smile, her hips, those glorious breasts. Squeezing out the last of his release, he collapsed, breathless, against the pillow.

He wiped his hand on the towel, took a picture of the evidence of the power she held over him, and texted, *This better not end up on your fucking Tumblr page.*

Damn it. She'd just blown his mind, and now he was thinking about that damn Tumblr page. She always blew his freaking mind, regardless of whether she was running scared or playing sexy, naughty games. He'd already spent too many days without her. How would he last for the remainder of her trip?

His phone vibrated again with a picture of Addy's sweet face. The moonlight glowed behind her, giving her an angelic appearance. Her eyelids were at half-mast, and the rosy flush burning her cheeks took his breath away. The unmistakable look of a girl falling hard for a guy glimmered in her eyes. A text bubble appeared below her image. *Another first with my boyfriend. Who needs Tumblr when I have the perfect cock to rock?*

Could she have said anything more satisfying? He needed her in his arms like a fish needed water. He walked into the bathroom to wash up, then put on a pair of briefs and called her. She answered on the first ring. "Hey, baby."

"Hi," she said in a sleepy, seductive voice that made him want to climb through the phone and hold her.

"That was only the hottest surprise ever." He tugged on a T-shirt and went out to the terrace. "How's my girl?"

"Better now," she said breathily.

Stretching out on the outdoor bed and wishing she was snuggled up against him, he said, "Yeah, me too, but I miss you even more now. What'd you do today?"

"Wished I had a hot tub to soak in."

"Sore? I could come up there and give you a good rub-down."

"I'm much more relaxed now," she teased. "But when I get back, I'll take you up on that."

"When you get back, I'll make you feel so good, you'll never want to leave again."

Silence filled the airwaves, and he uttered a curse.

"Addy, don't freak out on me. I'm not trying to tell you what to do. I'm just telling you how much I miss you."

"I don't freak out. I..."

He heard her moving around and feared she'd end the call. "You hide, Addy. Don't hide from us."

"I'm not," she said too strongly. He envisioned her beautiful eyes narrowed and wary. "It's freezing out here. Let me get in my tent. Hold on." A minute later she said, "That's better. I had to pull on some sweatpants. Sorry."

"No worries," he answered, even though he was worried. She'd gone from sex kitten to sweet girlfriend to clamming up in the blink of an eye. He needed to figure out how to bridge the gap between her need to be independent and his need for more. He'd give anything to be on that frigging mountain so he could look her in the eye and talk this shit out.

Pushing to his feet, he paced the terrace, the silence stretching between them once again. He stared out at the city lights, telling himself to back the fuck off and give her space. He'd waited months to get this far. What was a few more days?

"What are you doing right now?" she asked.

"Thinking about how much you've changed my life."

"I did not. How could I? We've only been together a few days."

Physically yes, but she'd been with him much longer than that. He'd learned a lot about Addy these last few days, most importantly, that when things got serious, she froze like a deer in headlights. He needed her to know how deeply she affected him, but he also knew better than to make her feel trapped.

"Seems like a lot longer. I was just thinking about how I used to hate coming back to the city after being away, and facing the incessant traffic noises and the stench of exhaust and crowds."

"Then why not stay at your cabin?"

"I stayed at my cabin almost exclusively until the night I met you." He let that sink in, expecting her to make a sassy remark, and when she didn't, he said, "I tried to write off my instant attraction—or maybe 'obsession' is a better word—as nothing more than you being a hot chick, but once you opened that smart mouth of yours, I was hooked." He paused again, counting down the seconds before the phone went dead.

"I think I was, too," she said softly, blowing him away yet again.

A guy could get whiplash trying to keep up with her emotions. "That's why I stopped staying at my cabin when I was in town. I wanted to be nearby so I didn't miss out on a chance to see you for drinks or dinner with the hopes of you coming to your senses and accepting one of my propositions."

"So you stayed in the city just so you wouldn't miss a

chance at having dinner or drinks with me? Why didn't you ask me out?" she challenged.

"Why didn't I…?" He laughed. "Are you serious? I offered myself up to you on a silver platter every damn time I saw you. The only way to get you in the same room with me was to ask Duke and Gabriella to meet me somewhere."

"You set up those get-togethers? I thought that was Duke, and Cash."

"*Hell* no. They never know when I'm coming into town. After that first night, which I didn't set up, I wasn't about to leave seeing you up to chance. You looked at me like a hungry wolf, but you blew me off at every turn."

She laughed. "Well, now I only blow you off when we're naked, so I guess it worked out for the best."

"Girl, you kill me."

"Nah. I make you happy and you know it. Speaking of hungry wolves, have you seen pics of Gab and Duke's honeymoon? She's been texting me, and the way Duke looks at her…"

"Is not hotter than the way I look at you."

She was quiet for a moment, and when she spoke, her voice was quiet but confident. "Nothing is hotter than the way you look at me."

He felt like he'd been given a gift. She was beginning to accept the way he felt about her instead of fighting it. "How are you really holding up, baby? Have you run into any trouble?"

"I'm okay. It's gorgeous up here, but admittedly a little rougher than I expected. The stream was numbingly cold this morning, so I doubt I'll be washing my hair much, and I had trouble navigating a few things on my hike this afternoon, but I'm doing fine."

He began pacing again, homing in on the part of her answer she probably hoped he would ignore. "What kind of trouble?"

"Nothing really. I just got a little turned around and had trouble finding my way back. But I did, and I'm fine, and you don't have to get all worked up over it."

Says the woman who gets worked up over words. "Did you use your compass?"

She went silent again.

"Addy, I showed you how to use it for a reason." There was no hiding the frustration in his voice.

"I'm fine, okay? I'll take it with me tomorrow. But I found my way back, and that's what's important."

"Yeah, except if you hadn't made it back I'd never know. No one would, until you'd been out there for days." He listened to her breathing and knew he was pushing all the wrong buttons again. "How much battery is left on your phone?"

"Forty percent. I meant to pack extra batteries, but I think I left them in the bag beside my couch."

"Keep it off but with you. If you get lost again, use the Find Me app I put on it. I programmed in Riser's Ridge. It'll give you directions back. Okay?"

"You did that?"

Her voice was full of wonder, and he was floored that she wasn't yelling at him for not trusting her hiking skills or some other bullshit. "Yeah, of course."

"You didn't think I could do this, did you?"

Here it comes… "Of course I did, but you can never be too prepared. It's easy to get lost up there."

"I'm not sure if I should thank you or be annoyed that you put a safety net around me when I wanted to do this by myself."

He pinched the bridge of his nose, smiling despite himself.

"Do you try to piss me off, or is that a bonus?"

"Piss *you* off? I'm the one being taken care of."

"You say that like it's a bad thing. It's a good thing, Addy. It means I care, so let's go with *thanking* me. Jesus, I'm going to start calling you 'stubborn girl' instead of 'sexy girl.' And make no mistake, you *are* doing this by yourself. You're the one on the mountain. When will you learn that accepting help from others doesn't make you weak? It makes you smart, and since you're already brilliant, you should be able to understand and deal with it."

"Fine!" she snapped. "I told you about my father, so cut me some slack."

He sank down to the grass as clarity dawned on him. "I'm sorry, Addy. You're right. I should cut you some slack. But maybe you should cut me some slack, too, because this is who *I* am. Just because you're miles away doesn't mean I'll close my eyes to your safety. I care about you, and I know you care about me, so stop backing off every fucking time I try to be your boyfriend."

His jaw tightened, and the muscles in his neck followed as silent seconds ticked by. He was sure she'd bitch at him or end the call, but the longer the silence stretched, the more his worries morphed into gut-wrenching guilt. The last thing he wanted to do was to hurt her, and he'd spoken so harshly...

"You still there?"

"Yeah." Her voice was husky and quiet.

"I'm sorry for getting mad. I just...Fuck, Addy. I care about you, and every time I say that you back off. I get it. I really do. You don't want to be told what to do. We've beaten that horse to death. But I need more or I'm going to lose my mind."

"I think I pretty much bared my soul to you tonight," she

said more confidently.

"We both did, but I want more than sex with you. I know you're sexy, but I also know you're smart, and stubborn, and capable. You are so much more than just sexy, and a big part of having more between us is not worrying that every time I say something like 'I'll make you feel so good you'll never want to leave,' you'll clam up on me. And I know now's not the time to discuss it, because you need to conserve your phone battery for the remainder of your trip, but just think about everything I said, okay?"

"Don't worry," she said, not unkindly. "I'm spending most of my time thinking."

"How can I help you believe that letting me into your life isn't going to negate who you are or take away your power to be the person you want to be? What do you need from me to get past this?"

"If I had the answers to that, we wouldn't be having this discussion."

They were talking in circles and getting nowhere, but at least she seemed to hear him this time. "Right. Listen, I had dinner with a few SAR buddies tonight, and they asked me to teach classes for the next two days. But I can run up a few cell batteries for you in the morning before I head over there."

"Jake," she said sweetly, "I need you to let me sink or swim on my own. I love that you want to take care of me, but until I figure out how to accept it, you're just going to push me away."

If there were a wall in front of him, he'd bang his head on it. "Maybe you should start thinking about how hard you're pushing me away." This time when the phone went silent, it was Jake who ended the call.

Chapter Twenty-One

WEDNESDAY ADDY HIKED all day, trying to get her arms around her inability to hold her tongue. She needed to get her act together. This was supposed to be a time of reflection and rejuvenation, to dig deep and discover just how strong she really was. So far, she wasn't impressed. Sure, she'd made it hiking five or six miles on a daily basis, and navigated back to her campsite without calling in search and rescue, but until Wednesday night she couldn't even make it a single night without hearing Jake's voice. What was that all about? She was determined to figure her shit out, and she hiked from sunup until sundown and had fallen asleep in her clothes without even eating dinner.

Thursday morning she forced herself to push through her aches and pains, which wasn't nearly as difficult as pushing through the all-consuming craziness going on inside her chest. The pit of her stomach knotted up thinking about how her call with Jake had ended Tuesday night, especially after it had started out so intimately. She knew it was her fault, but she was at a loss about how to make her stupid mouth stop spouting off before she had time to think through her responses. She needed to figure out why that was and what she wanted.

I want Jake.

But I also want my independence.

She was in dire need of straight talk from her bestie. And

yes, Gabriella was on her honeymoon and probably wanted nothing to do with Addy's relationship woes, but considering she'd never had any relationship woes before, Addy figured Gabby owed her one.

She powered up her phone to send her a text, secretly hoping she might have missed a text from Jake last night and refusing to allow disappointment to take hold when there were no messages from him. That was her own fault. His offer to bring her extra batteries for her phone *before* teaching a class was beyond sweet and generous. But was it stepping over a line? Infringing on her independence? Or was that just her insecurities from her past peeking its ugly head in where it didn't belong? Cognitively she knew the answer, but when he'd offered, her knee-jerk reaction had kicked in, and she'd treated him as if his motivation had been to invade her privacy or *fix* things for her, as if she couldn't deal with them on her own.

Her glaring screw-up was too painful to dissect. She sent Gabriella a quick text. *I set out to test my boundaries and find myself and now I'm more lost than ever. WTF? Please tell me I'm not so fucked up that I can't love and be loved.* She tossed her phone into her backpack, bound and determined to figure her shit out, and a six-mile hike to Pirate's Peak would provide the solitude she needed.

But first she needed to get her butt out of the tent and down to the stream, where she had another issue to conquer. How to manage getting in and out of the frigid water without muddy feet. Maybe she should skip rinsing off. She was just going to get dirty again during her hike.

Maybe I can get used to being smelly and having dirty hair. That was not a goal she wanted to achieve. She gathered her supplies and headed down to the stream. Along the way she came up with a plan for staying out of the mud.

She grabbed an armload of fallen branches with leaves and pine needles still intact and spread them out along the shore, creating a large enough area for her to stand on while she dried off and dressed. That was her first *win* for the day. When she returned to the campsite she remembered toilet paper when she had to pee. *Win number two*. And when she tripped and fell over a log, splitting open her knee, she cleaned and bandaged it like a pro. *Win number three*. Not wanting to push her luck on her hike, she put the damn compass in her pocket, stowed her journal, extra energy bars, water, supplies for dinner, the camping books she'd forgotten to read, and a hoodie in her backpack. She rolled up her sleeping bag and blanket, and secured them to the pack, dragging it the first few feet as she rolled her shoulders to loosen them up before her trek. A night at Pirate's Peak, a change in scenery, would give her a chance to clear her head.

The first few hours of her hike were a test of her fortitude, as the steep incline caused her muscles to fatigue. But she was determined to make it, and pushed on, crossing over bare areas of grass and rocks and into thick forests of trees. Prickly limbs snapped against her chest, piercing her clothing like needles. She stopped several times to rest, but she forgave herself instead of beating herself up for it. Like her relationship with Jake, sometimes she needed to slow down to move forward.

Her real adventure started in the late afternoon when she arrived at the bottom of Pirate's Peak. She dropped her pack to the ground, rolled her shoulders back to loosen the ache they were growing accustomed to, and gazed up at the incredible, intimidating sight before her. It looked like someone had plunked a mountain of rock on the ground, then split it with a few uneven swipes of a giant ax, creating a perfect slope of jagged rocks to make it possible to climb. Addy drew in a deep breath, second-guessing her decision to not only climb to the peak, but to spend the night there as well. She'd gotten comfortable in her tent. The ridge felt like her private oasis, but this was new territory, and she had no idea what she'd find at the top of those rocks. Jake's serious face appeared in her mind. She could almost feel his eyes boring into her. *Why, sexy girl? Why do you have to do this alone?*

She was beginning to wonder that herself. She took a long drink from her water bottle, wiped the sweat from her forehead, and turned to take in the views. *What am I really doing out here?* Until she figured out what was missing in her life, how could she embrace the idea of sharing it with Jake?

Beyond the tips of tall pines, rolling hills plunged to a cavernous valley. She could barely make out the structures, but a town was discernible by snaking roads and a flatter landscape. A lake lay still as glass, reflecting the late-afternoon sun. *Sweetwater.* Logan had told her all about the quaint town with cobblestone streets and old-fashioned storefronts. Maybe she and Jake could plan a trip together and visit the town. There was so much beauty outside of the city. Why had she waited this long to explore? The urge to call Jake and share her excitement with him fluttered inside her. As gorgeous as the view was, and as thrilled as she was to finally get this far on her journey, something was still missing. This trip had seemed like such an exciting and necessary idea when she'd seen all the places Jake had been and witnessed the things he'd accomplished. But now she realized it wasn't the places he'd been that had captured her attention. *Captured my heart.* It went so much deeper. It was his dedication to helping people. His loyalty to what he believed in, his loyalty to his family.

And your loyalty to me.

He never looked at the camera because he knew the secret to happiness. It wasn't in others seeing that he could achieve something, or that he adored his family. His happiness came from within, from doing the things he loved. Seeing those pictures sparked something bigger than just the need to prove she could get off her comfy couch and climb a mountain. But she'd spent so many years proving to herself, to her family, to anyone who might look at her like a girl born with a silver spoon in her mouth, that she was more, she hadn't seen what was right in front of her. It didn't matter what anyone else thought. Jake's voice floated into her mind again. *I know you're there with me. Nothing else matters.*

Her eyes drifted to Sweetwater again, and she imagined walking along the cobblestone streets with him. Sitting at the edge of the lake getting drunk on his kisses. The truth she'd been trying to outrun clung to her like a second skin. She *needed* him. She missed the way butterflies nested in her belly when he smiled, and the way he looked at her. *God*, the way he looked at her. He had a way of seeing parts of her that no one else had ever taken the time to see. *You need a man who can put up with your shit and slap your ass.*

Her eyes welled up and she swiped at the tears. When had she become a fountain of emotions? Laughing to herself, she turned back toward the last leg of today's journey. She couldn't stand there and daydream all day. The sun would soon give way to darkness, and when that happened she wanted to be set up on Pirate's Peak. Her body still wasn't used to the daily climbing, and even the thought of scaling that mountainous rock made her tired, but she wasn't a quitter.

I'm proud of you. Be safe, sexy girl. Jake's voice gave her the push she needed.

She'd missed him too much when she'd first read those words to feel the full impact of his praise. Now, as she stared up at the rock face, she was excited to take a picture at the peak and text it to him. She finally had someone to share her accomplishments with. She had Gabriella, but sharing her accomplishments with a girlfriend was different from sharing them with a man she liked. *Liked? I'm so far beyond* like *I can't even see it anymore.*

She gave her intimidating challenger a once-over. Having pored over articles written by hikers of all ages who had climbed Pirate's Peak without any equipment, she knew she could do it, too. She assessed the deep ledges and long stretches of uneven rock, allowing plenty of space for fingerholds. As she hoisted her pack onto her back, a wave of doubt washed through her. Her pack wasn't all that heavy, but it might make climbing something this challenging awkward. She stared at the rock face, which had gotten its name because of a darkened area of rock that resembled an eye patch, and the jagged horizontal crack about ten feet off the ground, which looked like an eerie sneer. *I've come this far. I'm not about to let a pirate-faced rock beat me.*

The rock was cold and unforgiving against her hands, stable and reassuring beneath each foot. Addy hoisted herself from one rock to the next, using upper-body strength she didn't realize she possessed, and undiscovered muscles came to life along her sides and at the junctures of her knees and quads. She felt powerful and confident. Adrenaline pushed her past the abrading on her hands and the weight of her pack bearing down on her shoulders. Sweat beaded her forehead and dripped between her breasts. By the time she reached the peak, stretching her arm over the cold, hard stone, her limbs were trembling. She pictured herself sliding back down and crashing headfirst into the ground.

Not helpful.

Wishing more than ever that she'd accepted Jake's offer to experience this with her, she ran her fingers over the ledge, blindly seeking something to grasp. Her fingers caught on a sharp edge, and she dragged her body over the ridge, scraping her thighs in the process. She dropped her backpack, pushed up to her hands and knees, and crawled away from the edge. Collapsing on her back, she lay with her arms stretched out, panting like she'd just scaled Mount Everest. Something dug into her butt. She reached into her pocket and withdrew the compass, remembering how she'd been a little offended when Jake had suggested she bring it. She was a fool.

"I did it!" she said into the air. An unstoppable smile formed on her lips, and her heart thundered so hard she was sure it was cursing at her, but she felt amazing! Closing her eyes and raising fisted hands to the sky, she yelled, "I fucking did it!"

Her voice echoed around her, reminding her of a philosophy class she'd taken in college. Her professor had posed the well-known thought experiment. "If a tree falls in a forest and no one is around to hear it, does it make a sound?" She'd enjoyed that class tremendously. It had made her question everything about life. Now, as she sat watching the sun dip from the sky, her voice no longer lingering in the air, she asked the same question of her achievement. If no one was there to share it with, did it really happen? Of course it did, and she took pride in that, but her mind continued down that path.

Tackling Pirate's Peak didn't fill the emptiness she'd thought it would.

It might have, if she and Jake hadn't become a *thing*. But despite the thrill of knowing she'd done something she never thought she would, she knew with her whole heart that it would mean more if they'd experienced it together.

She unzipped her pack and emptied it as quickly as she could, fishing around for her phone. The need to talk to Jake, to share this moment with him, was stronger than her need to breathe. She pushed the power button, and remembered he was teaching a class. She'd have to text instead of calling. Her phone didn't power on. She pushed the button again…and again. The damn thing was dead. She could have sworn she'd powered it off after texting Gabriella, but she'd been in such a hurry, she must have forgotten. Now there would be no pictures, no texts, just the mind-numbing reality of spending her big moment alone.

Her eyes sailed over her sleeping bag, the supplies she'd brought to make dinner, and finally, her journal. Shoving her useless phone back in the pack, she grabbed the journal. How could he have known exactly what she needed on this trip, when she thought all she needed was to be alone with her thoughts?

She opened the journal and read the note he'd written for her again. *Sexy girl, you can hike for miles, but everything you're looking for is waiting for you right back here. Your Neanderthal, J.R.*

She glanced at her supplies again, and realized she'd forgotten her lantern, pillow, and the firestarter to heat up her dinner. Her eyes drifted over the edge of the rocks at the branches and other pieces of firewood she'd need to start a fire. Sighing heavily, she clutched the journal to her chest. Jake would have thought this through. She wasn't about to climb back down Pirate's Peak.

Opening the journal once again, she wrote, *I wish I could share this with you. This beautiful view, the excitement I feel inside me, the—*

She fisted her hand around the pen, tears dampening her eyes. It wasn't the view or the excitement of what she had accomplished that she wanted to share with him. Those things seemed so insignificant compared to the love burgeoning inside her. She might have forgotten to bring the things she *thought* she needed to make herself comfortable, but none of them mattered. Even if she had remembered to bring every one of those items, she'd still left behind the most essential element of all.

My missing piece.

CHAPTER TWENTY-TWO

JAKE DOWNED THE last of his beer and set the empty glass on the bar, hoping the bartender, a buxom blonde who had spent more time vying for his attention than doing her job, wouldn't start flirting again. Jake wasn't in the mood to hang out at NightCaps, the bar where he usually met his brothers—and Addy. But after spending two days trying not to think about the fact that she hadn't texted or called, Cash's invitation had been a welcome one. Of course, while his phone was silent as a frigging stone, Cash had received three texts in the last thirty seconds.

Jake pushed his empty beer bottle away. He'd thought he'd get trashed and forget about the gnawing ache in his gut telling him to get in his truck, hunt down Addy, and talk some sense into her. He'd texted her this morning, and again this afternoon, and she hadn't returned either one. Knowing Addy, she'd turned the damn phone off to make a statement, but worry ate away at him that she'd run into trouble. He knew if he hightailed it up that mountain and she was fine, she'd give him hell for checking up on her. He was *this close* to saying fuck it and going anyway. *Time for Little Miss Independent to stop hiding behind her past.* Maybe when Cash finished texting he could distract him enough to make it through a few more hours. And hopefully by then Addy would come to her senses and call him.

Blondie returned, fluttering her lashes as she whisked away his empty bottle. He averted his gaze. It was only nine thirty on what felt like the longest Thursday in the history of the world, and the bar was packed. Normally he liked the eye candy that hung out in NightCaps, but the only eye candy he wanted was too frigging far away to see.

"Everything okay?" Jake asked as Cash returned another text.

"Yeah." Cash shoved his phone in his pocket. "You know my buddy Boyd Hudson?"

"Sure. He started med school, right?" Boyd had worked with Cash at the firehouse for a few years before moving away.

"Yup. In Meadowside, Virginia. He and his fiancée, Janie, just set a wedding date. Looks like we'll be going to Virginia for a wedding."

"Awesome. I'm happy for them."

Blondie returned with another beer for Jake. "Here you go. Anything else I can get you, just ask." Her sultry blue-eyed gaze told him she truly meant *anything*.

Before Addy, he wouldn't have looked past the ready-and-willing, no-strings-attached *opportunity* before him, but now he saw a lonely woman looking to fill a few empty hours. Jake wondered why she couldn't see that he was turned off by the idea of his hands on anyone other than Addy. He felt like he was so consumed with her he had a blinking neon sign that read PROUD BOYFRIEND OF STUBBORN, SEXY ADDISON DAHL on his forehead.

"Thanks," he said with blatant disinterest, and turned away.

"Damn," Cash said under his breath. "When did pigs start flying?"

"The night of Duke's wedding." His phone vibrated, and he withdrew it from his pocket, hoping like hell it was Addy. Duke's name flashed on the screen. "Shit. This can't be good."

"A guy on his honeymoon shouldn't be anywhere near his phone," Cash said, locking a serious gaze on Jake as he answered the call.

"Hey, bro. You okay?"

"Let's see," Duke said casually. "I'm in paradise with the most gorgeous woman on earth, doing our best to start our family. What do you think?"

That's hard to believe, because the most beautiful woman on earth is busy making me crazy up in the mountains. Jake heard a thread of something in Duke's voice that made him hold back the tease. "Then why are you calling me?"

"Because my thoughtful wife is worried about her best friend." Duke's tone turned serious. "Have you heard from Addy?"

"Not since Tuesday." *When we had a rough end to our call.* The hair on the back of Jake's neck prickled. He pushed to his feet as Duke explained that Addy had texted Gabriella and seemed upset, and Gabriella hadn't been able to reach her since. The thought of his girl alone and upset already had his insides twisting, but while she might pull stone-cold-stubborn silence on him, she'd never do that to Gabriella.

Cash rose beside him and tossed money on the bar. "What's going on?"

"Gabby's worried about Addy." *But not half as worried as I am.* Then to Duke he said, "Tell Gabby not to worry. Her phone probably died, but I'm going to find her." He promised to text Duke with an update, and ended the call as he pushed through the crowd toward the exit.

"Want me to come with you?" Cash asked.

Jake flagged down a cab. "No. I've got this."

Two hours later, armed with his SAR equipment, and as his mother would say, *enough piss and vinegar for four men*, he went in search of the girl who knew how to push all his buttons. Jake took the mountain at a fast clip, stepping over fallen trees, around bushes and rocks. Guided by a headlamp and his own keen sense of direction, with every step his protective instincts kicked in harder. He could kick himself for not leaving hours ago.

A quick glance at his compass told him he was heading in the right direction. Riser's Ridge was a few miles straight ahead. He had tunnel vision, his every thought consumed with Addy, the most sensual, smart, gorgeous, stubborn woman he'd ever met. If anything happened to her, he'd never forgive himself.

The miles passed quickly, and when the tree line thinned, revealing bright stretches of royal-blue sky, he sprinted into the clearing and followed tracks to her campsite. His heart beat faster as he approached the dark tent, taking in the rock-lined fire pit, the clothesline strung between two trees, and the area around her tent, which was free of debris. She'd listened to his advice, or her own good sense. He crouched by the front of the tent, taking a moment to get a grip on his emotions. Chances were, she'd give him hell for showing up, and he guessed that hauling her into the kiss he'd been dying for wasn't the best response to anger.

"Addy?" he said softly, not wanting to startle her. "It's Jake. I'm going to unzip your tent."

He unzipped it slowly and said, "I missed you, baby. I—" His stomach sank at the sight of the empty, almost barren, tent. In three seconds flat he cataloged her missing sleeping bag and gear. All of his search and rescue instincts surged forward.

"Addy?" he hollered, rising to his full height and scanning the area. She was out there alone somewhere spending the night without a tent. *Jesus, Addy.* He couldn't decide if she was brave or stupid. Not that a tent was critical, but it provided a modicum of safety from the elements—and predators.

He bent at the waist, assessing the footprints around the site. There were only his and hers, which was a relief. At least the probability of someone absconding with her was off the table. But where the hell was she? Inspecting the ground more closely, he noticed freshly moved dirt just beyond the tent. Leaves were pushed to the side, as if she'd dragged something off to the west. He envisioned her tugging her backpack, cursing under her breath about him and his need to be there for her. His smile faded quickly as reality hit. If she was too tired to carry the pack, then how far could she have gone?

Plowing forward, he kept his light on the ground and his mind on the search, mentally ticking off all the places she'd wanted to see on her journey.

ADDY STARTLED AWAKE, her eyes darting blindly into the night. She clenched her fingers around the sleeping bag, holding it beneath her chin and listening to leaves brushing in the breeze. It was cold without the protection of her tent, and sounds were amplified. She'd had a heck of a time falling asleep. Her mind had traveled to eerie places. Places she hadn't allowed it to the whole time she'd been on the mountain. But out here on the rocks, exposed to the elements, she'd conjured up all sorts of awful things. Mountain lions surrounding her, hungry wolves on the prowl, confused black bears with a craving for human flesh. *Great.* Now she was panicking again. She squeezed her eyes closed, pretending to have a tent around her, though she knew how ridiculous it was to think that scrappy little vinyl dome could protect her from any of those things. A loud *snap* of twigs brought her eyes wide open. She held her breath, listening to the very clear, ominous snapping of twigs.

She was *not* conjuring this up. Something was out there, and it sounded heavy.

Snap, snap, snap!

She was trembling, her mind racing through her options. *Lie still? Pray whatever it was couldn't climb?*

Snap! Snap!

She inched further down into the sleeping bag. Should she get up and try to scare it away? Could a bear see her up on that gigantic rock? What would she do if whatever it was charged up the rocks? There was no place to run.

The snapping sounds stopped.

She exhaled the breath she'd been holding.

Scrape, scrape.

It was at the base of Pirate's Peak. Addy lay frozen, too scared to move, listening for—

The unmistakable sounds of heavy breathing broke through her fear. She scrambled out of the sleeping bag and ran, hunched over—as if that might make her invisible—to the far edge of the boulder, where she crouched as low as she could and peered over the side. The way down was a straight drop. Holy fuck, she was cornered. Jake was right, she had no business out here alone. She couldn't fight off a wild animal.

Or a crazy mountain man.

Ohgodno. No, no, no.

Where was her Neanderthal when she needed him? Why did he have to listen to her? He should have known she needed him, just like he knew she needed the journal, the compass, and the goddamn slap on the ass. The next time she saw him, she'd give him a slap all right. Right upside the head for not being more stubborn than her! She'd never been one to pray, but she closed her eyes and begged, pleaded, groveled to whoever would listen. *I promise to stop being stubborn, to listen to Jake's advice, to appreciate all the things he does, and to make a bigger effort with my parents, and—*

The sound of flesh slapping on rock brought her eyes open. A gigantic arm curled over the edge of the boulder, and without a single thought, she bolted toward it and slammed her heel on his fingers. "Go away! I have a gun!"

"Fuck!" The arm flew backward and Jake's head rose into view, his face twisted in pain.

"Fuck! I'm sorry. I'm so sorry!" She stumbled back as he hoisted himself onto the boulder, rose to his feet, and glared at his injured hand. Her panic-driven words flew like bullets. "What are you doing here? You scared the shit out of me. I thought you were a bear. Or a killer." She hated her anger, hated every word she said, but she was shaking like a leaf and too scared to stop yelling. "Don't you ever listen? I told you I don't need you here."

"Gabby thought you were lost," he shouted, stalking toward her. "Damn it, Addy. I need that hand to touch you!"

"I'm not *lost*. What the hell is wrong with you people? Can't a girl be left alone?" She didn't want to say the hurtful words, but her mind was spinning with fear, and relief, and confusion so thick she could barely breathe. Tears burned her eyes.

He stepped closer, and she stumbled back, too upset to be

touched, stopping inches from the edge of the boulder.

"What the hell, Addy? She couldn't reach you," he seethed. "*I* couldn't reach you for two days. *Two* days."

"So you traipsed up here to drag me home?" *God I love you*, played in the recesses of her mind, fighting through the panic, through the anger, but it was trapped. *Why am I arguing?* Her knees were so shaky she crossed her arms around her middle and held on tight, hoping to remain erect and struggling to keep her tears from falling.

"No," he shouted. "I traipsed up the mountain to make sure the woman I love is okay."

"I'm *not* cutting my trip short. I'm fin—wait? What?" She couldn't have heard him right.

He wrapped his arms around her, inciting a flood of tears.

"You're scared, maybe a little in shock," he said firmly, holding her tight. "I'm not here to take you home. We were worried about you, and this is what you do when you love someone: You make sure they're safe, and you don't drag them away from the thing that means the most to them. I'm so in love with you, Addy, and you're too damn stubborn to see that I don't want to change you, or take away your independence or your search for who you are, or proving yourself, or whatever this is. I want to help you fill all those gaps, even if that means doing it from the other side of the state. But I can't make it through a single fucking day not knowing if you're okay."

He ground his teeth together, but nothing could hide the adoration in his eyes. Tears tumbled down her cheeks. She was unable to think, unable to speak. He pressed one hand to the back of her head, the other to her lower back, and held her, calming the panic inside her.

"Breathe, baby, nice and slow. Let all that fear out and let me in, sexy girl. Let me love you and experience life *with* you. I don't want to make all your decisions. I just want to make sure you're safe. And *mine*. Definitely *mine*." The last two words came with a smile that cracked her heart wide open.

She buried her face in his chest, trying to steal his courage, his strength, his ability to say the three words that seemed to come so easily for him—and carried a lifetime of anxiety for her.

"What took you so long?" slipped out.

He lowered his face beside hers. "What, baby?"

Smiling despite the nervousness whirling inside her, she said, "What took you so long?"

"What took me…?" He pulled back, annoyance simmering beneath his loving gaze. "Jesus you drive me crazy."

"I *know*. I'm sorry."

"No you're not. You're not goddamn sorry, but you're *my Addy*, and I wouldn't want you any other way." He brushed his lips over hers. "Except maybe naked."

He kissed her softly, a feathery tease of a kiss, rousing more than passion, more than pure lust. He roused her very soul.

"Do you love me, Addison?" he whispered. "Really, truly love me? Because I'm pretty sure all this hollering is *us*, and I'm not sure that's ever going to change."

"I don't want it to." A laugh bubbled up with more tears. "You're the key to my Pandora's box. You unchained my heart." Their connection sparked hotter, burned deeper. *A forever burn*. "You're my stormy night, and I am truly, deeply, and definitely *madly* in love with you."

"Then shut up and kiss me, stubborn girl, before I read you the riot act for scaring the shit out of me."

When his lips met hers, warm and soft but gloriously firm

and demanding, she surrendered to the love that had been building for months. Heat scorched through her, exploding like fireworks in her chest and setting free a world of deeper emotions, greedier desires. She tore at his shirt, covered his chest with kisses, touching every bit of flesh she was able. The next few minutes were a blur of clothing flying through the air and desperate kisses as they stumbled to the sleeping bag in a tangle of limbs, laughing and kissing and touching like they'd never get enough of each other. Jake came down over her, his thick thighs parting hers, his strong arms gathering her as close as he possibly could. He gazed into her eyes and she knew. She *knew*, without a shadow of a doubt, that he was her destiny.

"I *need* you, Jake," she confessed. "I need *you*. Not a conquest, not a good fuck, but the heart and soul of my stubborn, gruff caveman who knows exactly how to love me. I love you, and I don't want to explore without you anymore."

"You have me, baby, every minute of every day."

"Even when I get scared and ornery?" She clung to his arms, a little fearful of the answer.

"When you're scared, ornery, flirty, and even when you need a smack on that incredible ass of yours. I get you, Addy, and I always will."

Chapter Twenty-Three

JAKE STOOD IN the center of the stream, water swirling around his hips, sunlight reflecting off the gentle ripples as he soaped up his chest. The muscles in his back flexed and bunched even with the slightest of efforts. Addy licked her lips, hungry for him even though it had been three days since he'd arrived on the mountain and they'd made love so many times she'd lost count. He *got* her. Really, truly understood her. All those months of flirtation and friendship came tumbling forward on Pirate's Peak. They loved like they needed each other to breathe, and after three incredible, sexy, loving, truth-telling days, she was even more in love with him.

He glanced over his shoulder, flashing his cockiest grin yet, and like metal to magnet, her core flamed.

"Are you going to bring that hot little body over here, or just stare at my ass?"

"I'd rather stare at your front, but you're selfishly keeping that to yourself." She motioned for him to turn around, which he did, blessing her with an even more glorious view. Water slid like a river down his impossibly broad chest, over beautifully sculpted abs to that tempting vee that disappeared beneath the surface.

He stalked toward her with a predatory look in his eyes, reminding her of the way he'd approached her the night of

Gabriella's wedding. Her pulse spiked, and she glided backward through the water, teasing her man and taking great pleasure in the growing hunger in his gaze.

"Afraid?" he asked.

"Never," she said, and this time, unlike at Gabriella's wedding, she was being honest. She was no longer afraid of the emotions he stirred in her. She craved them, reveled in them, and she let him know every second she could.

"Then why are you running from me?" He moved swiftly through the water, and she continued walking backward.

"Running? I like to think of it as whetting your appetite."

He lunged, catching her and lifting her into his arms. She shrieked with delight, winding her legs around his waist.

"You can't escape us, sexy girl." He nuzzled against her neck and nipped at her earlobe, sending shivers down her spine. "You're *mine.*"

"Prove it," she challenged.

He lifted her up and drove her down on his eager shaft, filling her so completely, she could barely breathe. The forgiving water slid over her heated flesh, bringing rise to goose bumps.

Staring into her eyes with a look of pure possession as he masterfully lifted and lowered her onto his cock to a slow, torturous rhythm, he said, "We're playing by my rules now, sweet thing, and I see our future in your eyes."

She pushed her fingers into his hair and took hold of his thick locks. "Are you telling me what to do, Mr. Ryder?"

"Yes."

The single word hit her in the center of her chest. His face was a mask of anticipation and worry, but no longer did her past own her. It was no match for her incredibly full heart.

"Then you better make it worth my while, or my Neanderthal boyfriend will kick your ass."

With a groan and a toe-curling kiss, he carried her to the muddy banks, laid her on her back, and amid the mud and muck, he pushed into her.

"I love you so damn much, Addy."

"Not nearly as much as I love you."

"I know. I told you, I see our future in your eyes."

She drew him to her, kissing him deeply. Their lovemaking was raw and rough, sensual and sweet. And when he rolled onto his back, squishing into the mud as she straddled his hips, muddy handprints on his chest, covering her thighs, her breasts, their entire bodies, she'd never experienced anything as beautiful. How was it possible that every time they made love was more intense than the last? Emotions she once feared grew deeper, stronger, more consuming with every breath she took.

She gazed down at the sexual beast beneath her and froze. Still as a tree.

"*Move*, baby," he pleaded. "I need to feel you move."

A slow grin spread across her lips. "What do you see in my eyes now, Mr. Ryder?"

TORTURE DIDN'T BEGIN to describe the way it felt when Addy held Jake at bay. Her tight heat enveloped him. Her delicate hands played over his pecs. She knew her touch drove him crazy. She owned every ounce of him, and he knew by the look in her eyes that she didn't doubt it anymore. Her tangled, muddy hair clung to her shoulders and breasts, making her look even sexier than moments earlier. His muddy handprints were all over her, and like a beacon of their love, her tattoo remained clear of dirt. She was his fierce, passionate, smart, no-boundaries girl. His friend, his lover.

My soul mate.

He gazed into her eyes, loving the challenge she posed, but he wasn't giving in. He did see their future in her eyes. The night on Pirate's Peak had changed everything. All her walls had crumbled down, and she'd finally let him in.

"What do you see in my eyes now, Mr. Ryder?" she repeated.

He wasn't about to lie and say he didn't see their future, but he knew better than to push his girl. "The need to come," he finally answered in the low voice that he knew made her sex twitch. And *man*, did he like that tight little squeeze.

She pressed her lips together, obviously annoyed that he'd sparked a reaction she couldn't control. He clutched her hips, lifting her easily along the length of his cock. She dug her nails into his forearms, trying to put all her strength into remaining still, but he knew just how to torture the woman he loved, and love her he did. They'd spent the last three days hiking, talking, and making love. She told him about her parents' and her grandmother's stifling, loveless marriages, and how all she wanted was to be loved for who she was. *I don't want to wake up one day and find you looking at me differently.* She was so tough, but so vulnerable, with insecurities that were well founded, but not with him. He'd told her just that. *When you're old and gray, with wrinkles and boobs that hang to your waist, you'll still be my sexy girl with a sassy mouth that's spent fifty years giving me shit. And I'll love you fifty zillion times as much as I do now.*

Pushing aside the talks that strengthened their bond, he focused on pleasuring his gorgeous, stubborn girl. He brought one hand between them, teasing over her most sensitive nerves.

"You can do that all you want," she said. Her eyelids fluttered, belying her challenging tone.

He continued slow, rhythmic thrusts, moving in time to every stroke of his thumb. "Come for me, baby."

"I'm not going…Oh, *God…*" She bit her lower lip, and he thrust harder. "Not going to…come until I'm good and ready."

"Fuck me, baby," he said as sweetly as he could manage. "You know you want to." Their lovemaking, like the rest of their relationship, was a wild storm. A beautiful, powerful typhoon.

She moaned through gritted teeth, her slick heat tightening around his cock.

Forcing her eyes open, she glared at him. "What do you see now?"

He swept her beneath him again and drove into her *hard.* The air *whooshed* from her lungs, and he claimed her in a punishingly intense kiss. She returned the kiss with fervor, taking him higher with every stroke of her tongue, every sweet, needy moan.

He tore away long enough to say, "I love you so fucking much. Come for me, beautiful," before taking her in another electric kiss.

She broke their connection, gasping for air. "Say I make the rules so I can come," she begged. "I need to come, Jake. *Please?*"

"Not a chance." He slapped the side of her ass, earning another sexy moan and a sinfully hot glare that sent a bolt of lightning to his cock. "Come for me, Addy."

She shook her head. She was at the edge, her body trembling, her inner muscles tightening despite her resistance. She was as stubborn as stubborn could be, and she was *everything* he needed.

"*Fuck* me, baby," he urged, needing to come but not willing to let go until she did.

"Who's the boss?" Her cheeks were flushed, her words breathless.

She was so adorably sexy he could barely stand it. She wound her legs around his waist and pressed a muddy palm lightly to his cheek, stroking her thumb over his jaw. Her touch was his Achilles' heel. Her gaze softened, the love swimming in her eyes drowning the last of his resistance.

"Fuck, baby," he whispered, and touched his forehead to hers. "Why do I love you so much?"

"Because I'm the thunder to your lightning. Stop talking and make love to me."

"So bossy," he whispered as he lowered his mouth to hers.

"You love me bossy."

"Stop talking," he said, trying to kiss her.

"Are you telling me what to do?"

He glared at her.

She wrapped her hand around the back of his head, drawing his face closer. "Okay, you win. I'll come for you."

"Why do I feel like you won again?"

With a tender hand on his cheek, she said, "Don't dwell on it," and as they gave in to their passion, *dwelling on it* was the last thing on his mind. He had a heart full of pleasure to dole out—and a lifetime of paybacks to look forward to.

EPILOGUE

ADDY TRACED THE new tattoo on the inside of her wrist. *Taken.* It had hurt like hell, but the pretty script font and the pain were true symbols of her and Jake's five months together. Not that their relationship was painful in a hurtful way, but they'd endured the type of pain that comes with the cleansing of one's soul. She and Jake had no secrets, and the more she opened up to him, the more she learned about herself.

Jake squeezed her hand beneath the dinner table, furtively glancing at her wrist. They'd met his family and Gabriella for dinner after getting their *Taken* tattoos. His tattoo was bigger, bolder, but she knew it caused the same weighty emotions in him. He knew her so well that when he'd gotten down on one knee last week, she'd been shocked. And when he'd said, "Sexy girl, you are my sun, my moon, and my ever after, will you get a tattoo with me?" she'd burst into tears. Actual. Tears. She'd come a long way, thinking before she spoke, not arguing every time he made a suggestion, and moving into his incredible rooftop apartment. Their life was beautiful and passionate, but she wasn't ready to jump into the institution that had scared her for so long. But he'd been one step ahead of her on that, too.

He leaned closer and whispered in her ear, "You about ready to blow this joint so I can show you how *taken* you are?"

Was she ever. It was through his patience and insistence that she'd learned to let him in, and the scattered elements of her past had begun to piece together. While she had enjoyed a happy, sheltered childhood, she'd come to realize how deeply she'd feared falling in love. Her parents' marriage of…*comfort? Convenience? Circumstance?* She didn't know how to classify it, but it hadn't provided the same strong role model of endless love that Jake had grown up with. She'd never acknowledged the fear that had sparked to herself, much less anyone else. But Jake made her feel safe and genuinely, deeply loved. She never believed she *needed* anyone, but Jake had become her rock, and she wasn't ashamed to admit she needed him as much as she wanted him. She'd even deleted her Tumblr page and told her parents about Jake. They seemed genuinely pleased for her, and she and Jake were planning a trip to visit them as soon as her parents returned from her father's latest fashion show in Italy.

"Hey, you two," Gabriella said. "You are *not* blowing out of our baby announcement celebration dinner early to go have wild monkey sex."

"How did you even hear that, Miss Bionic Ears?" Addy teased. She was thrilled for Gabriella and Duke. They'd conceived on their honeymoon, and although she'd shared the news with Addy right away, they'd waited to share the news with the rest of the family until they'd passed their first trimester. Gabriella was cutting back her office hours as soon as the baby was born, and tonight Jake and Addy would reveal their plans, too.

"She didn't have to hear it," Andrea said, and mouthed, *It's all in the eyes*, as she pointed to her eyes, then winked.

Jake nuzzled against Addy's neck. "There's no escaping us, sexy girl. I told you that the night of Duke and Gabby's wedding."

"Speaking of weddings," Siena said with a mischievous glint in her eyes. "When are you two taking the plunge?"

Jake squeezed her hand again, flashing the I've-got-this look she'd come to adore and rely on.

"We're secure enough in our relationship not to need rings," Jake said, lifting their joint hands and revealing their new tattoos.

"Oh my gosh!" Gabriella laughed. "Only you two would do that."

"I love them," Siena gushed, reaching for Addy's hand and inspecting the tattoo more closely. "That must have hurt like crazy."

"It did," Addy said as Jake reclaimed her hand and pressed a kiss to her wrist.

"But all things worth their salt come with pain," Jake said, gazing into her eyes. A silent message of *I love you*s passed between them. "We do have our own announcement to make."

"You're pregnant!" Lizzie said hopefully.

"No, no, no, no, no," Addy insisted. She hadn't realized she'd been afraid of mirroring her mother's hands-off parenting style until she and Jake had begun discussing having a family of their own. He'd seen through her declarations of not being wired to be a mother, and like everything else, he'd gotten to the core of the issue and they'd faced it together, through talking, tears, and love. Addy knew their love was too big and they were too stubborn to let anything scare either of them away. They both wanted a family someday, when the time was right. Or as Jake put it, *When Addy finally realized she could never be the type of parent her mother was because her passion ran too deep, and that she'd instill the need for independence in their babies.* He was sure they were destined to have adorably stubborn children who tested them at every turn, and she looked forward to it. *One day.*

"SHE'S NOT PREGNANT," Jake said. "Jesus, you guys are in such a hurry. I've waited my whole life for this woman. I'm in no rush to share her." Although for a guy who hadn't wanted any ties or distractions, he was all in with Addy. And when she was finally ready to have children, he was all in for that part of their lives, too. And if they decided down the line that they didn't want children, that was okay, too. As long as they had each other, their life was complete.

Addy was looking at him so openly lovingly, his heart skidded. He'd experienced so many life-altering moments with her, he'd come to expect them. They hit every morning when he woke up with her in his arms and every evening when she walked in the door after work. And in a million moments like now, when a single glance reminded him of how far they'd come and how many incredible years they had to look forward to. No, he wasn't in a rush to share her, or to leave her for a single day, which was why he was thrilled with Addy's decision.

"Dude," Gage urged. "Are you going to share your news? Sally and I have a plane to catch. We have a meeting early tomorrow for the new community center we're opening."

"It's snowing pretty hard," Jake pointed out. It was mid-November and they'd been hit with an early winter storm.

"I'm sure the pilot will cancel if it's unsafe," Gage assured him.

"Can you share your news, please? Lizzie and I have a wedding to plan," Blue said.

Their wedding was taking place in just a few weeks, over the holidays. Jake was pretty sure it was already planned to the hilt, which meant Blue wanted to get Lizzie back to their hotel for some smokin'-hot loving. Not that he blamed him. He was dying to get Addy alone, too.

"Or do I have to take you out back and pummel it out of you?" Blue joked.

Jake scoffed. "First, I'd kick your ass, and second…I don't have a second, so I'd kick your ass again."

Everyone laughed. Addy leaned in to him and touched his cheek. He'd never get used to the way her touch sparked an avalanche of emotions inside him.

"We all know you're big and bad," Addy said, running her finger along his jaw. "So stop chest bumping and tell them."

"Yeah, *big, bad* Jake," Duke teased. "What's up?"

"Hey, that's for me to say," Addy said sternly. "Go rub your wife's belly or something."

"My girl's got my back, Duke. Watch it." He pressed a kiss to the back of Addy's hand. "My incredible girlfriend has decided to train for search and rescue. When Gabby reduces her office hours, Addy's going to go on SAR missions with me."

"We'll go on them *together*," she corrected him.

"I'm not trying to get the upper hand," Jake explained. But one look in her beautiful eyes, and he relented. This had been her decision, and he'd actually tried to get her to change her mind at first, explaining that he worked in all kinds of weather, in the middle of the night, and often in deleterious environments. But true to her stubborn nature, she'd wanted no parts of his excuses. And she was right. She wasn't merely tagging along. She insisted on being formally trained and certified, and he was proud as hell of her. "We'll go on them together."

"Addy? Is that true?" Ned set his fork down beside his plate, giving her his full attention.

"Yes," she said with pride in her eyes. "When I was on Pirate's Peak alone and scared, two things became very clear to me." That pride warmed to adoration, and she gazed into Jake's eyes. "The first was that I was madly in love with my big, brooding, possessive boyfriend."

She returned her attention to his father. "You raised such an incredible man, I was hoping you and Jake could both help me learn how to do search and rescue. Gabriella and I help others on a legal front, and I love the work we do." She smiled at Gabriella. "But so much changed while I was on the mountain. I fell in love with the wilderness. Everything felt bigger, more real, and natural. Like I could breathe better, and believe it or not, after I got past the pain of using muscles I didn't know I had, I missed the pain. It had meant I was pushing myself. And I really miss doing that." She smiled at Jake, and he nodded, encouraging her to reveal the other thing that had haunted her since her trip.

"There was this moment in the woods that made me want to do more with my life. I had kicked off my boot and found it lying in the woods outside of my campsite. All I could think about was how desolate that image was and what you and Jake must face with search and rescue. Being frightened and alone on Pirate's Peak put me *in* that boot and made me realize how terrified a person who is lost must feel. I want to help. I don't think I can know Jake's going out to help find someone and *not* want to be right there helping, too."

"You know, sweetheart," Ned said, "we don't always work in the best of conditions or during normal working hours."

"Boy, the apple really doesn't fall far from the tree," Addy said. "Jake already tried to talk me out of it."

"Waste of time, Dad," Jake said.

"Well, I for one am proud of you," Cash said. "It takes a strong person to be willing to drop everything to help others."

"Addy's the strongest woman I know." Gabriella smiled at Addy. "And I'm happy for you, Ad, but no SAR missions when I'm having my baby, okay? I need you there telling me to shut the hell up and push, because Duke would push for me if he could."

Addy's eyes glassed over. "You know I won't miss it. Andrea, I was also hoping you would consider teaching me how to cook. Jake's tried, but I think I need to learn from someone less bossy."

He knew she was only half teasing. Every time he tried to teach her to cook they ended up naked. Hell, when they were at home, they spent *a lot* of time naked, and he loved every minute of it. She and his mother had become as close as a mother and daughter. Addy needed that connection, and as he listened to his mother say she'd love to help, he had a feeling his mother needed it, too. Without realizing it, Addy had taught Jake that there was no such thing as being loved *too* much, although there was a fine line between love and possession. He was learning about that, too. As much as she was *his*, she'd always be her own person first, and he admired that about her.

"Thank you," Addy said to his mother. "I hear you make delicious cream puffs. Would it be okay if we started with dessert?"

When she shifted a wickedly naughty gaze in Jake's direction, his stomach dipped and heat flooded his veins. He'd once wondered if that crazy fluttering in his stomach would ever change, and now he knew, without a shadow of a doubt, that with his stubborn, sexy girl, it never would.

—Ready for more Ryders?—

Fall in love with Gage and Sally!

It's been years since Sally Tuft's husband died, years since she was left to raise her teenage son alone, and years since she'd told the only other man she wanted that they should be just friends. Now her son has left for college, and Sally has no distractions to keep her from thinking about her best friend and coworker, Gage Ryder, and what could have been.

Gage Ryder believed that one day Sally would move past the death of her husband and they would finally leave the friend zone and explore the passion that's simmered between them since the day they met. But it doesn't seem that's ever going to happen, and it just might be Gage's turn to move on.

When Gage and Sally are tasked with opening a new youth center, their close-knit world is expanded—and sexy new prospects move in. Sally and Gage are forced to confront their attractions, or let each other go forever.

Have you met the Bradens?

All Braden books may be enjoyed as stand-alone novels or as part of the larger series

From *New York Times* bestselling author Melissa Foster comes a new sexy romance, WHISPER OF LOVE, in which Tempest Braden, a music therapist, meets Nash Morgan, a reclusive artist, and single father, with a secret past.

Tru Blue, a sexy stand-alone romance

"Ms. Foster went for the gut with Truman and Gemma. Tru Blue is more than a romance, it is a story of love, a story of hope and a story of courage. 10 + stars." Night Owl Reviews

He wore the skin of a killer, and bore the heart of a lover...

He wasn't going to fail them. Not now. Not ever...

There's nothing Truman Gritt won't do to protect his family—Including spending years in jail for a crime he didn't commit. When he's finally released, the life he knew is turned upside down by his mother's overdose, and Truman steps in to raise the children she's left behind. Truman's hard, he's secretive, and he's trying to save a brother who's even more broken than he is. He's never needed help in his life, and when beautiful Gemma Wright tries to step in, he's less than accepting. But Gemma has a way of slithering into people's lives and eventually she pierces through his ironclad heart. When Truman's dark past collides with his future, his loyalties will be tested, and he'll be faced with his toughest decision yet.

MORE BOOKS BY MELISSA

LOVE IN BLOOM SERIES

SNOW SISTERS

Sisters in Love

Sisters in Bloom

Sisters in White

THE BRADENS at Weston

Lovers at Heart

Destined for Love

Friendship on Fire

Sea of Love

Bursting with Love

Hearts at Play

THE BRADENS at Trusty

Taken by Love

Fated for Love

Romancing My Love

Flirting with Love

Dreaming of Love

Crashing into Love

THE BRADENS at Peaceful Harbor

Healed by Love

Surrender My Love

River of Love

Crushing on Love

Whisper of Love

Thrill of Love

THE BRADEN NOVELLAS

Promise My Love

Our New Love

Daring Her Love
Story of Love

THE REMINGTONS

Game of Love
Stroke of Love
Flames of Love
Slope of Love
Read, Write, Love
Touched by Love

SEASIDE SUMMERS

Seaside Dreams
Seaside Hearts
Seaside Sunsets
Seaside Secrets
Seaside Nights
Seaside Embrace
Seaside Lovers
Seaside Whispers

BAYSIDE SUMMERS

Bayside Desires

The RYDERS

Seized by Love
Claimed by Love
Chased by Love
Rescued by Love
Thrill of Love

SEXY STANDALONE ROMANCE

Tru Blue
Bearing Her Secrets

BILLIONAIRES AFTER DARK SERIES

WILD BOYS AFTER DARK

Logan
Heath
Jackson
Cooper

BAD BOYS AFTER DARK

Mick
Dylan
Carson
Brett

HARBORSIDE NIGHTS SERIES

Includes characters from the Love in Bloom series

Catching Cassidy
Discovering Delilah
Tempting Tristan
Chasing Charley
Breaking Brandon
Embracing Evan
Reaching Rusty
Loving Livi

More Books by Melissa

Chasing Amanda (mystery/suspense)
Come Back to Me (mystery/suspense)
Have No Shame (historical fiction/romance)
Love, Lies & Mystery (3-book bundle)
Megan's Way (literary fiction)
Traces of Kara (psychological thriller)
Where Petals Fall (suspense)

ACKNOWLEDGMENTS

I really enjoyed writing about Jake and Addy and all their angst about letting go and falling in love. Theirs was not an easy story to write, but it was true to their nature and I hope you loved it. I'd like to thank Christopher Boyer, executive director/COO of the National Association for Search and Rescue, for patiently answering my many questions. Had it not been for you, I couldn't have given readers such a well-rounded book. Thank you. I have taken fictional liberties in this book. Any and all errors are my own and not a reflection of Chris's knowledge or expertise. Please also note that the Silver Mountains are a fictional mountain range, not intended to be the Silver Lake Mountains. All noted points of interest, such as Pirate's Peak, are also fictional.

A special thank-you to Lisa Bardonski and Christy Dyc for pulling me off the ledge and reminding me to go with my gut instincts. It really helped. I met Lisa and Christy through my fan club on Facebook. If you haven't joined my fan club yet, please do!
www.facebook.com/groups/MelissaFosterFans

The best way to stay abreast of Love in Bloom releases is to sign up for my monthly newsletter (and receive a free short story!).
www.MelissaFoster.com/Newsletter

Follow me on Facebook for fun chats and giveaways. I always try to keep fans abreast of what's going on in our fictional boyfriends' worlds.
www.facebook.com/MelissaFosterAuthor

Thank you to my awesome editorial team: Kristen Weber and Penina Lopez, and my meticulous proofreaders: Elaini Caruso, Juliette Hill, Marlene Engel, Lynn Mullan, and Justinn Harrison. And last but never least, a huge thank-you to my family for their patience, support, and inspiration.

Meet Melissa

www.MelissaFoster.com

Melissa Foster is a *New York Times* and *USA Today* bestselling and award-winning author. Her books have been recommended by *USA Today's* book blog, *Hagerstown* magazine, *The Patriot*, and several other print venues. She is the founder of the World Literary Café and Fostering Success. Melissa has painted and donated several murals to the Hospital for Sick Children in Washington, DC.

Visit Melissa on her website or chat with her on social media. Melissa enjoys discussing her books with book clubs and reader groups and welcomes an invitation to your event.

Melissa's books are available through most online retailers in paperback and digital formats.

CPSIA information can be obtained
at www.ICGtesting.com
Printed in the USA
LVOW12s1738020217
523021LV00004B/857/P